I don't want to remember. I don't know how long that hot, sensual dream lasted, or what Gabriel saw, or what he thought, or when he left the room, or why. I don't really know why he killed himself, why he threw himself off the balcony.

Even ten years later I found it hard to think about that day. I didn't want to think about it. It was over, and Gabriel was dead. The past would suffocate me if I let it. And the truth, whatever it was, didn't matter. I wasn't responsible for what Gabriel had done, or what he had thought. Even if he had lived, chances were good I wouldn't know him now, I thought.

Also by Lisa Tuttle in Sphere Books:

A NEST OF NIGHTMARES

Lisa Tuttle

Gabriel

SPHERE BOOKS LIMITED

SPHERE BOOKS LTD

Penguin Books Ltd, 27 Wrights Lane, London W8 5TZ (Publishing and Editorial)
and Harmondsworth, Middlesex, England (Distribution and Warehouse)
Viking Penguin Inc., 40 West 23rd Street, New York, New York 10010, USA
Penguin Books Australia Ltd, Ringwood, Victoria, Australia
Penguin Books Canada Ltd, 2801 John Street, Markham, Ontario, Canada L3R 1B4
Penguin Books (NZ) Ltd, 182–190 Wairau Road, Auckland 10, New Zealand

First published in Great Britain by Severn House 1987
Published by Sphere Books Ltd 1987

Copyright © 1987 by Lisa Tuttle
All rights reserved

Made and printed in Great Britain by
Richard Clay Ltd, Bungay, Suffolk
Set in Plantin

Except in the United States of America, this book is sold subject
to the condition that it shall not, by way of trade or otherwise, be lent,
re-sold, hired out, or otherwise circulated without the
publisher's prior consent in any form of binding or cover other than
that in which it is published and without a similar condition
including this condition being imposed on the subsequent purchaser

To Dianne
and, with thanks,
to Nann and Malcolm

chapter one

His hair – straight to his shoulders and gleaming like a raven's wing – was the legacy of an Indian great-grandfather; his sky-blue eyes and artistic talent came, he told me, from his Welsh granny, while his small, wiry frame was exactly like his father's. His temper and his passions were, I believe, all his own, like the scars on his left hand, like his violent, early death.

His name was Gabriel Archer, and he was my husband for eleven months. He died at twenty-three, a few days before my nineteenth birthday. Ten years later, on my twenty-ninth, he came back to haunt me.

Not that I was ever really free of him. But as the years passed the memories stopped hurting so much, and our brief marriage seemed as long ago as childhood.

I was living in Chicago then, by myself, working in a restaurant, hating my job, hating my life. My twenty-ninth birthday fell on a Saturday, the day my best friend Polly was getting married at her parents' house in Lake Bluff, so that morning I got up early, caught the train to Lake Bluff, and travelled into my own past.

Once on the train I curled up in my seat and closed my eyes. I never could reconcile myself to getting up early, and sleep was waiting for me, like my unmade bed. In a moment, the train became a plane, and I was sitting next to Polly's boyfriend, Dan. He was angry, but I knew I had the right seat. As I tried to explain myself, I realized that it wasn't Dan, but my father. My father didn't approve of my going to New Orleans, but he couldn't stop me. No one could stop me now, for I was on the St Charles Avenue streetcar, and I knew just where I was going.

I left the streetcar in front of a dark green house with black shutters, built, Louisiana-style, a full storey off the ground. The huge palm trees and ancient bearded oaks shaded and shielded it from the noise of the Avenue. As I climbed the steep, wide steps I felt myself moving up through layers of quiet. The deepest stillness waited at the top. Standing on the porch, I took the cool brass doorknob in my hand and felt peace settling on my soul. I had come home.

The door opened on silence: a long, shadowy hall. At the end was a room full of windows, filled with light. Someone was waiting for me there. I could see a man standing by one of the windows, looking out. I could see nothing but his form, silhouetted against the glare, but that was enough. I knew him by the way he stood, and by some other deeper sense. It was Gabriel.

The sound of my shoes against the parquet floor was like an avalanche, but he didn't seem to hear. He didn't look round. He began to walk past the window, out of my line of sight, and no matter how hard I struggled my feet could gain no purchase on the slippery floor, and I made no progress. The hall stretched before me, longer than ever. I tried to call his name, but the thick, heavy air pushed the words back into my mouth, choking me, until I woke, gasping for breath.

I straightened up, massaged my aching neck, and glanced around to assure myself that no one had seen me sleeping. My heart was pounding hard and, despite the frustration of the familiar dream, I felt an odd excitement, as if Gabriel really *was* alive, and might be waiting for me somewhere; as if I'd remembered something important, as if I'd been wrong about his death. Of course, I knew he was dead – I had seen his broken body – but the feeling of the dream persisted, making me hopeful. If it wasn't Gabriel who waited for me, perhaps it was someone else. Maybe I would meet someone at Polly's wedding, someone who would change my life. I was glad of the hope, however irrational. I needed something to sustain me.

Going home was always hard. Until I was thirteen, home had been in Worcester, Massachusetts, and I still thought of the house in Lake Bluff as 'the new house'. I had left it when I was eighteen to marry Gabriel, but less than a year later I was back. Back in the same house, in the same room, as if I were still my parents' pretty, clever, cheerful teenaged daughter, as if I'd never been married, never been grown-up, never escaped at all. My room was just as I had left it, even to the piles of *Glamor* and *Mademoiselle* under the single bed. Ten years later it was the same. My parents wouldn't change it – to them it was still my room. I wouldn't change it either (I'd felt a twinge just throwing out the old magazines), because it wasn't mine to change. It belonged to the girl I had been, the girl who had died with Gabriel. I don't think my parents expected or wanted me to move back in, but the room seemed to promise me that I could go back, could try again, and this time, maybe, get it right.

When my mother met me at the station, I told her I wouldn't be able to stay the night after all, but would have to return to Chicago after the reception, to work.

'Oh, dear,' said my mother. 'Your father and I had planned to take you out to dinner, for a birthday treat. How unfair for you to have to work on your birthday! Well, never mind. Another time.'

She was disappointed, but not in me. My father, I thought, would blame me – and he would be right, because I was lying. I'd arranged to have the night off, but now that I was here I didn't like the idea of going from my best friend's wedding to my parents' house. It was too depressing. I didn't want to be envious of Polly, starting her new life, but I was. It would only be worse if I stayed.

They had presents for me, which I opened as the three of us sat in the living room, making a formal occasion of it. My mother had bought me a soft leather shoulder-bag and a blue silk scarf. She knew my taste, and this year she hadn't risked getting my size wrong. My father gave me a cheque, as usual. It was all over very quickly, and I was uncomfortable, feeling that I owed them something now, although I didn't know what. I looked at my watch.

'I'd better get going.'

'But the wedding's not –'

'I know, but I told Polly I'd help her get ready.' I stood up, impatient now to get away.

'Well, we'll see you there,' said my mother. Then: 'Oh, I almost forgot. A letter came for you today.'

'Here?'

'I put it up in your room.'

Had I really expected – or wanted – to get away without so much as a glance inside my old room? I wouldn't have felt threatened if I hadn't felt the attraction of it. I didn't think much about the letter as I went upstairs – it would be advertising, or a plea for charity, my name picked off some ancient mailing-list.

The pale blue walls with white trim, the dark floorboards showing around the edges of the Indian rug, the blue and white curtains I had made myself from material which matched the geometric pattern of the bedspread, the furniture, the pictures, the keepsakes from childhood: all were the same, always as I remembered. It was like walking into my own brain.

The letter was on the pine table where I had once done my homework. Even before I picked it up I knew it wasn't junk mail. The envelope was square and white, and my name and address had been printed in a large, careful, rather childish hand. There was no return address, but when I saw the New Orleans postmark my stomach lurched.

New Orleans was Gabriel. New Orleans was the past. When I had left New Orleans, I hadn't kept in touch with anyone I knew there. Who, after ten years' silence, would contact me now?

I sat down on the bed with the envelope in my hand. I didn't want to know. I didn't want to open it. I had to.

It was a birthday card, pink and gold, neither attractive nor amusing, the sort of sentimental old standard which I would never buy for anyone nor expect to receive myself. A wreath of roses in garish pinks and reds embraced the words, in gold, 'To My Darling Wife'.

Inside, my name had been written above a printed verse.

My eyes scanned the sentimental rhyme without taking it in. All I could see was the signature beneath. I knew that signature. I recognized it immediately, almost physically.

Love, Gabriel.

My hands were shaking as I shoved the card into my bag, out of sight. The dream of Gabriel still alive had made me feel hopeful, but this card, implying the same thing, frightened me. For a moment I doubted everything I thought I knew, all my memories, my whole life. Then I felt furiously angry. Of course Gabriel was dead. The card was a trick, a cruel joke by someone who had known me in New Orleans, someone who still wanted to hurt me. I couldn't think about it now. Polly was waiting for me. I had to get through her wedding before I could let myself think about New Orleans.

The walk to the Bakers' house, only two blocks away, calmed me a little, at least on the surface. The confrontations with my past – with so many different layers of it – left me feeling somewhat detached from the present. I was no longer sure where I belonged.

I didn't ring the doorbell; I just opened the door and went in. Polly and I had been in and out of each other's houses throughout our adolescence, sharing our lives, closer than sisters. I hadn't been to the Bakers' house for five or six years, but as I stepped inside I felt the familiar atmosphere of my second home accept me as if no time had passed. I could hear, distantly, the sound of female voices pitched a little too high, and I followed the sound through the immaculate green and white living room, through the dining room, to the family room – now empty of its usual furniture – and through the sliding glass doors into the back garden.

Polly was standing with her sister Jan and their mother on the closely trimmed grass in a space between rows of grey metal folding chairs. Polly and her mother, both dressed in brightly coloured caftans and gesticulating wildly as they argued, looked like mythic figures: the tall, slim sky-goddess confronting the round, fiery sun. And Jan in her modern clothes was the mortal caught between them.

When she saw me, Polly let out a cry and rushed to hug me as if it had been years instead of days since we'd seen each other.

'Save me,' she muttered against my hair. 'Get me away from that woman before I kill her! Now she wants to turn the chairs round in the other direction!'

'Should I talk to her?'

'No, no, Jan can handle it.' Still clinging to me, Polly looked back and called, 'Mom, I'm getting dressed now. Don't forget you've got to change, too. Let Jan take care of everything else.'

We went arm in arm into the house. The soft fabric of Polly's caftan billowed out and teased my legs, and I could smell Aliage warm on her skin. It reminded me of the year we'd shared an apartment, when she'd had Aliage-scented soap, handcream and bath oil, and I had taken to using it too. It had come to seem like a physical link between us, a family fragrance.

'I can't take much more of this,' Polly said, shutting the bedroom door behind us, closing out the world as she had often done when we were teenagers. 'I can't wait till it's over.'

I looked around, trying to remember this room, but it was impossible. It was anonymous, a guest room, redecorated by Mrs Baker after Polly had left home.

'This is supposed to be *my* wedding, isn't it?' said Polly, going to the closet and taking out a dress shrouded in clear plastic. 'My special day? You'd think she could just shut up for once, keep her opinions to herself and let me have it my own way. But, no, everything I do is wrong, and she has to tell me so. Even my dress.'

'She doesn't like it?' I had helped Polly choose it.

'Extremely unflattering, she says. Makes me look like a hippo – might as well be a maternity smock, she says.'

Our eyes met and Polly shook her head. 'She was just saying whatever came into her head. Although I don't know what she thinks she could do if I burst into tears and agreed it was too awful to wear . . . a little late now to zap out to Lord and Taylor.'

She slipped out of the caftan and looked down at herself. 'Can you tell?'

I stared at her naked body. Polly was tall and big-boned, but she had never been overweight. Her stomach looked as smooth and flat as ever, but weren't her high breasts heavier, and wasn't her waist less defined? It might be only the passage of time, the approach of thirty, because I'd had similar thoughts about my own body recently. I shook my head. 'You look just the same. What does it feel like?'

She shrugged. 'It doesn't feel like anything. Except my tits are definitely bigger – I can't stand to go without a bra. That's all. No morning sickness. I guess it'll be different when I start to show, but most of the time I don't even remember.' She wriggled into a pale pink slip.

Somehow I didn't believe her. How could she even for a minute forget she was pregnant? I had the unpleasant feeling that she didn't want to tell me the truth, either because she thought I wouldn't understand, or because she no longer wanted to share everything with me. And why should she? We had grown apart, we had changed, we had let men come between us. Friendship always took second place to love. That was understood.

'Do you need help with your hair?' I asked.

'You could help me pin it up – I've got some little flowers to wear in it – but first I've got to get my face on.' She sat down at the dressing table, yanked open a drawer and picked out mascara, lip-gloss, eye-shadow and blusher. 'Talk to me while I make myself beautiful.'

I sank down on the edge of the double bed, covered now with a blue and green patterned spread. I tried to remember what the old one had been like, when this had been Polly's room and we had spent the nights together sharing secrets instead of sleeping. But the present pattern caught my eye and would not be dislodged.

I looked at Polly, her cheeks flushed and eyes bright, beautiful without make-up; beautiful in her pale pink slip with her dark hair tumbling down her back. She leaned into the round, lighted make-up mirror – it was the twin of mine, both of them gifts from our mothers when we were sixteen – her eyes wide and her expression intent.

'I need to fix myself up, too,' I said. 'I only had time for the bare minimum this morning.'

'Overslept again, huh? I'll do you – I'll do you something amazing. Want a make-over?'

'Do I need one?'

'Just for fun.'

I shook my head. 'There's no time.'

'There *is*,' she said. The distress in her voice tore at me. I saw that she was near tears. She went on looking in the mirror, but now looking at my reflection as she spoke. 'I've always got time for you,' she said. 'It's not going to change *that* much. Look at all we've survived already.'

'I know,' I said. 'I'm not losing a friend, I'm gaining a friend's husband.'

'You'd better not.'

'Hey, best friends – what happened to sharesies?'

But neither of us was really in a mood for teasing.

'Nothing's going to change,' she said. 'I'm not moving away, Dinah. And it's not like Dan and I – I mean, we've *been* living together. So why get so worried about the marriage? It's a formality. We'll still be friends, like always.'

She was right in a way. We would still see each other: I would be invited over for dinner, and we would meet up in town for shopping and lunch. The forms would remain as they had despite long separations and changes in both our lives. But something crucial was about to change for ever, and we both knew it. At the core of our friendship had always been moments like this, of casual, easy, ordinary intimacy. Two women alone together in a room. Talking, getting dressed, putting on make-up, simply being together. Despite everything, we always came back to this. But in the future when Polly sat in a bedroom in her underwear, putting on her make-up, she would be with her husband, or with the child she said she couldn't yet believe in.

I got off the bed and went and hugged her. 'Of course we will,' I said.

The ceremony, which Polly and Dan had written themselves, went smoothly and was quickly over. I thought that writing your own ceremony was a corny thing to do, but instead of being embarrassed as I had expected I was moved almost to tears. I'd never thought very much of Dan, but seeing the way he looked at Polly made me jealous.

After the formalities, most people made for the tables laden with food and champagne which had been set up in the family room, and I looked around a little desperately for someone besides my parents whom I knew. The long horsey face and bright curls of Marilee Higgins had never before seemed so appealing to me. At school she'd been a jock and I never had much to do with her, but she had been a room-mate of Polly's at college, and I had learned to like her. She managed a health spa in Chicago, and had done me a favour once by hiring me on a part-time basis to teach dance and exercise classes, letting me work whatever odd hours I could fit in between more lucrative waitressing jobs. I gulped some champagne and rushed across the room to greet her, startling her with my enthusiasm.

'Oh, hi,' she said. 'I was wondering what had happened to you – you haven't been in to work out for ages.'

'I know. I've been tired.'

She shook her head reprovingly. 'That's when you need it the most, when you're tired. You should know that.'

'Well, I do some routines at home, to music. How's the spa doing?'

'Not too bad. The recession doesn't seem to have hit us. People don't mind spending money to make themselves look better. The Big O says –' she interrupted herself, grasping my arm. 'Oh, hey, he's in town. You ought to come in tomorrow and give him a thrill.'

'What do you mean?'

'Mr Opacek – you know, the big boss, the owner.'

'Oh, I remember. I met him.'

'You sure did. *He's* never forgotten. He's crazy about you. He asks about you every time he calls. He can't understand why you don't work for us any more.'

'Tell him to make me an offer I can't refuse. It's only because of the money, you know. I'd *much* rather teach dance or work-outs than wait tables, but I need the tips.'

'You're still waitressing?'

I shrugged, not liking to admit how unhappy I was about my situation. 'Well, you know, jobs are hard to find. I never got a degree, I can't type, my only experience is as a waitress, so who else would hire me? It's not so bad. It's work.'

'But you'd do something else if you had the chance?'

'It depends. Well, sure I would. I don't want to wait tables all my life.'

'How would you feel about managing a health spa?'

I stared. 'Your job?'

'Not mine. The same job, somewhere else. It would mean leaving Chicago, though.'

'I don't have any reason to stay in Chicago. I'm just there because I don't have any reason to leave. Are you serious about this?'

'Are you interested?'

I paused to think. I'd never thought of managing a health spa, and I had no idea what the job would entail or what it would pay, but I wanted a change. This was the way change happened, out of the blue, unexpected, like love. You could turn your back or run away, or you could say yes, and see where it took you. 'I might be. Is this a serious offer?'

'It's not mine to offer. But, like I said, Mr Opacek is in town. Come over tomorrow, come to lunch with us. I can tell him you're interested. He's looking to hire somebody. I didn't have any more experience than you when he hired me. He likes you already – it won't be hard for you to sell yourself, if you want to do it.'

I felt again the building of irrational hope, of excitement, which the dream of Gabriel had brought with it earlier. Gabriel had taught me to believe in fate. I looked at Marilee's open, homely face and said, 'You think I could do it?'

'Why not? If you're interested, if you're willing to put in the time and effort. The big thing is customer relations. Yeah, I think you could.'

I thought about living in the suburbs, a single woman away from the city, and wondered what it would be like 'Where is this spa?'

'There's more than one. You could probably take your pick. The Big O has been expanding his empire down into the Sun Belt. He bought out some other company, I think . . . anyway, he's got four or five, maybe six or seven, new properties and he's going to need managers for each one. One is in Miami, I know, and there's one or two in Atlanta, and . . . where else? Name a Southern city.'

'New Orleans.'

'Yeah, definitely New Orleans. I don't remember where else, but they're all warm places. No more Chicago winters! What's wrong? You're not thinking you'd miss Chicago winters?'

'No . . . No, I was thinking about the New Orleans summer.'

New Orleans in the summer was where it started for me. That was where I met Gabriel, although he claimed we had known each other in another life and would be together after death. He said our meeting was fated, outside time, and I liked to believe him. But whoever we were in previous lives or might be in lives to come, there was a moment in real time when Dinah Whelan and Gabriel Archer first set eyes on each other, and that happened in New Orleans, in the Morning Call.

Polly and I had been wandering around the French Quarter all day, drugged and dazzled by the heat, the crowds, the foreign-ness of it all, and the heady excitement of being on our own for the first time ever. As we walked past the big, old-fashioned coffee house in the French Market, the door to the Morning Call swung open, and the hot, rich smells of chicory, coffee and frying doughnuts seduced us inside.

My feet were sore, my shoulder aching from a bag stuffed with necessities and impulse buys, and it was good to sit down. The very smell of the coffee revived me, but when I saw the plate of *beignets* Polly had ordered to go with our *café au lait* I groaned in despair.

'You're going to spoil our dinner!'

'Nothing is going to spoil my dinner,' she said. 'Absolutely nothing. I'm going to eat and eat and eat and enjoy every mouthful. And if you can't handle it, I'll eat all these myself.'

I tore a piece off one of the fresh, hot doughnuts, dredged it in sugar, and felt it melt in my mouth. 'Heaven,' I mumbled, and I meant not only the taste, but the whole glorious week of freedom stretching ahead.

'Don't look now, but somebody's in love with you. Or maybe he's never seen a girl with a sugar moustache.'

I wiped a paper napkin across my mouth before turning my head for a look at Polly's latest discovery.

Eyes like shards of noonday sky, pure colour. It was a physical sensation, as if he had touched me inside.

Under the table, Polly kicked me. 'Didn't your mommy tell you it's rude to stare?' she asked in a low voice. She suppressed a grin. 'Anyway, he's not *that* good.'

'His eyes,' I said. 'Did you see his eyes?'

'Blue. Like yours.'

I shook my head. His eyes weren't like mine. They were magic. I was overpoweringly aware that he was still looking at me. His gaze was like a beam of light heating the side of my face.

'How old do you think he is?' said Polly. 'Do you think he's in college? Is he a native or a tourist?'

We always spent a lot of time looking at strangers and speculating about them, but this time I couldn't play the game. Polly leaned across the aluminium table, speckled now with sugar, crumbs, and crumpled paper napkins. 'Are you OK?'

'Let's go.'

She stared, then patted my hand. 'We're going.'

Outside on the hot street again, our backs to the windows where I was certain he still watched, Polly said, 'What's wrong? Was it that guy?'

'No, of course not.' The lie came automatically. But she was my best friend. I could lie to myself, but not to her. After a moment I said, 'I don't know what it was. I just felt . . . scared . . . all of a sudden.'

'I guess he was kind of creepy-looking, those hollow cheeks –'

'*No he wasn't!*' My anger surprised us both. I sighed, and searched my memory, trying to understand. 'It was the way he looked at me. It was like he knew me. I felt like I knew *him*. But I don't. And then I just felt kind of shaky, and I wanted to get out . . .'

'It's probably low blood-sugar,' said Polly. 'My uncle has that. He has to eat every three hours or so, and lots of protein, or he gets all shaky and weak. Probably you need some protein.'

'It is almost dinner time,' I said. 'Maybe you're right. Probably it wasn't anything to do with that guy at all.' But if that were the case, why couldn't I stop thinking about him? Why did I feel lonely now for someone I had never met?

We had dinner in a French restaurant recommended by the guidebook. Polly declared everything excellent, but I wasn't hungry. The *beignet* I had eaten seemed to have expanded to fill my whole stomach, and I merely picked at my meal and sipped iced water.

'I hope you're not coming down with something,' said Polly. 'That would really be a drag, to come all the way to New Orleans just to get sick! Maybe we should have an early night – go back to the hotel right after we've finished eating?'

I tried to shake off the strange, foreboding sense of loss which oppressed me. 'No way,' I said. 'We've only got eight nights here, and I don't want to waste one. No parents, no chaperons, we can do whatever we want. We're eighteen, we can drink!' I dug out the guidebook, pushing aside my plate. 'We'll try Pat O'Brien's first,' I said. 'It's supposed to be a New Orleans tradition. It also says college students go there. Maybe we'll meet some men.'

I rolled my eyes at her and she giggled. We joked about running wild on this, our first adult vacation, but we knew we wouldn't. We were good girls, Polly and I, virgins still at eighteen, not drug users or smokers, cautious drinkers. Our parents knew they could trust us even far from home; the habits of obedience were strong. We might look, and fantasize, and flirt with sin, but after a week away we would return home and get ready to go to college. It was then, we imagined, that our real lives would begin.

Pat O'Brien's was a crowded, noisy, happy bar, a public party which shook me out of my self-preoccupation and cheered me up. We ordered the house speciality, a sweet, fruity punch called the Hurricane. On the patio, the tropical air wrapped round us like wet velvet. It was easy to talk to strangers, and we fell in with a college debate team from Minnesota. I forgot my earlier mood and was enjoying myself until I felt a large hand clamp on to my knee. I pushed it off. It came back, and began creeping up my thigh. I pushed it away again, and realized that it didn't belong to the boy I was talking to, but was attached to someone I hadn't seen before, someone who wasn't even looking at me. I moved away and caught Polly's attention. 'We'd better go,' I said. 'Stan and Jimbo are going to be really, really mad if we don't show up to meet them.'

'Gosh, you're right,' said Polly agreeably. 'Look at the time!'

But back on the street she pinched my arm. 'I refuse to have a boyfriend called Jimbo! What's he supposed to be, an elephant?'

'A professional wrestler,' I said. 'You can have Stan. Stan wears black turtleneck sweaters, and glasses, and has a crewcut.'

'He's studying to be an architect, and he does *not* have a crewcut. Just because he has a normal hair cut, not like those hippies you go for – where are we going, anyway?'

I paused to dig out the guidebook. It was night time, and far above us the sky was black, but artificial lights of all colours illuminated the street. It was like being at a fair, or indoors. There were people everywhere, laughing, talking, in groups and couples. Many had drinks in plastic cups as they travelled from one bar to another. 'You didn't mind leaving?' I asked.

'No, of course not. There's a million bars in the naked city, and we're going to check out every one. Where next?'

'How about the Old Absinthe House? Sounds different. Should be a lot quieter. Very historic. Or do you want to choose one?'

'No, no. You pick tonight. I'll be the boss tomorrow.'

We linked arms so we wouldn't lose each other as we made our way down Bourbon Street. Voices, laughter and loud, brassy music roiled the air which was thick with the smells of beer and garbage, food and people. I was drunk, but it was on the strange, rich atmosphere of the city more than on the punch I could still taste on my tongue.

'It's fairyland,' I said. I looked down, and even the beer cans and plastic cups rolling in the gutter glittered like treasure.

But Polly had been distracted by the photographs outside a strip club, photographs of the most improbable-looking women. 'That's not real,' she said, tugging me to make me look. 'Those *can't* be real. What do you think, Dinah?'

'Perhaps you young ladies would like to come inside and see for yourself?'

A man in an electric-blue suit was looming over us, leering.

'No, thank you,' I said hastily. 'Not tonight.'

'Any night,' he said as I hauled Polly away. 'Any night, you're welcome, you're all welcome inside, no cover, absolutely no cover at all!'

I started giggling, although nervously. Polly tugged at my arm and said, 'Oh, Dinah, let's *do*. Let's do go back and look! I didn't think they'd let us in. Wouldn't you like to see a strip show? I would! I've always wanted to. I didn't think they'd let us in!'

'Oh, they'll let us in,' I said, still giggling. 'The question is – will they let us out again?'

'They wouldn't want me,' said Polly. 'Not with *my* chest. Did you see those pictures? How could anybody built like that walk around? I mean, the laws of gravity . . .'

Walking into the Old Absinthe House – crowded, but cool, dim and quiet – was a relief after the hectic sounds, light and unrelenting moist heat of the street. I shivered as we entered, and I thought it was from the arctic blast of air-conditioning, until I saw a figure move away from the bar as we approached and heard a voice, low, mellow, Southern, say, 'May I buy you a drink?'

It was the man from the Morning Call.

I couldn't speak or move.

Polly put her arm round me and came to my rescue. 'No, thank you,' she said in her coolest, most adult voice. 'That's very kind, but her boyfriend wouldn't see it that way. He's about twice your size with a jealous streak as big as his fist.'

The stranger didn't say anything, but he didn't go away. He just watched me, waiting for me to speak, as if we were alone and no one else in the world mattered.

The knot in my chest finally gave, and the loneliness vanished. I realized that I had been afraid I would never see him again, and I was glad that he had found me.

'Yes,' I said. 'You can buy us both a drink.'

Polly gave me a sharp look, but dropped her protective arm, accepting my change of heart. 'I'll have some absinthe,' she said.

'Absinthe is illegal,' he said. 'But you could have Pernod, which is supposed to taste the same.'

'Illegal? Why?'

'Artists and poets and other disreputable Bohemian types used to drink themselves to death on it in the old days. They made it with wormwood, which is a poison. You can still drink yourself to death if you're determined, but it takes longer now.' He looked at me. 'What would you like?'

I couldn't think with his gaze on me. 'The same,' I said, and then was in agony when he looked away, trying to catch the bartender's attention.

The booths were all taken, and there weren't any empty chairs, so we remained standing after we'd been served. I wasn't sorry. I liked standing beside him at the bar, so close that any slight, casual movement might allow him to touch me accidentally. But we were both far too aware of each other for any accidents.

I still had only the most uncertain, confused impression of what he looked like. I had been struck by the blueness of his eyes from the first, but apart from that I was aware of him more as a presence than a person, as if he was some form of energy. The bar was dim, and I was shy of looking at him directly, so the physical details filtered through only gradually.

He was not tall – five-foot-six, my own height – and slender but sinewy. Later I learned how strong he was. Glossy black hair hung straight and shining to his shoulders. He was clean-shaven, tanned, with high cheekbones and rather full lips.

If Polly hadn't been there, I don't know that we would have said a word. I didn't have anything to say – I just wanted to be near him. But Polly's presence made things normal. We were strangers in a bar, and there were certain conversational conventions to be observed.

Through Polly's questions I learned that this stranger's name was Gabriel Archer, and that he was twenty-two years old. He had been living in the French Quarter for the past three years, and he said he was an artist. He made a precarious living doing pastel portraits of tourists, and he occasionally worked as a bartender. At other times he had been a student, a shrimper and a beer-bottler.

'I do what I have to to survive,' he said. 'Money isn't important, but you need it to live. Art is what's important. I work for money but someday I'll paint something that will make my life worth while. That's what I hope.'

I hung on his every word, hardly realizing that he never asked me about myself. Compared to him, I had no life. I had only just emerged from the cocoon of childhood, but he was an adult.

Polly was less impressed, and finally she dragged me off to the ladies' room to tell me so.

'I'm tired of that yellow liqueurish drink,' she said. 'Let's go somewhere else.'

I looked at my own dazed and dazzled eyes in the mirror. 'I like it here,' I said.

'It's almost one o'clock,' she said. 'We've been here since –'

'Oh, all right. We can go someplace else. Maybe Gabriel has a favourite bar.'

'I meant by ourselves.'

I looked at her, willing her to understand. 'Polly, I like him. I really like him.'

'That's what I was afraid of,' she sighed.

I frowned. 'And what does *that* mean?'

'It means: what am I supposed to do? I feel like a third wheel.'

'I'm sorry. I didn't mean for this to happen. Maybe he's got a friend –'

'No thanks!'

'I was thinking about you,' I said. 'I don't mind it being the three of us. But I can't leave him now, not when I've just met him. If you're really bored you could go somewhere by yourself.'

'I think we should stick together. You don't know this guy, and he's older and everything . . . Look, why don't we leave now, and you could make a date to meet him tomorrow, somewhere during the day, and if you wanted to be alone with him I could just go shopping or something –'

People often blame rude or irrational behaviour on drink, but if I was intoxicated it was solely on Gabriel's presence. I couldn't think beyond the urge to be close to him. Already, I was afraid I had been away too long, and that he might have vanished while Polly tried to reason with me. If he had, I'd never forgive her, I thought.

'I want to stay,' I said, 'I want to talk to him. You can do what you want.' And I pushed out impatiently through the heavy, swinging door.

He was watching for me, his figure tense as he leaned against the bar. When our eyes met, I felt his relief as my own.

Polly, bless her, did not abandon me. Despite my rudeness, despite her yawns, Polly hung on.

Gabriel cocked his head slightly to one side and looked deep into my eyes, seeing things no one else had ever seen.

'Do you ever have dreams about people you don't know . . . and then meet them?' he asked. 'Do you ever know what's going to happen?'

I shook my head, but unwillingly, wanting it to be true.

He nodded. 'I do. I dreamed about you before I saw you. I've been looking for you for a long time. You know that, don't you? You recognized me today, when you saw me in the Morning Call. I could *feel* it . So could you, and it frightened you. That's why you ran away. But I knew I'd find you again. It was fated.'

Was he crazy? He made me nervous, but I responded to his intensity. I wanted the crazy, wonderful things he said to be true. And there was a connection between us, a recognition. Whatever it might mean, it was undeniable.

Eventually Polly got tired of being the witness to our self-absorbed conversation. She said she couldn't stay awake any longer and, with or without me, she was going back to the hotel.

She was my friend, but I would have let her go. Gabriel, with less reason to be kind, said that we would walk her back. On the street he took my hand.

That was the first, physical touch. That was when I gave myself to him and decided that, unless he made me, I would never leave him. In a personal sense that, to me, was our marriage.

I thought it was that simple. I was eighteen, and I could decide what to do with my life. I married Gabriel, becoming a wife instead of a daughter. I thought it was for ever, until he died. Then I thought that was the end. Now I wasn't even sure about that.

chapter two

The dream, the card signed 'Gabriel', the talk of a job in New Orleans – coincidence was Gabriel's country. He would have called it fate. Befuddled by champagne and memories, I wondered, as the train carried me back to Chicago, if he would have been right. Maybe Gabriel was now and always had been my fate. Maybe I was meant to go back to him.

But Gabriel wasn't living in New Orleans. Gabriel was dead. Even if – by some impossible chance – I was wrong about that, his wife, the innocent eighteen-year-old who had loved him, no longer existed. I had grown up. I was different now. I had loved other men – loved them longer, more deeply, more seriously than I had loved the man who had so briefly been my husband. I could remember how Gabriel had seemed to me, and how I had felt about him, but what had seemed romantic then – his sullen, smouldering looks, his self-centred suffering – would simply turn me off today. I wasn't a moth to be drawn to that sort of flame anymore.

And yet . . . perhaps I still wanted to be. Maybe it wasn't Gabriel I really missed, but my own younger self. I missed the way I had loved him, and the person he had loved, and the endless possibilities life had held for her.

I didn't like my life now. I didn't like my job, or my solitude, my lack of hope, or my envy of Polly. I especially disliked the place where I lived – a shabby apartment in an old, wooden block of six just off Argyle Street. It had seldom felt less like home than it did to me that night, the balmy air of the suburbs still fresh in my lungs. Uptown, on that warm summer evening, smelled of exhaust fumes, gasoline, garbage and curry. The ageing hippies who lived opposite were playing heavy metal very loud, and I caught whining snatches of a country-and-western song floating on the breeze.

I locked my door behind me and hurried to establish my own atmosphere, putting a Joan Armatrading record on the stereo, making a cup of Red Zinger tea, and then settling on the couch, avoiding the broken spring out of long-established habit. I looked around at the familiar room, and wondered how I could have stayed so long in such a horrible place.

Eighteen months, before, I had grabbed this apartment eagerly, willing to overlook the unpleasant aspects of the neighbourhood and the sheer ugliness of the rooms because the rent was low and I didn't plan to stay long. I simply needed somewhere to live by myself when the two-month idyll with Anthony had become a purgatory.

I had covered the mottled walls with white paint and furnished the emptiness with discards, hiding hideous upholstery with Mexican blankets. I hated the sight of them now, because they reminded me of when I had been in Mexico, in love with John. That was over, as was my passion for Anthony. Since then, there had been a few brief encounters, mostly with married men. Nothing I cared to think about now. I worked in a restaurant and I slept alone, dreaming of being loved and waking up to loneliness. Lately – since I'd known of Polly's pregnancy – I'd been having fantasies about having a baby. I'd never given it much thought before, never when I was actually involved in a stable relationship, but now, alone and pushing thirty, I felt mistrustful of men and found the thought of my own baby more compelling than the idea of a new lover. Romantic love ended: men died, or changed or went away. But if I had a child, it would always be mine.

The record clicked off, and I could hear someone walking upstairs, and the low rumble of voices. Music from outside and the distant, neverending rush of traffic. I closed my eyes, imagining the solid, comforting weight of a baby in my arms. I felt as if someone was standing by the window watching me, but when I opened my eyes I was alone.

The baby was a fantasy and would remain so. Awake, I couldn't forget that babies had to be fed and clothed, and I had a hard enough time doing that for myself. I wasn't going to be a Welfare mother, bringing her illegitimate baby up in poverty. Without meaning to, I thought of my father, and how he would react. But nothing I could do now would please him. He had never forgiven me for marrying Gabriel and turning my back on the intellectual, committed career he had imagined for me.

Why shouldn't I go to New Orleans? I could make a new start there, with a new job, friendlier surroundings, a nicer apartment . . . Gabriel was dead; I couldn't undo or change my marriage, but I *could* go back. I could start over.

But that birthday card nagged at me – it was a warning as much as an invitation. I had to see it again. Maybe I had missed something, some clue or additional message. I wanted to check the signature against my marriage licence. I searched through my bag with growing impatience, finally emptying it on to the couch. Coins, a pen, lipstick, all rolled to the floor as I scrabbled. But it wasn't there. The card was gone, as if it had never existed.

Sunday morning I woke early, excited in a way I hadn't been for a long time. It was something like the way I felt in the early stages of a new relationship, before anything had actually happened, when it seemed that anything might. But this mattered so much more than another love affair.

I spent more time and effort dressing for what was supposed to be a casual lunch, a friendly meeting, than I had for Polly's wedding. I worried about how I looked and the impression I would create, and filled the hours before I could leave marshalling reasons for Mr Opacek to hire me.

It was a bright, warm day and I had plenty of time, so I walked to the spa. I was scarcely aware of the Chicago streets around me, already thinking ahead, living somewhere else. I fluctuated between self-confidence and despair: certain at one moment that the job was mine, the next moment all too aware that people without experience weren't given jobs simply because they wanted them. Marilee's confident smile and wink at me when I arrived at the spa tipped the balance: I was in. I could do it, I knew I could.

'Dinah! How good to see you! And you look marvellous!' As he hugged me, I felt the unused strength coiled and waiting in his arms, and caught a whiff of spicy cologne.

Paul Opacek was a small man in his fifties, almost aggressively fit. His skin was taut and tanned as leather, and his head appeared to have been shaved, as if he was too impatient to wait for baldness to come naturally. I had thought Marilee was teasing when she said he had a crush on me, but the look in his eyes told me she hadn't just made it up.

'Marilee tells me you might be interested in joining the team,' he said. 'Well! But we'll talk about that over lunch. I hope you like Greek food. That's the one thing I must insist on. I've been promising myself lamb and fetta cheese and retsina for weeks. You can't find good Greek food in Dallas.'

'I didn't know you lived in Dallas.'

'Just since recently. It's a good central location, with the international airport and all. Of course, it's all because I'm expanding into the South, as Marilee told you. Anyway, let's get going – we can start on a bottle of cold retsina.'

'Make mine beer,' said Marilee. 'That stuff is like turpentine.'

'And what's wrong with turpentine?' he asked in mock indignation. Then he glanced at me. 'I remember a good Greek restaurant in New Orleans . . . in the Quarter . . . very down-home and basic, with Greek music on the jukebox and the sailors dancing with each other when it got late – you know the place I mean?'

I shook my head. 'It's been nearly ten years –' I wished the words back, but it was too late. Probably Mr Opacek wanted someone utterly at home in New Orleans, not a stranger like me. I wouldn't have lied, but I could have given a different impression, I thought. But if the question had been a test he didn't give any sign of disappointment.

'It's a lovely city, isn't it?' he said. 'No wonder you'd like to go back.'

The restaurant was only a few blocks away. Mr Opacek joked with the waiters and ordered a feast, far more food than we were likely to be able to eat. I'd had nothing to eat since Polly's wedding, but I had no appetite. I hoped I would be able to swallow enough so that my nervousness wouldn't be too evident.

I expected some sort of inquisition, but he launched into what seemed like a sales pitch. As if I were an investor rather than a job applicant, he talked about the importance of keeping fit, and the growing awareness of this, and the willingness to spend money on their health, of the American public. He quoted membership figures, profits gross and net, and compared his own small but rapidly growing health empire with others. I tried to look attentive, but I didn't take very much of it in. He didn't have to impress me – I already wanted the job. It was I who had to sell him, and I worried about the questions he might ask.

After the appetizers, he got to the point. 'Marilee has told you I'm looking for people to manage the new properties. Basically, experience isn't the important thing. I'm looking for bright, capable, attractive young people; self-starters who believe in success, and don't need me to be checking up on them. Usually, I would hire from within; take somebody already working in the place and promote them. That's what happened with Marilee. So she already knew the ropes. You'd be coming in from the outside, which makes it a little more difficult.'

'She could spend a few days following me round and learn everything she needs,' Marilee said. 'It wouldn't be that different when she got to New Orleans.'

'Sure, sure,' he said. He was still looking at me, undistracted by Marilee's contribution. 'It's not the sort of job that needs a long apprenticeship. You could pick it up in no time; you're not dumb. And you're good with people – the clients like you. But you know the most important thing in a manager?'

I shook my head, chagrined at missing the very first question. But it wasn't a real question, because he wanted to tell me.

'Responsibility,' he said. 'The ability to accept responsibility. In some ways, managing is about delegating responsibility, because you have to pick out people who do all the little daily jobs, the teaching and the cleaning and the buying and the selling. But – bottom line – the responsibility is all yours. Because if somebody gets sick or doesn't show up, you have to be prepared to fill in, to keep things going. You have to take responsibility – there's no one else behind you. Some people can do it, and some people can't. But it's the hardest thing to judge, beforehand. You never really know until you give someone responsibility whether they can deal with it.'

He had been leaning forwards, but now he sat back and, oddly, it was as if he did so to look at me more closely. 'Do you believe in fate?' he asked.

I didn't know what to say.

'*I* do,' he said. 'Not like in the old Greek myths. You can make your own fate – it's not something predetermined and waiting for you. But there are moments when things happen, when things come together, and chances have to be taken . . . call it luck, or chance . . . do you know what I mean?'

Feeling almost hypnotized by his steady, brown stare, I wondered what he knew. What had I told Marilee? I nodded. 'That's why I went to New Orleans in the first place,' I said. 'That's why I want to go back.'

He smiled, triumphant. 'You want a job in New Orleans; I need someone for a job in New Orleans. It's timing, it's luck, it's fate. I consider myself a good judge of character. I like to trust my instincts. My instincts are telling me to take a chance. You want the job? It's yours.'

So I was going back to New Orleans.

'As soon as you can,' Mr Opacek had said, and that suited me. I quit my job on one day's notice, and informed my landlord I would be leaving at the end of the month. Then I set about stripping my life down to the bare essentials.

The first time I went to New Orleans I had one suitcase: a week's worth of clothes, a hairdrier, travel iron, make-up, guidebook and diary. Not much to start on a new life. This time I would have more, but as most of my possessions were second-hand and replaceable, I didn't want to spend a lot of money shipping them. The idea of a fresh start was more promising.

I sold my stereo system and many of my records, and bought myself a tiny cassette radio complete with headphones. After that it became easier to sell off books, clothes, dishes and furniture at junk shops around the neighbourhood. I liked the idea of myself travelling unfettered into a new life. The things I found there would all be so much better than what I had already.

For several days I followed Marilee round at the spa, observing, asking questions, and making notes to myself in a new blue spiral-bound notebook. I felt organized and energetic. I stopped thinking so much about Gabriel, and became more aware of the attractive men around me. It seemed ironic that they should be appearing just as I was about to leave, but perhaps it was a hopeful sign, like flowers in spring. If they were blooming in Chicago, there would be even more in the warm and sunny south.

Yet for all my positive thinking, I was nervous. Every day I doubted myself and wondered if I was making a terrible mistake. I longed to talk to Polly about it, but she was unreachable, on her honeymoon with Dan. I dithered about telling my parents and kept putting it off, afraid of their disapproval. I remembered my father's rage, and my mother's tears, from eleven years before. Their actual response when I finally phoned them was almost a let-down. They were surprised but not displeased. They wished me well. They offered no advice. I wondered, as I hung up, what it was I wanted from them. Forgiveness? It was too late for that. I had to live my own life.

My life, now, was packed into three suitcases and a box.

Alone in O'Hare, waiting for my flight to be called, I confronted my own freedom. I had never been so unconnected, so unanchored in my life. No one was waiting for me in New Orleans. No one would stop me, or even notice, if I missed my plane and went instead to Anchorage or London. True, I had an agreement with Paul Opacek, but that seemed a fantasy. The job didn't exist yet. It seemed to me I could fall out of my new job as suddenly and easily – even unintentionally – as I had fallen into it. But of course I would go to New Orleans. Whatever my doubts, I had less reason to stay in Chicago, and no reason to go anywhere else. My luggage had been checked through. I boarded the plane.

A man sat down next to me, and as we looked at each other I could feel his approving smile mirrored on my face. He looked interested in me, and I found him immediately attractive. He was a big man, with broad shoulders and a deep chest. His hair was curly, black sprinkled lightly with grey. His eyes, darklashed, were a deep, clear brown. I thought of chocolate, melting in my mouth. His voice was like chocolate, too, with a faintly bitter New Jersey edge to keep it from cloying. I guessed he was in his early thirties.

'New Orleans?' he asked.

I nodded.

'Business or pleasure?'

'Business – I just got a job there, so I'm moving.'

'Oh, hey, you won't regret it. It's a great place. You been there before?'

'Yes . . . but not for a long time. How about you?'

He had moved to New Orleans a few years earlier to work as a sales representative for a small but growing computer company. He didn't say very much about himself – instead, he asked me questions, and I responded to the sympathy in his eyes and told him far too much about my past, my early marriage and the fate that was taking me back to New Orleans. I told myself it was because he was a stranger, and that things said while travelling, between strangers, don't really count, but there was something else going on. He liked me – I could feel it – and I liked him. The initial spark of interest kept getting warmer as we talked.

'I probably shouldn't be doing this,' I said. 'I can't go back – Gabriel's been dead ten years.'

'You're not going back to Gabriel,' he said. 'Just to New Orleans. I can understand that; it's possible to fall in love with a city, too.'

'It must have changed a lot in ten years,' I said. There was a distant, stifled wailing: somewhere on the plane a baby was crying.

'Probably not as much as you think. Gotten bigger around the edges, of course, but it's a city of traditions, and the centre is still the same. It's a magic place; things happen there that couldn't happen anywhere else.'

The baby was still crying and it was making me tense. I felt its misery like an abrasive against my skin. The man beside me shifted in his seat, and I thought he felt it, too.

'Would you –' he said, and paused, then started again. 'Would you like to go out to dinner with me tonight? To celebrate your return. Somewhere in the Quarter, of course.'

I wanted to jump up and find the baby. Where was its mother? What was wrong with her? Couldn't she comfort it? I'd never let a child of mine go on crying like that.

'Am I completely out of line?'

'What?'

'I just asked –'

'The baby,' I said, unable to stand it anymore.

'We're descending,' he said. I stared at him. 'Can't you feel it? The pressure's changed. The poor little thing doesn't like it one bit.'

I realized then that I had been half-consciously coping with the change, swallowing to make my ears pop. 'Do you have any kids?' I asked.

He smiled. 'I'm not married, if that's what's worrying you.'

'No, I know, but you said –'

'Yeah, I *was* married once, for a little while. We didn't have any kids, thank God. Anyway, to return to my question – dinner? Tonight?'

But now that we were about to land, no longer in limbo, I became more cautious. Even if I might want to see him again, I couldn't share my first night in New Orleans with a stranger. A sudden image of Gabriel sitting at a table in the Morning Call made my skin prickle. I shook my head. 'Thank you, but not tonight. I think I need to be by myself. I want to get my bearings, indulge myself by looking at old landmarks.'

'OK. Another time?'

'Yes, I'd like that.'

'Do you have a phone number?'

'Why don't you give me yours. I'll call you once I'm settled.'

'Sure,' he said, reaching into his jacket for a notebook, and I could feel his withdrawal. He thought I was just being polite, and maybe I was. He was attractive, but all I could think about right now was New Orleans, waiting for me like a fickle lover.

New Orleans felt like coming home. As I walked out of the airport, the steamy, drunken air of a Gulf Coast summer embraced me, and I relaxed.

I didn't know the area around the airport, or any of the streets the cab took me along, but the sunlight, the heat, the pastel colours and the smell of the air made everything familiar. Eventually, as we drove towards the business district closer to the heart of the city, I began to recognize bits and pieces, or at least to imagine that I did. The street names chimed like a song learned in childhood: Magazine, Canal, Decatur, Chartres, Exchange, Royal . . .

I remembered that somewhere in the city were nine streets named after the Muses. I couldn't remember exactly where, but I remembered one silly, intoxicated night when we had invented Muses for the modern age: the muse of rock 'n' roll, the muse of the paperback original, the muse of comic books . . .

I smiled, remembering the girl I had been as if she were

someone I had known once and lost track of, someone I might find waiting for me among the euphonious Southern streets.

The taxi let me off at my hotel and I checked in without really thinking about it, taking my bags up to my room and then going back out again immediately, not even pausing to wash my hands or comb my hair. My stomach was tense, my throat dry, and the muscles in my thighs trembled slightly: I felt an almost sexual excitement as I walked through the French Quarter, as if I were going to meet a lover.

Like the rest of the tourists dawdling along the crowded streets, I moved slowly. Only my expectations did not slow. Every breath I took of the rich, damp, odiferous air recalled another memory. Ten years of experience melted and rolled off my skin, and I was a girl again, glancing shyly sideways into the open doors of bars and at the photographs of strippers and exotic dancers posted on walls, gazing with more open interest into the display windows of antique shops and art galleries, staring into restaurants and at the faces of the strangers around me as I imagined other lives for myself.

Weaving in and out of the crowd, evading looks and sexual remarks from men, holding myself apart from the tourists, I wasn't sightseeing but going where I belonged. Street people, we had called ourselves, those of us who worked in the bars and shops and restaurants of the Quarter. I passed buildings I remembered, and some which had changed, restaurants and hotels, small boutiques and old-fashioned row houses with lacy ironwork balconies, through the stale malt smell of beer and the hot burnt-sugar perfume of pralines, scents of food and drink and people rising off the pavement with the heat, moving towards the river, towards the French Market and – there it was. The Morning Call.

Going inside, I was disoriented. It wasn't the way I remembered, it wasn't the way I had dreamed about it – and yet it must be, for I couldn't say how it was different. A large high-ceilinged room glittering with window-light and mirrors and aluminium table-tops, the buzz of voices, flies and the distant sizzle of deep-fat frying. I had a moment's uncertainty, and then the room came into focus and there was no discrepancy, no memory, but only the present reality.

I ordered what I had first ordered eleven years ago, what everyone ordered at the Morning Call: *café au lait* and *beignets* which I powdered lavishly from the metal sugar cannister on my table. The sweet, burnt-chicory taste of the coffee brought the past back in a powerful rush, and I felt that I was being watched. I turned my head, but the table in the far corner was empty.

Eleven years fell on me like a heavy cape. Outside, a kid with a huge radio tugging at his shoulder walked past to the thumping blare of a disco beat, unmistakably of the eighties. There were other people all round me, tourists and locals talking, laughing, sipping coffee and eating doughnuts, but I felt as if I were alone in the bright, noisy room. I pushed away my *beignet* untouched, losing my appetite for a taste belonging to the past I couldn't recapture.

What had I expected? Did I really think I would find Gabriel again – a new Gabriel? Was I looking for Gabriel, or trying to lose him?

I had intended to spend my first day in New Orleans on a magical memory tour – after the Morning Call the Old Absinthe House, and then the apartment on Decatur Street where we had lived, but now the very thought made me too tired to go on. I had changed. The world had changed. Only Gabriel had stayed the same, and that was because he was dead. I could see traces of him everywhere, if I wanted, but I would never have him whole and living.

It was time to admit that, and to make my peace with New Orleans. This was going to be my city now, not Gabriel's. He was no longer a part of my life. He belonged to memory, and it was time to let memory fade in the bright colours of today.

Leaving the coffee house, I walked down to Jackson Square to look at St Louis Cathedral, the postcard image of New Orleans, the centre of the tourist's city. As usual the Square was filled with tourists snapping cameras and street people selling ice creams and pastel portraits. Paintings of furry kittens and big-breasted, doe-eyed women, the same old street scenes and landscapes and sunsets over water lined the iron railings of the park. They hadn't changed in ten years, although the paint was fresh and I thought they had proliferated: bad art was obviously profitable.

On the other side of the iron fence people with wild manes of hair and tattered bright clothing sprawled on the grass, smoking hand-rolled cigarettes or drinking beer while naked babies played beside them, all of them unaware that the seventies had gone out with the tide, leaving them stranded on the bare beach of the eighties.

I went past, on down to Canal Street where I boarded a streetcar. I had always loved the streetcar for the same reason that I liked the El in Chicago: it had a personality, and it was a part of the city in a way no ordinary bus or train could be. I liked the way it rattled and clanged along, noisy and friendly as a character in a children's book.

On St Charles Avenue I grew tense, and leaned closer to the smeared glass of the window. Among the beautiful houses I was searching for one in particular: an old green house with black shutters and a deep porch, raised high off the ground and surrounded by palm trees. Was that it? Or that one? Maybe it was painted a different colour now. I didn't know if I had already missed it, or seen it without recognizing it. I told myself it was only a dream, and whether it was a remembered house or an invented one could not possibly matter, but, somehow, it *did* matter, and I couldn't stop looking. My tension increased and the beginnings of a headache knocked at my skull.

I lurched to my feet and down the aisle as the streetcar clanged to a stop. Audubon Park. I got out and stood on the esplanade, blinking in the fierce sun. The streetcar rattled away, leaving me there alone. The trees in the park across the street promised shade, and there might be a water fountain. I knew I should take some aspirin before the headache became unbearable. Crossing the street, I swayed and almost fell. The heat, I thought, and then remembered I'd had nothing to eat all day, although I had been drinking on the plane.

Beneath the trees it was no cooler, but at least the leaves blocked the sun, which was some comfort. I followed the path towards the pond, remembering a huge old oak tree, hung with Spanish moss, and the bare, hard earth beneath it where Gabriel and I lay down together.

There were some pigeons on the grass beside the path, four or five of them standing together in a little clump. They didn't move as I passed, which struck me as odd. They weren't like birds at all, more like cows, bored and patient as they waited, motionless, for milking time.

I remembered the swans, gliding in pairs across the still dark water, mirrored in it, and doubly twinned. Or had there been swans? I remembered Gabriel telling me how swans mate for life, but had those large, white birds drifted on the water before us, or only in our minds? I couldn't trust my memory. As the years went by I was romanticizing my own past, changing it until I didn't know what was real, what wish, what fear.

There was the water, there the oak tree, and there, beneath it, stood someone waiting for me.

My heart thumped out of time with my footsteps, making me falter. But it wasn't a man – only some trick of perspective had made me think that. I could see now that it was only a child, a slight, short-haired kid in jeans and a white T-shirt, standing alone at the water's edge.

As I approached I saw his stance change as he heard my footsteps, and then he turned.

Blue eyes – my throat constricted – and black hair, short and sleek as sealskin. I thought he was about eight years old. He looked so small, and his face was so sad, that I thought he must be lost.

Angry with his unknown mother for leaving him alone, I wished for a moment that he was mine. He might have been. With those eyes, with that hair, he could have been Gabriel's son. I felt the old, familiar pain of longing cramping low in my stomach and tightening my throat as I stared at him.

His eyes widened and darkened slightly, as if he had seen something astonishing in my face. Then the corners of his full lips quivered and he said my name.

I took a step back.

He said it again, more certainly.

'What? What did you say? I'm sorry, do you know me? Who are you?' I asked.

The little boy dipped his dark head and cocked it slightly to one side, an oddly familiar movement. Then he looked up into my eyes as if he could see things there no one else had ever seen, smiled and said:

'Gabriel.'

chapter three

Ben stared at the gleaming, flat surface of the pond, imagining himself beneath it, sinking into the cool, dark, nothing. No more pain, no more loneliness, no more questions. He'd be dead, and they'd be sorry.

It would be some time before his mother missed him, though, and even longer before his body was found. No one would know where to look. He could hear his mother telling the police that he'd gone to see a movie. How many movie theatres were there in New Orleans? He could see policemen thronging every one, shining their flashlights beneath the seats, searching the rest-rooms, interrogating ticket-sellers, arresting suspicious characters like the strange men in raincoats his mother had warned him against.

They might think he had run away. After all, he had five dollars. They would go to the bus station and find out how many different places his money could have taken him to, and then they'd have to check out every one. Maybe they would call in the FBI. Maybe they would think he had been kidnapped, and set up roadblocks. The thought of traffic held up for hours, lines of cars stretching back for miles, all because of him, almost made him smile.

How long before they thought to drag the pond? It might be months. No one knew he liked to come here. If they thought of drowning they'd think of the river or the lake or even the lagoons of City Park long before this tiny, forgotten pond.

But maybe they wouldn't have to drag the pond. Did dead bodies sink or float? He couldn't remember. That was the sort of thing Alan would know.

At the thought of Alan, Ben clutched himself tightly, holding his pain, mourning the loss of his best and only friend. Alan would be sorry he was dead, if he ever heard the news. Well, it served him right for going away.

That wasn't fair. Ben knew it wasn't Alan's fault – he hadn't had a choice. Kids never did. Parents made decisions for them and moved them around like they were no more important than plastic soldiers. Alan's mother had taken him away, and that wasn't Alan's fault.

Except that Alan had *promised*. Ben and Alan had sworn an oath that they would never be parted, that they would be best friends and blood-brothers for ever and ever, until the sun stopped shining and the rivers ran dry.

Ben closed his eyes, hearing the words they had both spoken, seeing Alan crouching in front of him in the hide-out, scabby knees protruding through ripped jeans, the blade of a stolen steak-knife flashing as he cut first his hand and then Ben's. They had pressed their palms together so their blood would mingle, and they had promised that no one and nothing would come between them.

Only three months after that fateful day, Alan had come racing down the street and pounded at the door, rousing Ben from his early-morning television viewing. He was breathless and crying.

They were going, he said, and he didn't know where. He'd had no warning, but woke up to find his mother throwing their few possessions into the car. It was always like that. His mother had decided it was time to leave, and she wouldn't say where they were going. There would be no forwarding address in case bill-collectors tried to find her. It had been in this same way that they had come to New Orleans from Atlanta. It was the way they had always lived and probably always would, only Alan had believed his mother when she said New Orleans would be their home for good, and Ben had believed Alan.

The pain of loss turned to anger. It *was* Alan's fault, he had promised and then broken his promise by letting his mother come between them. He could have refused to go; he could have hidden; he could have stayed with Ben. He could have become Ben's real brother, been adopted by Ben's mother. Why not?

But Alan had gone away, promising to write. That was three weeks ago, nearly, and Ben had stopped expecting the letter to arrive. Alan had lied to him. Alan didn't care. Alan had never really been his friend at all.

Alan probably had a new best friend by now. Although he was just as small and bad at games as Ben was, Alan was smart. He could make people like him. He could tell jokes, and he knew all sorts of interesting facts, even if he did make half of them up. Necessity had taught him to survive as a newcomer in countless different schools, playgrounds and neighbourhoods. He was a survivor and had learned to adapt. Ben was not his first friend and would not be his last.

For Ben it was different; he had always been a loner. He preferred his own company, or that of adults like his mother, to other children. Before Alan he'd never had a friend, and he hadn't felt the lack. Alan had changed everything. Alan had taught him the meaning of loneliness.

No more. Ben stared at the pond, imagining cool water rushing to fill his nose and mouth. Then he shuddered and stepped back. He hated getting water up his nose. That was why he hadn't learned to dive, and why he would swim only in his own way, head up like a dog.

Drowning would be hard since he knew how to swim. He wondered how long it would take, and if he would be able to keep his head down once he felt the water up his nose. Maybe he should try to hit his head on something, to knock himself out first so he would drown without noticing.

It was easier to think of himself as dead than it was to imagine how he would do it. He liked thinking of his mother's distress, the tears running down her face as she sobbed his name and blamed herself.

But then Angus would put his arms round her. Even in Ben's fantasies he couldn't have his mother alone! Horrible Angus Purdy – even his name smelled – was always there.

He would tell her that Ben had had an accident, but that it wasn't her fault and she mustn't cry. He would comfort her, and they would go into the bedroom and close the door, and she would soon forget all about Ben. Angus would make her forget. She would be glad to have Angus to love.

Ben realized he was grinding his teeth. She had to know. She had to realize that Angus was to blame. Ben's death must make her hate Angus and send him away. He would have to leave a note and tell her why he was killing himself – he would tell her it was because of Angus; tell her that if she told Angus to go away and leave them alone he would –

But what could he do if he was dead? What good would it do him? What would it matter?

He didn't really want to die, he just wanted things to be different.

He wished he knew where people went after they died. He had been told about Heaven by his grandparents – and Hell – but he didn't really believe in those places. His mother had told him once that people who died were born again, years later, in new bodies in this world; but another time she had told him that death was like going to sleep for ever. Neither of those things sounded too bad – at least they would be a change, an end to this lonely life.

Before he met Alan, Ben had not been lonely. For long before he had known Alan, for all his life, there had been Gabriel.

Gabriel was always there, an intangible presence, his closest friend, his other self. No one but Ben knew about Gabriel, but he was real all the same.

Usually Ben was aware of Gabriel's presence in a kind of passive way, as if Gabriel was very near but sleeping. Then there were the times when Gabriel woke up.

It happened most often when Ben was drawing. Sometimes Gabriel took over his hand, to draw what *he* wanted, and Ben was usually happy to let him. Occasionally, whether or not he had a pencil in his hand, thoughts would come into Ben's head which he recognized as Gabriel's because he didn't always understand them. Certain places, people or things would prick his attention unexpectedly, and like a dog catching a scent he would be alert, ready for something that never happened.

At night when Ben lay in bed, not quite asleep, images filled his mind, vivid and alive, a mixture of dream and life, wish and memory. Gabriel told him stories about his life, and Gabriel – a grown-up man, an artist – had the freedom and adventure that Ben longed for. Sometimes the dream-memories were enough, but at other times a powerful frustration built up in Ben, a breathless, hot, trapped feeling which forced him to try to escape.

Lying in bed he would struggle to rise and then he would feel a sudden loosening and know he had succeeded: he could slip out of Ben's body as easily as he could get out of bed.

He would rise into the air, feeling the most delicious freedom, and from the ceiling he would look down at the little boy far below before continuing up through the now-insubstantial roof and out into the night.

He was free, then. He could go wherever in the world he wanted, unconstrained by time, matter or distance. Sometimes he had adventures in far-flung parts of the earth, but most of the time he remained in the familiar confines of the French Quarter, drifting along the streets he walked by day, looking for something, although he didn't know what.

That was wonderful, a secret life he never told even his mother about.

But sometimes in waking life, when Ben felt Gabriel hovering near, the frustration would build up again because he couldn't do or say what he was thinking, the things Gabriel was telling him about. Then it would spill out into a violent rage, and Ben would go away somewhere, and Gabriel would do things over which Ben had no control, of which Ben had no memory.

Ben remembered the last explosion. It had happened more than a year ago, several months before Alan came. He couldn't remember what exactly had happened, or why, but there was broken glass on the floor and his hands were bloody and sore. His mother was standing over him, her terror changing into anger as he tried to tell her that it wasn't his fault, he hadn't done it, it had been Gabriel.

She had swatted him hard on the hip. 'Stop that! You can't get out of it that way any more. I don't mind your games, but you're not a baby now. You know the difference between right and wrong, and you should know the difference between make-believe and real life. Just look around! There's no one else in this room and there never was. *You* did it. Not me, and not some imaginary friend, but you.'

'Gabriel is real!'

'No.' She seized his cut hands, making him cry out. 'That's right, *you* feel it, don't you? Not Gabriel. There is no Gabriel, not any more. These are *your* hands, *your* blood. You did it to yourself. You. Gabriel is *you*.'

It was true that Gabriel had no body of his own, that he was not like anyone else, that no one but Ben could see him, but he was real. Ben had never doubted it before: he knew what Gabriel looked like, what he felt like when he was near (and the difference when he was away), what his voice sounded like. But for the first time his mother's insistence made him doubt what he knew.

And a few months later Ben met Alan, and as he had less time alone, Gabriel slipped into the back of his mind, into the past, like a game he had outgrown.

Was it possible that Gabriel had never been real? Had he only been make-believe, as his mother said? If that was so, then Ben knew there was no point in wishing for him back. But if he was real . . .

More and more as the boring summer days dragged on without Alan, without anything to do, Ben found himself thinking about Gabriel trying to remember everything he'd known about him in an attempt to find him again and bring him back.

Where had Gabriel gone? Maybe he was sulking. Ben thought he might have hurt Gabriel's feelings by forgetting about him for so long while Alan was his friend. He understood, and longed for a chance to make things up to Gabriel. If only he would come back. If only he could find him.

In the past, drawing pictures had brought Gabriel close to him, and there was one subject which unquestionably belonged to Gabriel and which, through Ben's fingers, he had drawn again and again: the portrait of Dinah.

That very morning Ben had taken his sketch pad – one of the real, high-quality artist's pads he received every Christmas – and sat cross-legged on the end of his bed, pencil in hand, gazing up at the painting on the wall. A fragmentary recollection drifted through his mind of what it had been like to hold a brush in his hand, to smell the oils and turpentine, and his heart pounded with hope.

The blank page glared at him, worse than a test at school. His hand was uncertain, his movements clumsy, and he marred the page again and again. The fluid contours of her body, the features of her face were distorted beneath his hands, a series of awkward, laboured lines. Where was Gabriel? Why didn't he take the pencil away and do it right?

He started again and again. The outline grew darker as he despaired. He couldn't do it. He could draw only the copy of a copy of the real thing.

With a grimace of anger, Ben hurled the sketch pad across the room. Its edge clipped the head of a plastic robot, which cluttered noisily to the floor.

'Ben? Is that you?'

The door opened and his mother frowned in at him. 'I didn't know you were still here,' she said. She walked across the room and gave the curtains a straightening tug. 'Why don't you go outside and play? It's a beautiful day.'

'There's nobody to play with.'

'Don't be silly. Go outside and look for somebody.'

'Do you have to work today?'

'I do tonight, but not until after you've had your dinner. Mrs Pym will come over.'

He made a face, but his mother was looking out of the

window and didn't notice. 'Go on, Ben,' she said. 'Don't waste the day. You'll be sorry when school starts if you haven't done anything.'

'It's too hot to go out. Why don't we play a game?'

'I don't have time.' She turned away from the window, suddenly brisk. 'Come on, Ben, I mean it. You've been moping around the house long enough. I know you miss Alan, but you're only making things worse for yourself. There must be something you can do – you used to get along perfectly well by yourself. I wish I had signed you up for day-camp . . . if I'd known Alan wouldn't be here . . .'

'I hate day-camp!'

'How do you know? You've never been to one. It would probably be good for you. At least you'd be out in the fresh air, getting exercise, instead of sitting around here all day. It might not be too late to sign you up for the second session.'

He knew he would hate it. He would be out of place, despised and tormented by the other children. His mouth was dry at the very thought. She could do it, too – she could send him away without a second thought. And it wouldn't do any good to argue. The mood she was in, he knew she would call it whining and get mad. But she hadn't done anything yet. Maybe she would forget, leave it until it was too late. He'd better distract her. He hopped off the bed and tried to look cheerful.

'Want me to wash the windows?'

She smiled but looked vexed. 'I don't want you to do any housework, thank you. I want you to enjoy yourself. Isn't there something you'd like to do?'

'Uh . . . could we go to the beach?'

She sighed. 'Oh, I didn't mean with me, honey. I meant something you could do by yourself, or with a friend. Isn't there a movie you'd like to see? I could give you money for a ticket.'

His heart sank. He knew what that meant. She just wanted to get him out of the house. She didn't care about fresh air, exercise, or what he would enjoy – she just wanted him out of the way. That meant Angus was coming over. Angus was always offering him money for the movies, and she'd picked up the habit from him. Didn't they realize how few movies there were which children were allowed in to? He and Alan used to sneak in sometimes, but he wasn't interested in doing that on his own, and he'd probably seen every movie worth seeing that was on in the area.

But obviously she was going to make sure he went out whether he liked it or not. So he might as well get some money out of it.

'I think there might be a movie I could see . . . and can I get a hamburger afterwards, and some ice cream?'

Her relief was obvious in the way she moved. She doesn't care, he thought, stuffing dollar bills into his pocket and suffering himself to be hugged. She wouldn't care if I disappeared, just like Gabriel.

Because he was thinking of Gabriel, when he left home Ben let his feet take him where they would, not bothering about direction. It was no great surprise to find himself eventually on Decatur Street, gazing up at the narrow ironwork balcony and curtained window behind which, he knew, Gabriel had once lived.

It was an upstairs apartment in the middle of a block of row houses dating back nearly 150 years. The white plaster front of the houses was beginning to chip slightly, but the black doors and shutters gleamed as if recently painted.

Ben went on staring up at the balcony, waiting for the familiar tug at his attention which meant Gabriel, but nothing happened. He had looked at the window so many times, although not recently. He had once made a habit of walking past the house no matter where he was headed – it was a kind of secret with himself, a way of saying hello to Gabriel.

Then he thought of something that made his heart beat faster. Was Gabriel *here* – was Gabriel here *now?* This was where he had lived once, long before Ben was born. It was the place he thought of as home, the place he had shown Ben more than once during his night-time visits. Ben didn't even have to close his eyes to see every detail of the two-room apartment, for his memory of Gabriel's stories remained vivid.

The walls were white, and the only decorations on them were Gabriel's own unframed canvases. The room with the balcony was the bedroom, furnished only with a mattress and a stereo, the speakers of which, on either side of the mattress, served as bedside tables, supporting two mismatched lamps, one yellow and one white. Placed to catch the best light from the window was an easel, and a metal folding table held paints, brushes and other working clutter: the room always smelled of paints despite the large window and electric fan.

The other room, the living room, had one cluttered corner which was the kitchen, and another which held Gabriel's large wooden drawing table and adjustable chair. The rest of the furniture was an eclectic, elderly jumble including, most prominently, a green velvet *chaise-longue* with one leg replaced by a fat volume of the *Reader's Digest Condensed Books,* and a glass-fronted wooden bookcase which Gabriel had sanded down, stained and varnished himself.

Ben's heart was pounding almost painfully hard. He could see it so clearly. Of course, where else would Gabriel have gone? Where else could he possibly be? Why had it taken him so long to figure it out?

He hurried down the street to the end of the block where a door in the wall led into a central patio shared by all the houses in the row. The only entrance to the upstairs apartment where Gabriel had lived was at the back, at the top of a wooden staircase.

The door was unlocked, so Ben went through, and then stopped short, disturbed because it wasn't what he expected. Instead of cracked pavement, weeds and a lot of garbage cans he found the patio full of glossy, luxuriant greens: date palms, banana trees, bamboo and closely cropped grass, with a smooth concrete path running round the edge. It was all changed, and for a moment Ben wondered if Gabriel would be equally changed. Maybe Gabriel wouldn't even remember him.

There were the stairs, and there the back door. Ben drew a difficult, shaky breath, grasped the wooden railing and began to climb slowly. The steps seemed firm beneath his feet, but he kept his eyes fixed on the door ahead, trying to ignore the fearful flashes at the edge of his mind, the sense of falling that threatened to overwhelm him whenever he went too high. He knew the ground wasn't far away but, because the steps were open, not safely enclosed in a building, he felt he was climbing into the air, and he didn't like to think about that.

Almost as soon as he knocked, the door opened. A man wearing faded cut-off jeans and rubber sandals stood there. He had blond curly hair and a darker moustache, and a smile which vanished as he saw Ben.

'Yeah? What do you want?'

'I'm looking for Gabriel. Doesn't he live here?'

But hope had already died. The door swung wide, revealing the interior. Ben saw pale grey walls, and a floor covered in black and white tiles. The furniture was all very modern, in black and white, plastic or aluminium. Gabriel didn't live there; he wouldn't.

'Never heard of him.'

Leaving, Ben tried to forget that black and white room, but it was real and it stayed with him. The other room, the peacock feathers, glass-fronted bookcase and three-legged *chaise-longue* faded into dreams until they were gone, like Gabriel. Had he made it all up? Had there ever been an apartment like that? Had he ever really known Gabriel?

He wanted to go home, to curl up in the comfort of his own room, or in front of the television. But he couldn't. Angus would be there, and he left no place for Ben.

With no real plan in mind, Ben caught the streetcar and let it carry him away. He loved the streetcar: its rattling, swaying motion; the comforting fact that it held always to the same course, stuck on a track. There could be no unpleasant surprises; everything was always the same.

Usually he liked to watch the city passing by the window like his own private movie, but today misery, loneliness and self-pity locked him inside himself. He rested his hot cheek against the glass and stared at the seat in front of him, imagining death and revenge. They'd be sorry, all of them. He'd find Gabriel, and then . . .

In Audubon Park the scent of water drew him, the urge for coolness, and it was there, staring at the water and thinking what a blessing it would be against his skin on this hot day, that he began to think of suicide.

They would be sorry, but it would be too late. He thought of wading out and sinking. Maybe he could tie stones to his feet, to make certain he couldn't struggle to the surface.

Why shouldn't he kill himself? What was there to live for? Even Gabriel didn't care. Alan had left him, his mother had Angus, and Gabriel was nothing but a dream. He closed his eyes, seeing the black and white room of a stranger.

Oh, Gabriel. With all his heart, Ben called to Gabriel, prayed to him to answer, to give some sign that he was real, that he cared, that Ben should go on living.

He heard footsteps behind him and tensed, defensively, expecting trouble. He turned round, ready to run if he had to.

But it wasn't another kid. It was a woman. Ben stared, not quite believing. Then she came closer, and he knew. She was older now, her hair was shorter, her face not so soft and vulnerable, but he recognized her through the superficial changes. He had stared at that face and tried to sketch it too many times to be mistaken. He felt new hope as the emptiness inside him began to fill. Gabriel had given him a sign.

'Dinah,' he said, and stepped towards her.

chapter four

He couldn't have said what I heard. He was probably foreign, saying hello in Hungarian or begging spare change in Greek. He couldn't possibly have known my name. He had not said 'Gabriel.'

Lying on the hotel bed, soaked with sweat and shivering in the air-conditioned room, safely locked in, I could still see those brilliant blue eyes – Gabriel's eyes – and hear him say my name. No mistake. I was terrified.

Desperate for contact with someone who knew me, someone who would tell me I wasn't crazy, I tried to telephone Polly. But she was still away on her honeymoon. I listened to the telephone ring and ring inside her house in far-away Chicago.

Why was I here? New Orleans had been a mistake, both times. New Orleans was bad for me. But I hadn't even unpacked yet. I could check out, call a taxi, go to the airport and catch the first plane back –

Back to what?

No job, no apartment, and no excuse for Mr O.

I could run away, disappear, go somewhere else – anywhere else – and start afresh: Albuquerque, Houston, Los Angeles, New York. It didn't matter; I would be a stranger wherever I went.

One hand clutched the edge of the mattress and gripped tight, to reassure me I was not falling. I was dizzy because of the heat, the shock, and the fact that I'd had nothing to eat all day. I was lying on my back on a bed in a hotel room and I was perfectly safe. The room was not spinning and I had not moved.

But who would catch me if I fell?

How old was I – four? five? – when I learned that the earth was a ball whirling in space and that gravity kept us on it? I asked my father what would happen if the gravity stopped.

'It won't stop,' he said.

But if the gravity wears out? If it doesn't work any more? If it gets turned off?

It won't wear out; it won't stop working; it can't be turned off.

Gently, carefully, using simple words and analogies, he tried to explain, but the worry continued to plague me.

But if it does, if it wears out just on me, if it stops for me, wouldn't I fall off? I remember, clearly, how I saw it: myself flying up in the air, out of control, then spinning away, past the clouds, out into the empty dark, beneath me my parents, everyone, everything shrinking in the distance until our house looked like a piece in a Monopoly game.

My father knew the limits of logic. Reason wasn't enough at such a moment.

'I won't let you fall,' he promised. 'I'll hold on to you.'

I wanted that promise renewed. I wanted someone close to me, holding me. Of course I knew it didn't matter what anyone said. I wasn't a child, and I knew that lovers died or went away, and even fathers changed their minds. You could only save yourself. Still, I would have given a lot for someone to say that to me, meaning it, just then.

I sat up, reaching for the phone book. It opened, as if of its own accord, to the *N*s, and there she was:

Neal, S. Emmet.

Still here, although at a new address, still single and styling herself S. Emmet Neal to conceal from strangers the fact that she was a woman alone.

Semmet, Gabriel called her sometimes, teasing. Semmet, or Sem-Met, Goddess-Queen of ancient Egypt. She claimed to remember a past life in Egypt, a time when she and Gabriel had first been together. I could see her so vividly, striking an Egyptian pose, looking the part with her darkly outlined eyes and full lips.

Sallie. I was shaking, my stomach churning with longing, regret and hatred at the mere thought of her. I pushed the directory away. No, I couldn't call her. I wouldn't break the ten-year silence. I didn't want to get involved with Sallie again. I wished I had never known her. And yet she was my last, my only, link with Gabriel.

Sallie was Gabriel's friend. Spiritually, he said, she was his sister. They had been lovers, of course, but only briefly. According to Gabriel, the love they shared had never been passionate, only affectionate. In a past life, in Ancient Egypt, they had been brother and sister. In present New Orleans they were casual lovers but serious friends. Because she was Gabriel's friend, she had to be my friend, too.

But friendship is a matter of choice. Sallie and I were stuck with each other, like sisters. We weren't allowed to be jealous. We were told to love each other. She was the witness to our wedding. From that first moment until the very last she was always there, third party to our marriage.

Loving Gabriel was all we had in common. Under any other circumstances, Sallie and I would not have been friends. For one thing, she was four years older than me which, at eighteen, was a huge difference. Like Polly, Sallie often appeared scatter-brained and helpless, but whereas with Polly it was an affectation covering an acute mind and determined will, in Sallie the confusion went deeper, reflected in every aspect of her life, from the torn and ill-fitting clothes she wore to the men she became involved with: men who beat her, stole from her, lied to her and disappeared; men who couldn't love her as she loved them.

Yet in spite of a life that sometimes seemed a chronicle of pain and bad luck, Sallie remained cheerful and good-natured, always optimistic. It was easy to be annoyed with her, but difficult to dislike her. I was a little in awe of her because she was older and because she coped with things which terrified me. I felt superior sometimes because Gabriel had chosen me, not her, but I was deeply envious of her relationship with him, of the time before I had come to New

Orleans when she had known him. She had something I could never have, memories of a Gabriel I did not know. Jealousy and curiosity drew me to her; sometimes it felt like love.

Physically, Sallie was very different from me: a couple of inches shorter and a good bit heavier, with large, full breasts and wide hips. She was always slightly overweight, complaining about it and embarking on useless diets. I told her she should exercise, but however enthusiastically she might begin, she lacked the self-discipline to continue. Her hair was wild and so dark brown I thought it black except when I saw it next to Gabriel's. Her face she thought marred by a nose too big for beauty, with an almost imperceptible bump in the bridge, but she had wide-set, clear grey eyes, and a beautiful smile.

She wasn't Gabriel's type. He liked cool, slender blondes. He'd been in love with someone like that – someone, said Sallie, who looked very much like me – when she first met him.

It was in a life-drawing class, where Gabriel and Sallie were both students. She had fallen for him immediately, but he didn't notice, having eyes only for one of the models. This model had yielded to Gabriel's determined pursuit to the extent of going out with him twice, but then she had told him that her boyfriend was coming back from Vietnam and she wouldn't be able to see him any more. This revelation took place at the end of a class. All round, the other students were cleaning their brushes, putting things away, preparing to leave, while the model gave Gabriel a quick, dismissive kiss, and left him.

Sallie, aching with sympathy, witnessed it all. She hovered by the door, unable to approach Gabriel, yet equally unable to leave with the others while he still remained.

But Gabriel appeared to be in no hurry. He made no effort to clean his brushes or put things away, but simply stood gazing at the painting on his easel, as if considering how best to finish the portrait of the woman who had rejected him. Finally he reached for a brush, then set it down. His hand next closed upon the jelly jar with a quarter-inch of turpentine at the bottom. As he stood there with the jar in his hand, still staring at the painting, he began to shake.

Suddenly he swung his fist at the painted face. And in his fist was the jar, which broke as he punched his hand through the canvas. He made no sound, even when the blood spurted and poured down his arm. It was Sallie who screamed, and Sallie who ran for help.

Afterwards, after the emergency room and the stitches, Gabriel let Sallie take him home with her, let her tend his hand and try to mend his heart. He stayed with her no longer than most of her lovers did, but perhaps he was kinder than most. At any rate, she accepted his interpretation of their relationship, became his loving sister, and undertook to love me, too.

If she hadn't been so accepting, so damned easy, Gabriel might still be alive.

I had spent the last ten years not thinking about Sallie, but now I had to admit it was she, far more than Gabriel, I had to confront in New Orleans. I had always blamed Sallie for Gabriel's death, but if she was to blame, so was I. She knew from experience how violent and self-destructive his anger could be, but I also knew about his jealousy.

During our marriage I never gave Gabriel cause for jealousy. I didn't flirt with other men – I scarcely even saw them. If I was sometimes jealous of Sallie, and the other, unknown, women in his past, that feeling was almost a luxury, or a game. His attention and his interest were focused on me so absolutely that I knew there could be no room for anyone else.

We had been married less than a year, but it seemed like a lifetime. For me it *was* a lifetime – my whole adult life. When I met Gabriel I broke with my past, my parents, my friends, my home, everything I'd ever known. I was no longer my father's daughter, no longer a schoolgirl. I was Gabriel's wife. I was a grown-up, with a job as a cocktail waitress and grown-up concerns like money and sex.

Gabriel had a two-room apartment in the Quarter. I moved in and, accepting it as uncritically as I accepted Gabriel, made no attempt to change it in any way. Anyhow, we never had money to spend on inessentials like furniture, and the only visitor was Sallie. When Gabriel and I were there together all we needed was the mattress on the floor and the stereo. We spent most of our time making love, talking or listening to records. And we cooked for each other, another act of love. Our tastes, like our culinary skills, were pretty basic. Red beans and rice, biscuits and gravy, chilli, scrambled eggs, sandwiches, tuna casseroles made with potato chips and cream of mushroom soup. We drank cold beer, munched corn chips and watched the late movie on a little black-and-white television set, or smoked dope and listened to Jefferson Airplane, Jeff Beck and the Beatles. There was no one to tell us what to do. I worked five, sometimes six, days a week, but the waitresses were always swapping around, so my hours were changeable. Gabriel set up his easel in Jackson Square some days and made money from the tourists, and other times he would fill in for acquaintances, bartending. We had everything we needed. When we were together in our apartment, the world outside ceased to exist. It didn't matter what time it was, or even what city we were in. We wanted nothing and no one else.

But there was always Sallie. Sometimes she would vanish for days or weeks at a time, absorbed by some new man, but she would always turn up again, usually wanting comfort.

One night, or maybe it was morning, Gabriel and I were at home. He was lying on the *chaise-longue* reading a science fiction novel, and I was sewing something at my hand-operated Singer. Jeff Beck was playing, and in another hour or two, I knew, we would go to bed. Then Sallie was at the door. She was crying – I knew that even before I saw her. I hugged her and then tried not to recoil, for she smelled strongly of sweat and sex. Gabriel fetched her a beer from the refrigerator, and after drinking half of it she calmed down and told us what had happened. She had been in bed with her new man, at his house, when the police had come and arrested him.

'Drugs?' asked Gabriel.

Sallie shook her head. 'Bad cheques. But I was so scared they'd search the place, and take me in, too. I had – I have some acid in my purse, you see!' She cried a little more, in relief at her own escape and regret for the fate of her boyfriend. After a while, she went to the bathroom. She was gone a long time, so I went to check. I found her lying in the middle of our bed, under the sheet, sound asleep.

Gabriel thought it would be unkind to wake her, so we shared the bed with her, one of us on either side. I couldn't get comfortable, and lay awake for hours. Gabriel and I nearly always made love when we went to bed together – now, because of Sallie's presence, we couldn't even talk or cuddle. I had never shared a bed with anyone but Gabriel, and the heavy, warm, sleeping mass of Sallie beside me made it impossible for me to relax. Finally, hearing from Gabriel's breathing that he, like Sallie, was asleep, I fell into restless dreams.

None of us talked about it afterwards – although Sallie seemed embarrassed in the morning. It was just something that had happened, I thought. But it was after that night that Gabriel started talking more pressingly about LSD.

The thought of drugs – even marijuana, which Gabriel had taught me to smoke – always made me nervous. It wasn't so much the illegality as other dangers which haunted me. The thought of being out of control. The fear of things changing. I'd heard a lot of scare stories about LSD, and even Gabriel, promoting its wonders to me, admitted he'd had one very bad trip. I couldn't believe that the experience could be worth the risk. But my fears didn't count for much. I could never hold out against Gabriel when he set his heart on something. I agreed: we would drop acid together. We would see visions. We would be closer than ever. Gabriel was worth the risk, to me.

I could feel the tension in him, humming through his bones like electricity, when he told me that Sallie had scored some acid. I thought he was remembering his bad trip, afraid it would happen again, and somehow his nervousness cancelled out my own. If he needed me to be strong and certain, I would be. I would protect him. I wasn't afraid.

On our way over to Sallie's we stopped at a grocery store and bought provisions: bags of tortilla chips, potato chips, cartons of dip, chocolate chip cookies, candy bars, six-packs of beer, crackers, cheese, bananas, apples and grapes, everything that appealed to us until all our cash was gone. It was a muggy, overcast afternoon. Gabriel sang 'Follow the Yellow Brick Road' and 'Lucy in the Sky with Diamonds', and we giggled conspiratorially whenever our eyes met. I hugged my sack of junk food as if I were hugging Gabriel.

Sallie lived in a modern high-rise building not far from the Quarter. As we waited to cross the street, I looked across at it and tried, as always, to pick out her window. This time it was easy, for one of her brilliant, tie-dyed caftans hung limply to dry on her balcony.

She was wearing another caftan, her usual musky perfume, and nothing else. She greeted me with a big hug, ignoring Gabriel who edged past us to put the beer in the refrigerator.

'Oh, God,' she said. 'I'm so excited. Aren't you? It's almost like it's *my* first time to drop, only better, because I'm not scared. I'm so happy for you, Dinah. God, you're going to love it, I just know. We won't let anything bad happen, so you don't have to be scared at all.'

It was only then that I realized that Sallie was coming along on our trip. I should have known, I should have guessed, but I hadn't. I felt like crying.

Gabriel came out of the kitchen with an open can of beer in one hand, and a wary look on his face. He looked ready to fight.

I couldn't say anything. If I said what I was thinking, Gabriel would be angry, Sallie would be hurt, and I would be in the wrong. I would spoil this day for all of us, and in the end, faced with Gabriel's disappointment, I would give in. I told myself that maybe it was better this way. Sallie had had more experience with drugs than Gabriel. If something started going wrong she would probably know better than I how to cope.

'You got the stuff, Sallie?' Gabriel asked. 'Are you girls ready? What are we waiting for?'

'I want Dinah to be comfortable,' Sallie said. 'That's all. It's her first time, after all! We'll sit down and have a beer and listen to music. You don't have to be nervous,' she said to me. 'Just relax, and let it come on. It might take a little while. What record do you want first?'

' "Nights in White Satin",' I said, and felt approved of when Gabriel went to put the record on. I looked around at the rather empty apartment. I had never spent much time here, and neither, I thought, did Sallie. The white walls were still bare of decoration although she had lived there for nearly six months, and her only furniture besides the stereo was a folding table and two folding chairs. There were a lot of cushions on the green shag carpet, though, so I sat on one of those.

Gabriel settled on to a nearby cushion. I saw that he had his sketch pad.

'Are you going to draw?' I asked.

He shrugged. 'I might. Sometimes there are things you can't put into words . . . they don't always look so good when you come down, but maybe sometimes . . .' he laughed. 'Once I drew a picture of the inside of my brain. It was a sort of diagram. It seemed really important when I did it, but later . . .'

'I tried to paint the face of God once,' Sallie said. 'You know what I'd really like? Finger paints. They're so sensual, and it doesn't matter if the pictures don't look like anything – it's probably better if they don't. Hey, do you think I should go out and buy some? It wouldn't take me long to run down to the dime store.'

'Yes, do,' I said. Anything to get her out.

But Gabriel said no. He said to Sallie, 'Don't go.'

We sipped our beer and talked. We listened to music. We waited. Gabriel held my hand, toying with the fingers, tracing secret messages on the palm and the inside of my wrist. I moved closer so that I could kiss him. Our kisses, at first rather perfunctory, grew more passionate. I was quickly aroused, as always, and I didn't try to stop him when he began to caress my breasts. I couldn't forget Sallie's presence, but maybe, if we ignored her, she would go into the other room. I kissed Gabriel open-mouthed, I pressed against him and strained to meet his caresses.

It took me a little while to realize that not all the hands I felt belonged to Gabriel. Sallie's lips were on my neck, and then her breath was hot in my ear as she squeezed my breasts. I opened my eyes. Gabriel was watching me.

'It's all right,' he said to the question in my eyes. 'It's all right. Just relax, go with it. It'll be good.' I let myself believe him because it was the easiest thing to do.

I wasn't sure what was really happening, anyway, what was real and what fantasy. Something had changed, either in me or around me. We kissed and hugged a little longer, until Gabriel said we should take our clothes off.

The mood changed as Sallie undressed me and we undressed Gabriel. I thought it was like playing with dolls, and as we struggled to undo his jeans, our fingers colliding, we began to giggle like children.

But Gabriel was serious. He was the teacher, he was the parent. He looked from me to Sallie and back again, touching our breasts, our hips, our faces. 'Kiss each other,' he said.

Sallie and I bit back smiles and stared owlishly at each other. It was like being in school, being afraid to laugh. We did what he said. We kissed each other, on the mouth, but like children, without passion.

'Not like that,' he said. 'Like lovers. Like you kiss me. Like this.'

He held my head in his hands and brought his mouth to mine, opening my lips with his tongue and probing deeply, slowly. He kissed me until I felt something melt inside, until I was breathless. When he pulled away, I could still feel the kiss. I could feel him kissing me as I watched him kiss Sallie. I knew the feeling of his tongue in her mouth.

She's the same as me, I thought. I imitated Gabriel and kissed her, slowly and carefully, and I wondered if this was how it felt to Gabriel, kissing me.

Everything we did was to please him. He told us how and where to touch each other. We were making love to him through each other. It was a game, not serious, and I did it for him. When he did things to Sallie, I knew it was still me he was loving. I wasn't jealous. This was just another fantasy, another bed-game. Even as I held her, and felt him thrusting into her, not me, and heard his soft, orgasmic moan, I knew it was for me. Although that sound – so private, *mine*, I'd always thought – gave me a pang, I conquered it, and kissed Sallie as if I were Gabriel. I was Gabriel. She was Gabriel. We were all the same.

After Gabriel fell away, sated, Sallie and I went on touching and kissing each other, lying on the floor in each other's arms. I hadn't come yet, and didn't know if I would be able to. I still thought Sallie and I were performing for Gabriel, but for the moment, without his direction, we could set our own pace and find our own rhythms.

It was different. Not better or worse, but different from any sex I'd ever known. Maybe that was the acid, which made everything – the carpet, the hum of the air-conditioning, Sallie's slightly asthmatic breathing – intensely erotic. Everything we did to each other was sexual. It was also, somehow, very private. I didn't have to wonder what she would like – I did what I liked, and so did she. After a while, I couldn't tell where her body began and mine stopped. There were no boundaries. We spoke inside each other's head, in some other language. I didn't know my own name. I forgot about Gabriel.

I don't know what we did, exactly. I don't want to remember. I don't know how long that hot, sensual dream lasted, or what Gabriel saw, or what he thought, or when he left the room, or why. I don't really know why he killed himself, why he threw himself off the balcony. I've always assumed it was in a blind, furious fit of jealousy, because he felt left out, because Sallie and I had turned to each other and didn't notice him. But maybe it wasn't our fault. Maybe I shouldn't blame myself. Maybe it was a mistake. Maybe Gabriel was in another world, just as I was. Maybe it was the LSD. Maybe he thought he could fly.

Even ten years later I found it hard to think about that day. I didn't want to think about it. It was over, and Gabriel was dead. The past would suffocate me if I let it. And the truth, whatever it was, didn't matter. I wasn't responsible for what Gabriel had done, or what he had thought. Even if he had lived, chances were good I wouldn't know him now, I thought. How many brides of eighteen were still married to the same man eleven years later?

Forget the past. I thought about the man I'd met on the plane, focusing for some reason on his mouth, remembering how vulnerable his upper lip had seemed, as if until recently he'd worn a moustache. What was his name? I dug into my purse for the piece of paper he had given me, with his phone number. Max Cullen. Without stopping to reflect, I dialled the number.

'Hi, this is Dinah Whelan – we met on the plane today?'

'Oh, hello!' He sounded surprised but pleased. I was encouraged.

'I – I wondered if I could change my mind,' I said. 'I know I said I wanted to spend this evening getting reacquainted with New Orleans by myself, but actually, thinking about the past has been kind of getting me down and . . . it would be nice to have dinner with you. I mean, I know it's late, and you've probably already made plans and all – I really don't mind – I just thought –'

'Hey,' he said, and his voice was very warm. 'Hold on – you'll talk yourself out of it again, and that would be a shame. I'm glad you called. I haven't made other plans. I'd love to have dinner with you. Where are you, and what kind of food do you like, and what time shall I pick you up?'

Calling Max had been the right decision. He wasn't just company, he was good company, and I liked him. There had been a spark between us at first meeting, and during the course of the evening it developed into something stronger and steadier. I was physically attracted to him, of course, but I also felt at ease with him. After my memories of Gabriel, Max's ordinary niceness positively glowed.

'I was going to bring flowers, but then I thought this would be more useful,' he said. He'd brought me a new street map of New Orleans, and also the name and phone number of someone he knew who had a furnished apartment for rent.

We had a leisurely, elegant meal in a French restaurant. The food was good, and so was the wine, but the approving warmth in his eyes nourished me even more. We talked about ourselves, although less intimately than we had on the plane. We talked about food, and movies, and cities where we had lived. He told me about hitching through Europe; I told him about living rich and poor in Mexico, and made it sound like a romantic adventure and not the disaster it had really been. I didn't tell him about the boy in the park – I was no longer sure there had been such a boy.

We didn't spend the night together. The possibility was there between us when he took me back to my hotel, but neither of us pushed it. I liked that. We would be civilized, and get to know each other, first. And we *would* get to know each other: I would stay in New Orleans, and put the past behind me.

Late that night I heard a baby cry, and I hurried down the corridor in search of it, trying one locked door after another without success. My father watched, cold and disapproving. He knew which room, but would not tell me: suitable punishment for having been so careless as to forget my own baby. I woke on my feet, halfway across the room, naked, hand outstretched for the doorknob.

I went back to bed, wishing I had asked Max to stay. Later, someone scratched at the window. I could not move, but I could see her: a woman with bat-wings and a skull face and long, greedy fingers. When she flew away, she had a small white bundle tucked against her side, something she had stolen from me, and her laughter shivered my soul.

I woke thinking of the boy I had seen in Audubon Park, wondering if I had dreamed him, too. I felt wrecked and hungover, but the first thing I did was to phone the number Max had given me. The apartment turned out to be a luxury flat which tourists rented for a week or a month at a time – beyond my means. Over breakfast in the hotel coffee shop I scanned newspaper ads, concentrating firmly on the present. After Chicago, prices didn't look too bad, although things had changed since the days in which Decatur Street was a haven for hippies, young artists and other members of the nouveau poor – it was full of desirable residences now.

Back in my room I made a few more phone calls, and went out to look at a possible-sounding apartment on Esplanade. It was on the wrong side of Rampart, which meant I'd have a longish walk to work in the business district every day, but I didn't mind walking. I wouldn't have to battle snow and freezing temperatures in the winter, and by next summer perhaps I would have a car.

The apartment was in an old house, built in the usual tall, porched Louisiana style. It had once been blue or grey, but there wasn't much paint left on the weather-beaten boards, and the porch railing looked as if it would crumble under pressure. The steps, at least, were new, which seemed a sign that the owners might be making repairs, as did the varnished front door and shiny new knocker.

A woman I guessed to be about my own age, blue-jeaned, T-shirted and barefoot, with long brown hair pulled back in a ponytail, answered the door. Her round face blossomed in a smile. 'Hi! Dinah, right?'

'Right.'

'I'm Morgan.' She shook my hand powerfully and beckoned me inside. 'I hope you don't mind stairs, because the one for rent is right at the top.'

'I don't mind.'

'The first person who came was a little old lady. She took one look, and that's all she wrote.' Morgan laughed. She had an odd accent, one I had forgotten but now recognized. It sounded like Brooklynese, but it was pure New Orleans.

'Do you own the house?' I asked.

'It belongs to my husband's aunt. She won't live in it – thinks the neighbourhood's gone downhill – but she doesn't want to sell. She lets us live on the first floor for free, as long as we take care of the place and rent out the others.'

Morgan was panting slightly as we reached the top of the stairs, but still talking. 'It's furnished, but if you want to get some of your own stuff, that's fine. Just tell me if you don't want anything. If nobody else wants to take it we can always put it under the house. There's nothing wrong with the furniture, but it's all pretty old and beat-up.'

'Sounds like every other apartment I've ever lived in.'

'Yeah, I've never bought anything new,' Morgan said, sounding proud of it. She dug into her pocket for the key.

From the first sight I liked it better than my old place in Chicago. It looked cleaner, for one thing. The walls were white, the woodwork dark blue, the curtains on the two windows blue and white chintz. The furniture was basic and unobjectionable: a foam couch covered in navy blue corduroy, a round wooden table and four cane-bottomed straight chairs, an elderly green armchair and a couple of rickety occasional tables, on one of which rested a small television set.

'You can re-paint if you want, as long as you let us OK the colours,' Morgan said. 'We had a tenant once who painted her kitchen a horrible reddish orange. You can't imagine. Going in there was like being inside a stomach. It was so oppressive. It took four coats of paint to cover it.'

I laughed. 'I like blue and white.'

'Then you'll like the bedroom.'

I followed her through one of the two doorways in the far wall. It opened on to a reasonably sized room, the walls pale blue, the window offering the same view of the street I'd glimpsed from the living room. There was a double bed – stained, grey-striped mattress on a plain metal frame – another rickety little table beside it bearing a china lamp, a solid chest of drawers, and a big old-fashioned wardrobe of dark varnished wood beside a closed door.

Opening it, I was surprised to see a bathroom instead of a closet.

'That's the drawback,' said Morgan.

'What's wrong with it?'

'I mean, the only way into the bathroom is through the bedroom. Also, no closets.'

'That's OK. I live alone. I'll take it.'

'Don't you even want to see the kitchen?'

'You think that will change my mind?' But I felt embarrassed, and annoyed with myself for doing exactly what I had done in Chicago: why did I have to take the first affordable place I saw? I was still rushing at important decisions without stopping to think.

Following Morgan back into the living room and through the other door, I considered making a joke of it, telling Morgan that the kitchen wasn't big enough and I'd have to think about it. But why should I spend more time looking at apartments just to prove a point to myself? I could do a lot worse than live here.

The kitchen was white with yellow trim, stuffed with a huge refrigerator, a narrow and ancient gas range, a table with a mottled yellow formica top and two wooden chairs. I squeezed past the table to look out of the window, but the view wasn't worth the effort: the grey plank side of the house next door and, very far below, a strip of grass.

'There's some stuff in the cupboards,' said Morgan, opening them. 'Pots and pans, plastic dishes. And a wok. We got two as wedding presents, so I put the other one in here. If you don't want it, just say. Same goes for everything else. You probably have your own kitchen stuff.'

'No, I don't. I moved down from Chicago, and I didn't have a lot of space for things like that. I figured I could buy what I needed, but all this will help.'

I told myself that I could look all over New Orleans without finding another apartment furnished even to kitchen utensils, and made the decision. 'When can I move in? Tomorrow?'

'You could move in today,' Morgan said. 'If you don't mind signing a six-month lease and giving me a month's rent for deposit.'

Reckless again, I said, 'I don't mind signing a year's lease. I'm here to stay.'

I spent the next few hours shopping in Maison Blanche and the other department stores along Canal Street until – bulkily if not heavily laden with necessities – I had to take a cab back to the hotel.

There I had a much-needed shower and reflected ruefully on the fact that in this three-shower-a-day climate I had just rented an apartment equipped only with a bathtub. Just as I had finished dressing the telephone rang.

It was Max, just wondering how my day had gone.

'One major goal accomplished,' I said. 'I found an apartment.'

'Hey, that's great! When do you move in?'

'Anytime I want. It's mine.'

'How about two hours from now? I'll come get you.'

'Oh, Max, you don't have to –'

'I know I don't have to. I want to. I'm going to. You get to say when.'

It would have been ungracious to refuse. 'That's very nice of you.'

'Not at all. Y'all have heard of South-run hospitality?'

I laughed, because he meant me to. 'OK, Aunt Jemima. In front of the hotel at . . . what, six o'clock?'

'Six o'clock it is. And after we've moved you in, I'll take you out to dinner.'

'Oh, no, that's too much. Look, I've got a fully equipped kitchen – everything but food. If you bring steaks or something – the least I can do is cook for you.'

'Is that the least? It sounds like a lot. I'll see you at six.'

Only two hours . . . I decided I wouldn't have time after all to visit the spa. It would have to wait until morning. Although

I wouldn't have admitted it to anyone, I was nervous about my new job, the unaccustomed freedom and responsibility of it. As if I was about to sky-dive for the first time, naturally I delayed the moment when I would have to jump.

Packing took about two minutes. After that I ordered a drink from room service, informed the desk I would be checking out, and stretched on the bed to watch junk television.

When I went outside at six o'clock the streets were damp and smelled of beer, and there was a hot dirty wind that instantly blew away all comfort, all residual coolness from my skin, making me feel sticky and irritable.

A piece of paper blew along the gutter, and the wind caught it up and slapped it against my bare legs. I snatched at it, meaning to crumple and hurl it away, but something about the feel of the paper – heavy, good-quality artist's paper – made me look at it, and the drawing on it caught my attention.

Sketched in soft pencil strokes was a face, a head, the beginnings of a figure. It was unfinished, not quite all *there*, but I recognized it: the artist's style as well as the subject.

'Ready to go?'

So absorbed, I hadn't even noticed the car drive up. Max grinned through the open window and got out. 'What's that you're reading?'

My fingers tightened on the page. I could still deny it, wad it up and throw it away. But then I held it out, curious to know what he would make of it.

'What is it?' he asked.

'What does it look like?'

'A sketch for a portrait. Where'd you get it?'

'Who does it look like? Does it remind you of anybody?' I watched him, waiting for some recognition to appear as he studied the drawing.

But he shrugged. 'Not really. Some girl. A pretty girl with long hair.'

'Me?'

He laughed. 'No, not you. A girl, I said. Some teenager. Why all the questions? Is it somebody you know?'

Did I still imagine myself a long-haired teenager? How embarrassing. 'No,' I said uneasily. 'It just reminded me . . . I found it blowing along the street. It doesn't matter. Let's get going – you shouldn't be parked there.'

The move, including driving time, took only about fifteen minutes. Max raced up those daunting stairs with my heavy bags as if in competition, and would hardly let me lift anything more than my own purse. He was showing off, and the realization made me feel fond but also superior, as if I should pat him on the head and thank him for being such a good boy.

On his last trip upstairs he carried a bottle of champagne. 'Do you have glasses, or do we drink out of the bottle?' He was out of breath and trying not to show it.

'Oh, Max –'

'Don't say I shouldn't have.'

'Of course not. I'm very glad you did.' In one of the kitchen cupboards I found some stocky, heavy-stemmed glasses. As I carried them out I heard the unmistakable, joyous pop of the cork.

Sitting on the corduroy couch, we toasted each other.

'May you be very happy here,' he said.

Raising the glass to my lips, I realized that I was happy, and it was because of Max. I felt comfortable with him, relaxed and safe as if, without even touching him, I was leaning back against his broad chest and feeling his arms around me. And it wasn't only boring safety he gave me. When, at last, he touched me – taking the empty glass from my hand and pulling me close for a kiss – it was more intoxicating than the champagne. I forgot everything else, all doubts and fears and memories, and knew I had come home.

chapter five

The A-Plus Health and Fitness Club was on the roof of an office building in the heart of the business district. It was an unlikely location for a spa, but Mr Opacek had told me that the bank which owned the building had installed a swimming pool and sauna in the penthouse as part of something called the Executive Club. Special perks for executives had vanished in the recession and, when approached by Mr Opacek, the bank had proved eager to sell A-Plus a very long lease on the whole top floor. In return, all the bank's employees had been offered a year's free membership in the club.

I gazed up at the stone and glass of the skyscraper – pretty modest as skyscrapers went these days – as if trying to see the health club. I still felt too nervous to go in and actually start my new job. Marilee had told me I had nothing to worry about. She had given me a lot of advice, but I couldn't recall any of it at that moment. Away from Mr Opacek's belief in me, with no one but myself to impress, I was paralysed.

The club had been open already for two months, serving members of the suburban branches of A-Plus who occasionally found this location more convenient, and some of the bank employees. I imagined secretaries swimming lengths and doing push-ups two days a week to atone for fattening lunches. New Orleans was such a sybaritic city, a place for eating and drinking and all the pleasures of the flesh. Had that changed in ten years? Had the fitness craze reached even New Orleans? Maybe there were enough snowbirds like myself living here now to make a difference, to make my branch of A-Plus a success.

My branch. I clung to the idea. Positive thinking. I *would* make it a success. I found some encouragement in the reflection that it had been running for two months without any manager at all – I couldn't possibly be worse than that. Anything I did would have to look like an improvement.

Time to jump. I pushed through the revolving door into the icy chill of the marble-floored lobby, and took the elevator straight to the top.

The doors opened to reveal an alcove in bright yellow, the A-Plus logo in blue on the wall above a long, high, curving desk. There was a girl sitting behind the desk, while leaning against it, talking to her, was a young man in a blue and yellow jogging suit. He came to attention at the sight of me.

'Yes, ma'am. May we help you?'

His bright, efficient friendliness, his clean-cut, youthful presence, made me feel old and dowdy. He wasn't handsome, but his aura was such that no one would ever notice that. His body was strong and athletic: not beefy enough for football, but sure to be good at five or six other sports. He looked like a college student – almost too good to be true.

'I'm Dinah Whelan,' I said. 'The new manager?' It came out weakly – I found it hard to maintain my confidence in the presence of his.

He didn't stop smiling, but it changed: there was no liking in his eyes. His voice was friendly enough, though, as he said, 'Well, I sure am glad to meet you, Miz Whelan! I'm Richard Potter. Call me Rick.'

Because he thrust out his hand, I shook it, half expecting him to show his strength by squeezing my hand too hard. But that, probably, is something men try only on other men.

'Well, Rick, are you –'

'The acting manager,' he said. 'I'll tell you everything you need to know. You take us by surprise, though – we sure weren't expecting you this morning. I thought you'd call, first.'

'I'm sorry,' I said, on the defensive now, feeling my confidence crumble.

'Oh, that's perfectly all right. Of course you were right to come in just as soon as you could. It's only that we're not really ready for you. My things are still in your desk. But don't worry about it – I'll get them cleared out in a jiffy.'

'Oh, don't. It doesn't matter – there's no hurry – I really didn't mean to put you to any trouble.' I felt as agonized as if he were my boss and I'd done something wrong on the first day.

'It's no trouble. But I'm being rude. I haven't even introduced you to Faith. Dinah Whelan, Faith Leasor. Faith has been helping me out by coming in a few hours a day to answer the phone, show people around, fill out exercise charts and so on. She's invaluable, as I'm sure you'll find.'

He might have meant it or not – impossible to break apart his smooth, charming sincerity to discover how much of it was real.

Faith was easier. She was a pretty little blonde girl, soft curls, pink T-shirt, heavily made-up eyes, and she looked about twelve years old. From the way she gazed at him, it was obvious she thought Rick was God's gift to women.

'I'm glad to meet you, Faith,' I said and, feeling my confidence creeping back, I asked, 'You're working part-time for us? Any chance you might want to make that full-time? We'll probably need some more people, once we really get going.'

A nervous, sideways glance at Rick. 'Uh, I don't think so ... see, I'll be starting college in September, and I really would like to keep working here part-time, if you'll let me. Richard has been really nice, really flexible on hours, which is good for me.'

'I'm sure we can work something out.' I glanced up at Rick. 'If you don't mind, I think I'll have a look around.'

'I'll give you the guided tour.'

'Oh, please, don't go to any trouble –' I stopped, reminding myself that I wasn't an imposition – he was working for me now.

'It's no trouble. As you can see, we're not exactly tripping over clients today.'

'No . . .' I craned round the edge of the alcove to see the empty exercise room. 'Is it always like this?'

'We get a crowd in at lunchtime. Secretaries and people who work in the building, mostly. Then there are some more in the evenings. Well, we haven't had a real launch, so people don't know we're here. I'm sure you'll have plenty of ideas for a grand opening.'

My stomach clenched at this reminder of my responsibility. 'Oh, yes,' I said lightly. 'Lots of ideas. We'll have to talk about them. I'm sure you'll be a big help, knowing New Orleans and the people here . . . my experience was in Chicago.'

'You were managing an A-Plus in Chicago?'

'Not exactly . . . could I . . .' I began moving towards the exercise floor and, as I had hoped, he followed me, the conversation dropped.

The atmosphere in the exercise room was familiar to me; the air even smelled just as it did in the spa Marilee managed. It was a long, broad room carpeted in the dark red, with mirrors on the walls casting bright, glittering reflections of the shiny new exercise machines. There were weighing machines in one corner, and racks of weights with jump-ropes dangling, padded benches and, above all, space – to lie down, to run on the spot, to dance and to do sit-ups. The emptiness of the room glittered and waited to be filled with noisy, perspiring people.

Catching sight of myself in the mirrored wall, I stepped closer. I looked better than I had imagined: calm and in control despite hair that needed combing. I touched it, wondering if it made me look too young and unprofessional the way it fell straight to my shoulders. Maybe I should get it cut and styled.

'I can show you the ladies' room if you want to fix your hair,' he said.

I glanced up, catching his eyes in the mirror, seeing his face before he could mask it. The contempt – or anger? – I saw there jarred me, and it hurt. To him I was probably middle-aged, too old to be attractive. But why should he dislike me?

'Vanity of vanities,' I said, trying for contact, smiling at him. 'No, I'm all right. I don't think I'll scare anybody who comes in – that's the important thing. Tell me, how long have you been working here?'

'Since it opened – just two months.' The easy, practised friendliness was back on his face. I might almost have imagined the other, except that I could still feel the jolt. 'I was working out at the Gentilly branch, and Mr Opacek wanted somebody to look after this place until he found a manager, so I volunteered. I thought it would be good experience for me, and it has been.'

He had hoped, I realized suddenly, to get the job permanently. Of course he resented me. I'd displaced him, taken his power away, stolen his job. I felt guilty and very vulnerable. What right did I have? I hoped he didn't know how little experience I had, afraid that would make him hate me more.

'I hope you'll help me,' I said. 'You must know everything about this place. You must have lots of ideas for improvements. I hope we can work together . . . or were you planning on going back to, where was it?'

'Gentilly. No, I'd like to stay here.'

'Good.'

We smiled falsely at each other, and he said, 'Let me show you your office. I'm sorry it's not ready for you, but like I said . . .'

A plain wooden door at the end of one mirrored wall led into a tiny, over-furnished office. There were two three-drawer filing cabinets of gunmetal grey, a matching desk and two chairs of moulded vinyl. Three of the walls were covered with imitation wood panelling, and the wall beside the door was hidden by a heavy brown- and gold-flecked curtain. Behind the desk there hung a vaguely impressionistic landscape, one of those paintings displayed in their dozens against the iron railings of Jackson Square.

Rick walked in but I hesitated, feeling the hint of claustrophobia. There hardly seemed room in that shoebox of an office for two people.

He looked at me, then grabbed the heavy curtain and

pulled it aside. Curious, I stepped in and saw that it was a window of tinted glass through to the exercise room.

'The mirror?'

He nodded. 'They never know when you're watching. So you can keep an eye on things while you're sitting at your desk. And you can preserve your sanity by keeping the curtain closed when the uglies are out.'

I had a mental image of friendly, smiling Rick sitting snug in this office, sneering at the customers, rating the females on a personal scoresheet and muttering obscene suggestions while they puffed and sweated in innocence. I realized then that I disliked him and didn't want to work with him.

'How about the rest?' I asked.

The locker-rooms and showers were like all other locker-rooms and showers; there was also a room with hairdriers, make-up mirrors and a vending machine selling fruit juice.

'You don't have separate rooms for men and women?'

He shrugged. 'There are two sets of showers . . . unfortunately, you can only get to them by coming through the locker-room. It wasn't planned very well.'

'So what do you – what do *we* do about it?'

'What I've been doing is having Monday, Wednesday and Friday for the ladies; Tuesday, Thursday and Saturday for the men.'

'And Sunday?'

'Sunday we're closed.' He held up a hand to forestall my objection. 'I know. I know. And it's a big day in Gentilly, too. But not here, not in the business district. People aren't going to come in from the suburbs just to work out. They're going to come here because it's close to where they work.'

'What about people who live in the Quarter?'

He shrugged. 'I don't think too many of our clients will . . . I could be wrong. If you think opening on Sunday is a good idea, that's your option, of course. And if you think it would be better to have women and men here on the same day – I'm sure not saying splitting the week is the greatest thing – the locker-room could probably be divided in two, with separate entrances. I don't know what that would cost, but you might want to look into it. It might be worth it in the long run. Let me show you the pool.'

He opened a door marked 'Swimming Pool' and I saw a flight of stairs.

For a moment I was disoriented; then I remembered it was on the roof. Going up, we emerged into heat, bright sunshine and the strong smell of chlorine. But the air was still and seemed stuffy to me – the pool wasn't open to the air as I had imagined, but protected from the elements by walls and a roof of glass. Through it, the sun scorched my bare arms. There were reclining chairs displayed on the white tiles around the pool. The blue water looked slightly murky.

'Filter probably needs changing,' Rick said. 'And it's stuffy up here – the ventilating system should be looked at. Maybe I should make out a list of trouble spots, the current situation, operating procedures – the way I've been doing things. Do you think that would be helpful?'

'That would be very helpful,' I said, feeling a little warmer towards him. It wasn't fair to blame him for imaginary thought-crimes, anyway.

'OK. I'll do that, and I'll clear out my desk – my things – and leave it on your desk tomorrow. Or – I guess you'd like to get settled in your office now?'

'Maybe we could go sit in the office and talk a little more, and you could tell me the things you think I should know. Maybe Faith would like to join us, at least until the lunch bunch comes in. We could have a "getting to know each other" meeting. After all, we're in this together.'

Rick Potter was helpful, but always with a grudging undercurrent. He didn't like me, and knowing that, I found it impossible to like him. But we'd both had plenty of practice being charming, and we were never less than polite. An outsider, listening in, might even have thought we were friends. I thought he would probably start looking for another job, and he'd drop me flat as soon as he found something better. In the mean time, though, he was good at his job and – like it or not – he was helping me. I knew I'd better learn everything I could from him, and as quickly as possible.

Faith was suspicious of me, and I knew why. It was an odd and awkward feeling, being on the other side for the first time. In the past I'd been one of the girls, but now I was the boss, and she might find it perfectly acceptable to lie to me, trick me, laugh at me behind my back. I made an extra effort to reach her, but although she thawed slightly, the barrier remained: I was of another generation and – more daunting – I held all the power in our relationship. But at least she didn't resent me as Rick did, and I could tell she didn't actually dislike me. It would be possible for us to work together amicably even if we couldn't be friends.

Later in the afternoon, when Faith had left, my first customer arrived.

I was sitting in my office, alone and not liking it much. Although I could hear the gentle sound of air from the ceiling vent, I felt the air in the room was still and hot. Panic crept up on me; I was finding it hard to breathe. Feeling ashamed of myself, I gave up and went out to talk to Rick.

He was behind the front desk, leaning forwards on his elbows to talk to a young woman with frizzy brown hair, in a sleeveless yellow dress. He was smiling his famous smile and pouring on the charm. Even from a distance I could practically see his eyes twinkle. They dimmed when I came in sight.

'Oh, here's our manageress,' he said.

The term grated on my ears like an insult. I felt I'd been demoted to something like a waitress.

'I'm the manager,' I said to the girl. 'Dinah Whelan.'

'How do you do? I'm Mary Schroeder.'

'I've just been telling her a little about what we offer,' Rick said. 'Mary is considering joining us.'

'I hope you will,' I said, smiling with all my might at her and ignoring Rick. 'Would you like to come back to my office to discuss terms, or shall I show you around first?'

She gazed at me with slightly protruberant eyes. 'Oh, Rick

has already shown me everything. It looks real nice. Only, I'm not sure I can afford it.'

'Well, we can talk about that in my office, where it will be more private. We do have several types of payment plan, and different categories of membership. We're very flexible here at A-Plus. I'm sure we can come up with something to suit you.' I was imitating Marilee, feeling a sense of relief because this was a part I could slip into without difficulty. Here, at last, was something I understood.

'I thought Rick was the manager,' she said as we walked away.

I looked at her sharply. 'Did he tell you that?'

She shook her head. 'Oh, no. A friend of mine who comes here told me I should talk to Rick Potter, and so I just naturally thought . . . he *seems* like he's the manager.'

'He was in charge for a while,' I said. 'He was acting manager until I arrived.' I put an emphasis on the word 'acting', as if it wasn't very nice – my childish revenge for his 'manageress'.

I spent more than half an hour with Mary Schroeder in my office. She said several times that she would have to think about it, and rose to go, but each time I made her stay. I was determined not to let her get away. I offered her special discounts: the first month, then the first two months, and finally three months absolutely free. And, in the end, she signed.

'Tell your friends,' I said. 'If you sponsor two new members you'll get another month free.'

I felt exhausted when she left, but triumphant. My first tiny success. Maybe I could do something more than show people to their tables and take orders.

Just before five o'clock Max phoned. I recognized his voice at once, and it made me feel warm and pleased. We chatted for a few minutes, renewing contact, and then he asked if he could have dinner with me.

'Oh, I don't think so . . . the spa doesn't close until nine.'

'I don't mind waiting.'

He was too eager, I thought. Although I liked his company

and disliked eating alone, something made me draw back, even if it was belatedly. How involved did I want to be?

'Not tonight,' I said. 'I still haven't finished unpacking. If you remember, somebody distracted me yesterday.'

He laughed, sounding shy. 'Can't I come over and try again? I'll help this time – I'll be good, I promise.'

'But I might not be. No, I want to do it myself.'

'How about tomorrow, then? For dinner?'

'Saturday,' I said, and we agreed on a time and left it at that.

I had already decided not to stay at the spa until closing time – it wasn't necessary, with both Faith and Rick on hand, and I felt restless. I left a few minutes after five, crossing Canal and submerging myself in the French Quarter once again.

It was still hot and sunny, but the streets were wet and there was the ozone tang of freshness in the air which spoke of a brief, hard shower of rain.

Just walking with nowhere in mind to go, I enjoyed myself. Already the nostalgia I'd first felt had given way to a sense of discovery. Even in the old Quarter things changed, and memories couldn't always be trusted. There was a particular bar I remembered where we used to eat muffaletta sandwiches and drink cold beer while watching passers-by through the open door. I remembered the view from the door distinctly – it was on the corner of Conti and Dauphine. Except that it wasn't. I went back and forth and round the block and the bar simply wasn't there. Fifteen minutes later, when I'd given up and decided the bar must have closed down, I found it – not on a corner, not even on Conti, but on Bienville. The smell of the muffalettas, at least, was just as I remembered. But I didn't order one, didn't even stay long enough for a beer. I was no longer interested in recapturing the past; I didn't want to brood and compare and yearn. My experience in the Morning Call had been enough.

But when I came to the bar called the Old Ship, I went in, as if I couldn't help myself.

It was the bar where Sallie had worked for most of the time I had known her.

A small, corner bar, cool inside and quiet, with no music. The clientele had always been locals, a lot of them street people. I remembered it as a dark, shabby place with a vaguely maritime décor of fishing nets, glass balls and anchors, but that had changed. A blackboard behind the bar advertised imported British ales, and there was a darts board in one corner, and framed oil paintings of ships in full sail.

Looking around, I felt tense, expecting Sallie to appear from behind the bar. But the bartender was a man with a huge old-fashioned handlebar moustache, and the only other person in the place was a middle-aged woman at the far end of the bar.

I sat down and asked for a whisky sour. The bartender was friendly and wanted to talk.

'Have you worked here long?' I asked.

'For ever. Two months,' he said.

No point in asking him about Sallie. I didn't want to see her, anyway. If I did, I could have phoned her. 'They must have hired you for the moustache,' I said.

'No, that was my last job. I used to be an Italian waiter. For this job, I had to learn to talk proper, love.'

A bad attempt at Cockney. I widened my eyes. 'Doesn't sound very Italian to me.'

'English, that was an English accent! All right, it's not very good. I'm better at mixing drinks.'

'Much better,' I said taking a sip. I gestured at the board behind him. 'What about those English beers? Are they any good? Do you have to heat them up before you pour them?'

Some people came in and he had to go away to serve them, but he came back and we continued our idle, meaningless, teasing conversation. He kept giving me sudden, intense looks which disoriented me slightly. Was he very interested, or was that just a mannerism? He might even be gay, with that moustache. He wasn't bad-looking, and he was easy to talk to. I wondered if I could be attracted to him. I looked at his bare arms – he wore a plain white, button-down shirt with the sleeves pushed up – and the contrast between the white cloth and tanned flesh gave me a *frisson* of desire. I raised my eyes to his, and something registered.

'Hey,' he said. 'Don't I know you?'

'Am I supposed to guess what movie that line comes from?'

'No, I mean . . . I think, I'm sure we've met before.'

'I told you I just moved here,' I said, feeling a sinking sensation. I didn't want him to know Gabriel's wife.

'But weren't you ever in New Orleans before? Or maybe it was San Francisco . . . no, I think it was here. Mardi Gras?'

'It was a very long time ago,' I said reluctantly.

'You don't remember me?'

I shook my head.

'What's your name? I'm usually good with faces – how long ago?'

'You must be thinking of somebody else,' I said. 'I was here, but that was ten years ago.'

'Ten years, wow, yeah, could be, could be – What's your *name?*'

'Dinah –'

'Of course! Dinah! Gabriel's wife!'

Caught and no denying it. I nodded.

'You should have said! But you don't remember me, do you? Of course, it's the 'stache, my own mother wouldn't – I'm Jeff, Jeff Alpers.'

A voice, a face in the background. Someone Gabriel had worked with. 'Uh . . . the Chart Room? Did you use to work in the Chart Room?'

'Hey, right! You remember ! That's great. God, that was a long time ago. So you came back. I always wondered what had happened to you. After Gabriel died, you just disappeared. Nobody knew where you'd gone. Even Sallie didn't know.'

Even Sallie. 'I went back to the Midwest, to my parents.'

'You look just the same, you know. Maybe even prettier. But tell me what you've been doing all these years? What made you come back?'

'I got a job. I'm managing a health spa . . . could I sell you a membership?'

'Nothing wrong with my health, darlin'.'

'It's for exercise – keeping fit, you know? Working out?'

'I don't believe in exercise, except in bed.' He leered. 'But tell me about yourself. You get married again, or what? Have you seen Sallie?'

I gulped down the rest of my drink as an excuse not to answer, but he wouldn't let me be.

'It's really great seeing you again,' he said. 'Why don't we get together sometime . . . I'm off at eleven. Do you like jazz?'

I shook my head. 'I can't. I've got to get up early in the morning, and –' I looked at my watch without registering what it said. 'I've got to go now, I'm meeting somebody for dinner.'

'Maybe some other time – you know where to find me.'

I couldn't get away fast enough. The beginnings of interest I had felt had been for a stranger, for someone new, not for Jeff Alpers. When I thought of the past it was Gabriel and Sallie I remembered, not the peripheral figures. But I had known other people and some of them, like Jeff, might still be around, ready to recognize me, and keep me chained to the past.

As I hurried home through the darkening streets, my skin prickled and my heartbeat was irregular. Sallie would be next, I thought. I might run into her round the next corner, before I had time to plan what I would say. If Jeff, whom I scarcely remembered, could recognize me, Sallie wouldn't be fooled. I would have to confront her, but I wanted it to be in my own time, on my own terms. I didn't want any more surprises.

As soon as I was home I switched the television on – Chicago reflex habit. I wanted a drink, but there was nothing in the house – shopping was something else I had to do.

I turned the television off – new habits started now – and threw myself into the serious business of unpacking, promising myself I'd think of nothing else until I was finished.

At the back of the wardrobe I found a stack of magazines

and pulled them out into the light, more than half expecting pornography. But they were interior-decorating magazines, the glossy, well-produced journals I loved, an expensive luxury I rarely allowed myself. It was a treasure trove and, my good intentions forgotten, I leaned happily back against the wall with one in my hands. I felt more warmly towards the unknown tenants who had gone before. The orange kitchen Morgan had told me about was explained: probably it had been terracotta, a misguided but understandable attempt to recreate the Tuscany kitchen that positively glowed out of page 98. The photographs were magnificent, each room a work of art. Dark wood and cool blue fabrics set off against roughly whitewashed walls; classical doorways, carpets I could almost feel against my fingers; stonework and crystal and warm red brick. One, which I gazed at for long minutes, was a view through a doorway into an old-fashioned English kitchen: fire glowing in the grate, a wicker basket near by full of kindling; pale sunlight falling from an unseen window on to the red-tiled floor. On the stone mantelpiece, a row of glass and pottery jars; above, a mirror reflecting the doorway. I stared and stared, longing to walk through that doorway, to feel the tiles cool against my feet. I took an almost tactile pleasure from the mottled blue-white colour of the fireplace surround, and from the way the shadows fell. I could imagine the face of one of Vermeer's self-possessed Dutch housewives reflected in the mirror.

But this wasn't art, only an artful photograph. A glimpse into the lives of strangers, into rooms and houses I could never own, never live in, never even visit except in my imagination. A mixed pleasure, such pictures, and the mixture was pain.

Letting the magazine slip away, I looked at the stranger's room I now found myself in, imagining it as a series of photographs. But the furniture was cheap and bare and gave no comfort, no promise of beauty, under the glaring electric light. It wasn't art and it wasn't mine.

Would I live in cheap rented rooms all my life? This wasn't

home – it could never be my home. I closed my eyes, conjuring the fine, high, wooden house in the Garden District, imagining quiet rooms with shuttered windows and polished floors, the hum of a ceiling fan, antiques and fine art gleaming softly and, in the background, turning away from the window, was Gabriel.

No. I opened my eyes. It was my dream, not his. Gabriel was dead and I didn't need him. I wasn't going to think about what might have been, but only what would be.

There was a telephone beside the bed. The telephone book next to it had been left by the last occupant.

I had to get it over with. I couldn't put it off forever, and I didn't want to wait, cowardly, for her to find me. I looked up *Neal, S. Emmet*, and dialled the number without even imagining what I would say.

A soft, young voice – not Sallie's – answered on the second ring.

'Oh – could I speak to Sallie?'

'She's not here right now. Do you want me to give her a message?'

It was a child. Why had a child answered Sallie's phone? She couldn't be married. My hands were sweating. 'I wanted to talk to Sallie Neal,' I said, slowly and carefully. 'Is this the right number?'

'Yeah, but she's at work now. Can I tell her who called?'

'No. I'll call back later. When do you expect her?'

There was a silence. Probably Sallie was sharing a house, I thought. This could be her housemate's child. Then the child said, very softly, 'Dinah?'

I was back in the park, beside the pond, and a boy with terrifyingly familiar blue eyes was staring at me. He knew me. He said his name was Gabriel.

'Dinah?'

I hung up the phone. I sat very still on the edge of the bed, afraid that if I moved I would be sick. So he was real, that little boy. He was Sallie's. Gabriel had a son.

chapter six

It puzzled him that she had run away. She should have known him and been glad to see him – hadn't Gabriel sent her? She was the sign he had been waiting and praying for, and he had to find her again.

She gave a purpose to Ben's days. He no longer sat alone in his room, mourning the past, but began his search the first thing every morning. He wandered all over the French Quarter, looking for her, and even went back to Audubon Park, to stand by the pond for more than an hour, hoping the first meeting would be repeated. When it wasn't, Ben refused to be discouraged. He knew it had not been a dream: Dinah was real, and she was in New Orleans, and soon they would be together again.

But where was Gabriel?

At night in bed Ben was eager to feel Gabriel's presence, to hear his stories again, but he was as alone as ever. At first he couldn't understand it, thinking Dinah's appearance must signal Gabriel's return, and then he knew. Of course. Gabriel was with Dinah. That was where he'd always wanted to be, and where he belonged.

In the closet, where they had lain untouched for months, were all his plastic figures: the cowboys, Indians, soldiers, horses, cows, buffaloes and dinosaurs that he had once loved to play with for hours, creating another universe on his bedroom floor. Now he dug through the box until he found his favourite soldier, a Confederate general he always used for Gabriel, and then again until he found the saloon girl in the ruffled, full-skirted dress, her moulded plastic hair long and straight down her back, which he called Dinah, and, with a feeling of deep contentment, he took them to bed with him, settling them together beneath his pillow and closing his eyes to listen to their conversation.

He continued to draw pictures of Dinah – not as she had been when he saw her beside the pond, but as Gabriel had known her; the Dinah who looked down at him from the portrait above his bed. He felt that if he could draw exactly as Gabriel had, he would become Gabriel. But it never happened, no matter how he longed for it, no matter how blank he made his mind. The drawings were his own.

His mother had known Dinah long ago. He thought about telling her that he had seen her in the park, but he never had a chance. She was always either with Angus, or thinking about him. Ben had never had much use for his mother's boyfriends, and he positively hated Angus. Their very first encounter had settled that.

It was a Saturday morning, and as usual Ben was up long before his mother, looking after himself. He fixed a bowl of milk and cereal, turned on the television and sat on the floor to watch cartoons while he ate. His mother's bedroom door was closed, and Ben knew from experience that no matter how loud the television got, it wouldn't disturb her until she was ready to get up.

It was a surprise to hear her door open about five minutes later, and Ben turned round, smiling and pleased, until the sight of what had come out froze the smile on his face.

Not his mother. A big, naked man with dead-white skin everywhere except for his reddish face and tanned arms, with tangled masses of hair sprouting here and there like diseased growths. It was a monster, growling words Ben couldn't understand, and coming straight for him on big, pale feet.

He had kicked Ben. It was a badly aimed kick, and Ben rolled away as soon as he saw the intention, so he wasn't really hurt, but it shocked him. He didn't understand what was happening, not even when the monster turned off the television and shambled back to the bedroom, slamming the door behind him.

'Oh, Ben, of course he didn't mean to hurt you! The TV woke him up and he was grumpy, that's all. You should know better than to have it on so loud when people are trying to sleep.' That was what his mother said when he told her, and her response shocked him almost as deeply as the kick. A horrible monster had appeared in his life, and his mother liked it! And how could he have known about keeping the television turned down? He hadn't even known of the monster's existence before. But now he knew, of course, and he knew a lot more. The kick had taught him to be wary of Angus, and no amount of false smiles or pretended kindness or dollar bills from the man could change his feelings. One irritated, sleepy kick had revealed the truth about Angus, and if his mother couldn't see that, Ben knew he had no hope of convincing her. He could only pray that in time Angus would disappear from their lives like so many other men. Already, though, Angus had lasted longer than most, and that made him even more of a threat.

Ben was lying in bed, musing sleepily about Gabriel and Dinah, when he heard the front door open, and his mother's voice. The background sounds of the television suddenly ceased, and then he heard Mrs Pym's elderly giggle. Female voices went back and forth, and then there was the sound of the front door opening and closing, and then silence. Ben held his breath, scarcely daring to hope, but could hear no sound of Angus. Swift footsteps – his mother's alone – and then his door pushed open, and a weight on his bed. The smell of beer and cigarette smoke and her own musky-sweet perfume as her face came down close to his.

He lay still, eyes closed, pretending to sleep, until the bed began to shake slightly and something wet fell on his cheek. She was crying.

'Mom?'

'Oh, my darling, precious Ben. Did I wake you? Oh, I'm so sorry. But I love you so much, you see. You're all I've got in the world, the only one, the only thing.' She pulled him up into her arms, clung to him and sobbed. She went on about how she loved him, how miserable she was, gulping for air and crying while Ben kept quiet, hugging her tightly and waiting for the storm to pass.

Eventually the tears ended. She pulled away from him and fumbled with her clothes, taking off her shoes and her dress but leaving on her underwear.

'Move over, sweetie.'

'What's wrong?'

'Nothing. Nothing's wrong as long as I've got you.'

He moved over and they lay together, wrapped in each other's arms. 'Oh, I love you, Ben.'

'I love you, too.'

'And you won't ever leave me?'

'Never.'

'Then everything's all right.' She gave a deep shuddering sigh, kissed him several times, and fell asleep.

Angus was gone, he thought, and felt a deep, sweet thankfulness. Things would be better now. Maybe she would even be able to help him find Gabriel – maybe he could tell her and she would understand.

The familiar warmth and smell of her relaxed him profoundly, and within a couple of minutes he had followed her into sleep.

In the morning he woke first, and the sight of her face on his pillow reminded him that he was happy. He was careful not to disturb her as he got up, sliding gently out of her embrace and slipping off the edge of the bed. He stood beside the bed for a moment and leaned down to look closely at her face in the dim light of the curtained room. There was no sign of injury – no black eye, no cuts or bruises this time – and he let out a sigh of relief. He pulled the sheet carefully up over her shoulders even though the room was warm, and stood a moment longer watching her protectively.

There was half a lime in the refrigerator. Ben sliced a neat wheel from it, then put it in a glass with ice and water. He got the Alka-Seltzer from the bathroom cabinet and added it to the glass. It fizzed up in his face, making him blink and grin.

'Benjy? Ben?'

She was sitting up in bed, her face puffy and confused.

'It's OK,' he said soothingly. 'I'm here. Everything is OK. I brought you something to drink.'

She took it from him like an obedient child and sipped, then recoiled, spilling some of it on to herself. 'Ugh! What is it?'

'Alka-Seltzer.'

'And you made it look like something good ... little sneak.' But she smiled at him lovingly, and drank the rest of it down, making a face. He took the empty glass from her hand and she lay back with a deep sigh. 'Hope that does some good ... I'm sorry I woke you up last night, baby.'

'That's OK, I like to know when you get home. I worry about you.'

She laughed a little, ruefully. 'It's supposed to be the other way around. You make a better parent than I do.'

'You're a great mother! You're the best mother anybody could have!'

The way she looked at him made him shiver with pleasure. She hadn't looked at him like that for too long. And she knew it, too, because she said, 'You mean when I'm here. When I'm acting like your mother, and not out getting drunk or having fights with – Come sit with me, sweetie.'

He perched on the edge of the bed and let her hold his hand.

'I'll do better, you'll see,' she said. 'I'll spend more time with you this summer. We'll go places. I know you miss Alan, I know it's hard, being by yourself. That's why I –' Her voice trembled and she bit her lip. He squeezed her hand, to remind her she wasn't alone.

'Oh, dear,' she said. 'I don't want to start crying again. Why does this always happen to me? Is it something about me, personally? Why don't I remember what always happens? Why do I keep hoping, making the same old mistakes? Men aren't any good. You can't count on 'em for anything. None of them are any good.'

Very softly, not sure whether or not he wanted her to hear, Ben said 'Gabriel'.

She heard. She gave a shaky laugh and there was scorn in her voice when she spoke. 'Oh, Gabriel! He wasn't any better. He didn't want me – he married somebody else. And then he died. That's got to be the biggest cop-out of them all. He jumped out a window. He didn't stick around any longer than anybody else I've ever been in love with.'

He bit his lip to keep from speaking. He didn't dare interrupt her. His heart was pounding with excitement. If only she would go on talking about Gabriel!

'He's gone,' she said wearily, the flame of scorn already extinguished. 'They're all gone. No sense thinking about it. At least I've got *you*. We've got each other. I should get up.'

'No, stay there. It's early still. You rest.'

'All right, sweetie. Just until my headache goes. Mmmm, you know what I'd love?'

'Some coffee.'

'You are a mind-reader!' She smiled up at him.

Ben loved taking care of his mother. It almost made up for the disappointment of hearing no more about Gabriel. Maybe later he could lead her back to the subject, he thought, as he hurried off to the kitchen.

While he was watching the coffee-maker, waiting for the water to drip through, the telephone rang. He snatched it up before the second ring.

'Let me talk to your mother.'

Ben stiffened at the familiar, hated voice. 'She's asleep.'

'Well, go wake her up. Tell her –'

'I'll tell her to call you back.'

'Now, you listen to me –'

Ben hung up. He stood very still, his teeth clenched, and then he made himself relax. No. Angus was out. He wasn't coming back.

He clambered up on to the counter to get down his mother's special coffee cup. It really looked more like a soup bowl, but she told him that in France everyone drank their morning coffee from cups that size. She had never been to France, but there had been a Frenchman one Mardi Gras time who had given it to her. The cup was blue and white, decorated with tiny, hatted figures round the rim.

The phone rang again just as he got down. He had expected it.

'Ben, I want to talk to your mother. She'll want to talk to me. She's going to be very angry with you if you don't tell her –'

'She told me she doesn't want to talk to you ever again.'

'So she's awake.'

'No. She told me last night. She's asleep now.'

'Wake her up, Ben. She won't be angry. She'll be glad, I promise you, I'll give you –'

'No, I won't tell her. So quit calling.' He hung up and waited, trembling. He counted to one hundred. He turned away from the telephone, poured out the coffee, waited again. Then he drew a deep breath and took his mother's coffee back to his bedroom.

'Who was that on the phone?'

'Nobody.'

'Mr Nobody?'

'Wrong number.'

'Oh.' Was she disappointed? She smiled at him. 'The coffee smells heavenly. Just put it on the table. I can't quite make myself sit up yet . . .'

'Just rest. Want me to get a wet washcloth to put on your eyes?'

'Do they look that bad? No, I'll be fine. Do you want to lie down next to me again?'

Of course he did. It was just the sort of wordless comfort that he craved, and that he missed on all those mornings when her bedroom door was closed. But he was still half expecting the phone to ring and couldn't really relax enough to enjoy the next few minutes of warmth and closeness.

Finally she stirred. 'I'd better drink my coffee before it's stone cold, especially since you were so sweet to make it for me. Can I sit up now?'

He rolled off the bed. 'I'll hand it to you. You don't even

have to sit up – want me to get some more pillows from your bedroom, to put behind your back?'

'You think of everything. You really know what I like, don't you, Ben? Yes, I'd love some more pillows.' When he returned with arms full she sat up and let him settle them behind her head, shoulders and back, and as she snuggled against them he put the coffee cup into her outstretched hands.

'You'll make somebody a wonderful husband someday,' she said, and stopped smiling.

Ben looked up at the painting of Dinah, looked from her blonde hair and cool, painted face to the dark, tousled hair and real, tired face of the woman below. For a moment he hesitated, clinging to his secret, afraid she would misunderstand. But he felt so close to his mother now, and he longed to cheer her up.

'I saw Dinah the other day,' he said.

'Who's Dinah?'

His mouth dropped, as he had imagined hers might. 'Oh, come on! You know!'

She laughed and shook her head. 'Nope.'

'Her!' He waved at the portrait above his mother. 'How many other Dinahs do you know?'

She frowned and cocked her head. 'Dinah? Ben, what are you talking about? How could you have seen her? *My* Dinah?'

'Gabriel's Dinah,' he corrected. 'I saw her in Audubon Park, by the pond, the other day when you told me to go out because –'

'But I don't understand. What do you mean?'

'She's come back to New Orleans.'

'What did she say? Was that her on the phone just now?'

'No. She didn't say anything. I just saw her. She ran away, I don't know why.'

'No, Ben, no, no . . .' She shook her head and set down the coffee cup on the bedside table. 'You never met Dinah in your life. She doesn't even know you exist. Even if she was in New Orleans and you passed her on the street, how could you possibly know her?'

'From the picture.'

'But that was painted ten, eleven years ago. She wouldn't look like that now.'

'She *does*, she looks just the same.'

'But it's not a photograph – I never thought the portrait looked that much like her. It's not the way I remember Dinah.'

'I recognized her,' Ben said stubbornly, aware that he was losing. He regretted having told her – it had never occurred to him that she would argue, that she might not believe.

She smiled and shook her head. 'You couldn't have.' Her smile was completely disbelieving, superior. 'Oh, Ben, I wonder sometimes what goes through that head of yours . . . you see some blonde who reminds you of a picture and you think it must be her. Children live in another world, honestly.' She twisted round to look up at the painting. 'Imagine you thinking that – I didn't even know you knew her name.'

'If you'd seen her you'd have to believe me.'

'Ah, yes, but I didn't see her. And that's how I know it couldn't have been her. If Dinah was back in New Orleans, she'd call me. She'd get in touch.'

A pounding at the front door made them both freeze. From the weight of the blows Ben knew it could only be Angus. 'Let's pretend we're not here,' he whispered.

'No, no, we can't do that.' Her eyes were bright.

'I'll go tell him you're sleeping,' he offered, although the thought of facing Angus frightened him. But to protect his mother he would do anything.

'He sounds angry, doesn't he? It wouldn't be safe for you –'

'We could hide.'

She laughed breathlessly. 'And make him madder?'

'He couldn't break down the door. Could he?'

'I don't think so. Oh, of course he wouldn't, even if he could. But he knows we're in here. It's silly to hide. It's not fair.' She got up. 'Oh, dear, where's my robe? I can't answer the door like this.'

'Don't. Don't open it.' He caught her arm, trying to pull her back. 'Please don't. He might hurt you.'

'Ben. Sweetheart.' She bent down and kissed the top of his head. 'It's sweet of you to worry about me, but he won't hurt me. He never has, not physically. I think he must have come to apologize.'

'Doesn't sound like it. Sounds like he's mad.'

'He must think I'm asleep. He's trying to wake me up, that's all.'

Now they heard his voice. 'Sallie! It's me! Open this door and let me in!'

'I'd better let him in.'

'Don't!' Anguished, he clung to her, held on with all his might.

'Stop it. Stop acting like a baby and let me go.' All the love and gentleness fell away. Her voice was as sharp and cold as her irritation. He wasn't her sweetie any more.

Still he gripped her, forcing her to peel him away, forcing her to push him off physically. She left the room quickly, giving him no second chance, not even bothering to get dressed. She went to the front door just as she was, in her underwear.

Ben felt sick, too miserable for tears. He closed his door and leaned against it. He didn't want to see.

But he couldn't help hearing her soft voice and Angus's loud one, the closing of the front door, the silence, and then murmurings, and his mother's throaty sigh, and nestling, nuzzling noises. Ben looked up at Dinah's painted face and felt ashamed, wishing he had not mentioned her to his mother. It seemed now like a betrayal, and he was glad she hadn't believed him.

His own belief was not shaken, but as he sat on the edge of the bed and stared up at the portrait he did wonder why Dinah had come to New Orleans. Was it really to find him, as he had imagined? Was she here at Gabriel's command? Was it possible – his stomach clenched with anticipated pain – that she had already left again? Or that she would leave soon if he didn't find her first? Why was he wasting time when he should be out there looking for her now?

He had his hand on the front door when he realized he was still wearing his pyjamas.

He didn't find her during his whole long, prowling search of the French Quarter, but it was that day it occurred to him that he might never find her if he only looked in the daytime. He might have a better chance at night.

When his mother worked at night, elderly Mrs Pym from next door came over to 'sit', despite Ben's protests that he was old enough to stay alone.

'How come you let me stay alone in the daytime but not at night? What's the difference? I'm not a baby – I don't need a sitter!'

'I know you're not a baby, but you should have a grown-up around just in case. What if a fire breaks out while you're asleep? What if you feel sick, or there's a burglar?' his mother responded.

It was a stupid argument: fat lot of good old Mrs Pym would be if any of those things happened!

Every night she settled herself in front of the television, and every night she fell asleep long before Ben did. Ben was surprised his mother hadn't realized how useless Mrs Pym was, finding her asleep like that night after night when she came in. He never said anything about it because he didn't want some younger, more alert babysitter who might impose restrictions. Mrs Pym's sleeping habits were useful – it was almost as good as being left alone.

Hand on the door, he turned to look at her as she sat snoring in the easy chair. Her glasses and shoes had fallen off, and the blue and white cotton of her dress moved up and down with each long wheezing breath. He knew that the only thing which would wake her was turning off the television set, but still he felt a little thrill of daring as he stepped out into the night, closing the door behind him.

The warm, heady-scented air enveloped him, and he walked towards the noise and colour of Bourbon Street. As always, the streets were filled with people. They might be the same people who were out by day, but Ben imagined them to be another race. Small people were a rarity here, so Ben was careful not to draw attention to himself, merging with the shadows when he could, never running and never lingering in one spot for too long. Once a man kept pace with him and started asking friendly questions, but Ben didn't answer and managed to lose his follower by mingling with a loud, laughing crowd in front of the Famous Door. Most of the time, though, Ben, well below the adult line of sight, was the observer, not the observed.

But having to be so careful, plus the fact that he couldn't go into any of the bars, made looking for Dinah a daunting task. Ben was tired. He had been walking around the Quarter for most of the day, and now he felt he'd been walking half the night as well. He began feeling sorry for himself, with the ache in his chest that meant tears. It was so unfair, being a kid, being alone –

Suddenly he realized where he had walked to. His mother worked in the bar right across the street. He paused and, because he was so tired, leaned his back against the wall and stared across at the open doorway, where smoke swirled beneath yellow lights like a veil hiding the interior. He heard the rise and fall of voices, the occasional burst of laughter. His mother was in there, behind the bar, serving drinks and smiling at strangers. Talking to them. Ben strained for the sound of her laugh – that rich, distinctive note. Tears pricked behind his eyelids. He was so lonely and tired, and did she care? Did she even know? What would she say if he walked through the door and asked for a Coke with lots of ice? She would be amazed – she would be angry, he knew. But she couldn't just throw him out. He wasn't a stranger, he was her son, and she would have to take him home. Then she would punish him, but he didn't care if she took away his allowance or made him stay in his room all day, or even if she smacked him one. He just didn't care, as long as she *knew*. Once she saw him she would have to talk to him. She would ask him what he was doing, and maybe he could make her understand this time about Dinah, and Gabriel, and how horribly lost and lonely he felt. And when she knew, then he could rest.

She was so near, closer than she ever was at home, behind the bedroom door with Angus. There was nothing to stop him. All he had to do was cross the street.

He had just pushed himself away from the wall when he saw Dinah.

Her white dress caught his eye, seeming to glow against the night. Even before he saw her face he knew her by the way she moved.

He stepped out of the shadows, into the pool of light cast by a streetlamp, right in front of her. She stopped, drawing herself up as sharply as if a pit had opened in the street before her. He still couldn't see her face well enough to read her expression, but he could see the tension in her stiff shoulders, and in the way she held her arms close to her sides.

'Don't run away,' he said. 'Please.'

'You're Gabriel?'

A hard, electric surge of joy shot through him, and he shivered and could not speak.

'Sallie's little boy?'

'She wouldn't believe me,' he said softly. 'She wouldn't believe it when I said I'd seen you.'

She moved her head and a strand of hair fell across her face, gleaming like gold. She pushed it back behind her ear, and he felt the gesture as if she had touched him. He knew that habit of hers. 'Well,' she said. 'She'll believe it when I go in there. I was just on my way to visit her. That is where she works?'

'Don't go yet. Talk to me first. I've been looking for you for so long . . . Why did you run away?'

The air was hot and sticky, a typical summer night, but Dinah shivered and rubbed her bare arms, holding herself. 'I thought you were a ghost,' she said.

Ben did something then that he had been wanting to do since that first moment beside the pond. He stepped closer to her, reached out, and grasped one of her arms. The skin was smooth and warm. 'Nope. We're both real,' he said, and finally felt her relax, as if his touch had drawn the tension out of her.

'Isn't it awfully late for you to be out by yourself?'

'I couldn't have found you if I'd stayed in.'

'How old are you?'

'Nine and a half.'

Some of the tension returned at that – he didn't know why. 'Of course,' she said, and pulled away from him. But he didn't let go. 'Excuse me – am I your prisoner?'

'Promise you won't run away?'

Raising her eyebrows, shaking her head, talking down to him. 'I won't run away.' Ben knew he was acting like a baby, but as he let go her arm he felt he was giving up his greatest advantage. He could only be sure of her when he held her.

'Does your mother know you're here?'

Ben rolled his eyes. 'What do you think?'

'I think that if you want to talk we should go somewhere and sit down. Not a bar, of course . . . She caught her lower lip between her teeth and looked around, hesitating.

'*I* know.' He took her hand and led her away, to the Morning Call. But she baulked at the door.

'Let's go to the other one. Café du Monde. It's just down there.'

'Why?'

'I prefer it.'

He had either to follow her or let her go. So it was the Café du Monde for a pile of hot, sugary *beignets* and the fragrant drinks which were more milk than coffee. They sat across a small table, close enough to touch, and at last he could look at her, gaze to his heart's content.

Her arms and shoulders, left bare by a plain white sundress, were lightly and evenly tanned. She wore a fine gold chain round her neck, and on her left wrist a man's watch on a brown leather strap. In the bright artificial light of the café, Ben could see that her face was a little more angular, not as soft as it looked in the portrait, and she had fine lines just becoming visible around her eyes and at the corners of her mouth.

'Why are you staring?'

'To see what you look like now.'

She grimaced, shook her head, and looked down into her steaming cup, holding it with both hands as if she needed the warmth. 'What do you know about me?' she asked suddenly, not looking up. 'How did you recognize me in the park?'

'The picture, the one of you that Gabriel painted. I have it in my room. I look at it all the time.'

'Do you? . . . So she kept it. I'd wondered – But I can't believe you recognized me from a painting done more than ten years ago!'

'That's what *she* said. But I did.'

'Yes, you did,' she said thoughtfully.

Encouraged, he leaned forward, the edge of the table cutting into his chest. 'Gabriel sent you,' he said in a low voice. 'Gabriel sent you to me, didn't he?'

She jerked back, jarring the table, splashing milky coffee. 'Gabriel's dead.'

'No! He's not – he's *not* dead!'

She glanced around the café, but no one was paying any attention to them. She pushed her hair back behind an ear, fingers trembling slightly. 'Look, I don't know what Sallie has told you, but –'

'*She* doesn't know anything about it! It's only us – it's you and me – *we* know about Gabriel. You know where he is.'

'Look, are you talking about . . . when you say Gabriel, do you mean my husband?'

'Of course.'

'Well, my husband is dead. He died ten years ago. I'm a widow. Do you understand that?'

She was treating him like a baby again; maybe she was testing him? Maybe he had to prove that he knew something. 'If he's dead, then why did you come back to New Orleans?'

She frowned slightly and looked at him sharply as if she'd just remembered something. But then her eyes evaded his; she shrugged and said, 'I got offered a job that just happened to be here. That's all.'

'What about Gabriel?'

'What *about* Gabriel?' Her voice was as sharp and cold as a knife, and there was no friendliness in her look.

Tears of frustration blurred his sight of her. 'You know,' he said. 'Please.'

'It's late,' she said. 'You shouldn't be here. You should be home in bed. Does Sallie leave you by yourself when she's working?'

He shook his head miserably, the tears spilling over.

'Oh, don't. Wipe your face.'

She thrust a paper napkin at him, and he rubbed it ineffectually at eyes and mouth.

'You're hopeless. Let me.'

He sat very still, warmth spreading through him like a healing balm as she brushed away sugar crumbs and dabbed away tears. She cared about him. He was close to her, and that was all that mattered.

'I'll take you home,' she said. 'Isn't anybody going to be worried about you?'

'There's Mrs Pym, but she was asleep. She's always asleep.'

He could feel her stifling a laugh in order to sound disapproving. 'Well, you shouldn't sneak out of the house. If she ever wakes up she'll be frantic. You wouldn't want to give her a heart attack, would you?'

'If you came to stay with me I wouldn't sneak out. I'd never want to run away.' He had thought she would be pleased, but again he had said the wrong thing. He sensed her cool withdrawal, although she said nothing.

Outside in the dark, warm street, though, she didn't object when he took her hand. He was content just to walk along with her in silence. He could imagine that she was going home with him, that they were married and living in the apartment on Decatur Street. Words weren't necessary. He didn't want to fight, or to make her angry. He just wanted to think about Gabriel and Dinah together.

'Where do you live, anyway?'

Reluctantly he came back to the present, and realized how close they were to home. 'Oh, just down here.'

'Is the door unlocked, or do you have a key?'

'I left it open. It's OK, I can sneak in and she'll never know.'

'Oh, great – the making of a criminal.'

'When can I see you again? Can I see you tomorrow?'

She didn't reply. He could see the yellow bug-light shining over his door and knew he didn't have much more time. '*Please?*'

'Which one is yours?'

He sighed and admitted to it. 'This one.' Then he perked up. 'Now you know where I live. You can come visit me!'

'Sure. Go on, now, don't hang around outside.'

'Will you come see me?'

'Yes, of course I will.'

'When?'

'Soon.'

'Tomorrow?'

'No. I don't know. Look, I know where you live. I'm not going to run away. You'll see me again, I promise.'

'But when?'

'Would you let go my hand and go back where you belong?'

He wanted to say that he belonged with her. 'Would you kiss me good-night?'

She sighed exaggeratedly. 'What a blackmailer! All right. But first let go. Now, close your eyes.'

He closed his eyes and turned his face up to her, felt her coming close, and then a kiss, butterfly-light, on his forehead. He opened his eyes. 'That wasn't a *real* kiss.'

'You don't deserve one. Now get inside.'

'All right.' Then he paused in the doorway. ' 'Night, Dinah.'

' 'Night, Gabriel.'

chapter seven

He was Gabriel's son all right. Not only his eyes, but other, less physical traits told me so. He had the same core of stubbornness, and the same trick of establishing his claim on me with touch.

I thought of his tearful denial that Gabriel was dead, and remembered my dreams – but that was idiotic. He was just a child. All children had fantasies.

I was emotionally drained when I left him, not up to a confrontation with Sallie. But I didn't want to put it off. I didn't want her hearing about me from her son. My slight advantage, knowing things she didn't, wouldn't last long. I had to make use of it while I could. So, trying to recharge, I went back to the bar where Sallie worked.

I was worried that I might not recognize her right away, that she might see me before I knew her, and take me by surprise instead of the other way round. She was bound to have changed, I thought.

And she had. She looked thinner, prettier, and more ordinary. She used make-up now, and her nose wasn't as big as I remembered. Her wild hair had been tamed by a good cut – still thick and wavy, but it was much shorter and looked manageable.

There had been no need to worry about not recognizing her. She might have changed much more and still, as soon as I saw her, I felt a tiny internal jolt. It was, to a lesser degree, what I had known when I first met Gabriel's eyes, and when I had returned to New Orleans. A sense of coming home.

It drew me like a magnet to the bar, towards her. She was

talking, casually friendly, to another customer. When I leaned up against the bar she turned towards me, the smile for him still on her face.

'What can I get you?'

I watched her eyes: first nothing, then a spark of wonder.

'Hello, Sallie,' I said, to make her sure.

Her pupils widened, darkening her eyes, as she really saw me. 'Dinah?'

She lunged forward – I suppose she meant to hug me, but there was the whole bar between us. Glad of it, I drew back a little. 'Yes, it's me. I'm back. I'll have a whisky sour, please.'

She went on staring at me, and the smile trembled on her face. 'I don't know what to say.'

Inside I was shaking, but I knew that to her I would seem totally in control. 'Why don't you start by making me a whisky sour? Get yourself something, too.'

'Oh, OK, thanks.'

I watched her get the drinks, and she was a stranger to me. No matter how important we might once have been to each other, I had known her less than a year, and that was ten years ago. When she came back with my whisky sour and a beer for herself Sallie looked a little more relaxed, and I thought she'd probably gone through the same mental routine I had, reassuring herself that we were little more, or less, than strangers: acquaintances meeting in a bar.

'Well, what brings you back to New Orleans?' Her Southern accent was stronger than I remembered.

'I'm managing an A-Plus health and fitness club,' I said. 'It's in the business district, not a long walk. Maybe you'd like to take out a membership?'

'I *should*. I never get any exercise, out of bed. How'd you know where I was working?'

'Jeff what's-his-name, down the street. He recognized me . . . I barely remembered him. He told me where to find you.'

'Well,' Sallie said vaguely, staring past me. 'It sure is nice to see you again. About the last thing I expected, though. I thought you were never coming back.'

'I thought that too, once. But I thought Gabriel might have told you I was here.'

She gave me a frightened look. 'Gabriel?'

'Yes. Didn't he tell you? I tried to call you, but he told me you were at work.'

'Who did?' Now she was looking at me as if I was crazy.

'Gabriel.'

'Uh huh. You talked to Gabriel.'

'What's so odd about that?' I was getting irritated. 'I called your number, and Gabriel answered, and I thought he might have told you that I called.'

'Gabriel.'

'Yes, Gabriel, your son, remember?'

'Oh!' She looked relieved. 'You mean you talked to Ben!'

'Ben?'

'My son.'

'His name isn't Gabriel?'

She smiled, shaking her head. 'Benjamin.'

'But his father was Gabriel.'

She looked into her beer. A man further down the bar was trying to get her attention. I didn't say anything. 'I've got a customer,' she said. 'I'll be back.'

'You don't have to tell me,' I said. 'I know. It's obvious, just looking at him. He couldn't be anybody else's.'

'Just hang on.'

I finished my drink while she was gone, and she brought back another one.

'All right,' she said. 'Before he was born, I wasn't sure . . . there was another guy it could have been. But you're right. All you have to do is look at him to see Gabriel.'

'Thanks a lot for letting me know.'

Her eyes flashed. 'Now you just wait a minute. I didn't run away – *you* did. Just how was I supposed to let you know?'

'You knew where I was. You knew I went back with my parents.'

'If you'll remember, I did get your address from Gabriel's parents and wrote to you. You never wrote back. You never gave a damn about me, so why should I about you? Why should I keep trying after you went off without a thought for me? When I found out I was pregnant – well, I couldn't afford to go up to New York for a legal abortion, and I couldn't face the thought of Mexico. Also, I knew there was a good chance it was Gabriel's. I didn't want to kill the only thing left of him in this world. So I decided to have it.'

'You should have told me,' I said, still sullenly harping on the same note.

'Why? It wasn't anything to do with you.'

'He was my husband.'

'Well, I loved him too!'

We glared at each other across the bar. Then Sallie laughed, a little shakily. 'Oh, God, that's all in the past. Isn't it? Does it really matter now what I should have done? I didn't do it to hurt you, you know. I didn't get pregnant on purpose.'

'I thought you were on the Pill.'

'I thought I was, too. But you remember how I was in those days – I'd forget my own head, if . . . I was always forgetting to take them. And my bag got stolen, with a month's supply . . . Oh, it doesn't matter how, it just happened. You think I should have had an abortion?'

'No, of course not. I just wish it had been me who got pregnant. It *should* have been me. I should have had his child. It would have meant so much to me, to have something of Gabriel left. You don't know how miserable I was. I wanted to die. A baby would have been something to live for.'

'But you did live,' Sallie said. 'That was ten years ago. You survived. *You* don't know what it's like, bringing up a kid on your own – you can't tell me it ruined your whole life, not having a baby when you were a teenager?'

I shook my head and knocked back the last of my drink. 'Not ruined it, no. But everything would have been so different. Sure, maybe it would have been rough – but better. There's never been anyone who meant as much to me as Gabriel, and there never will be, now. But if I'd had his *child* . . . why was it you? Why not me?'

'I didn't stop you getting pregnant,' she said sharply. 'You didn't want a baby then, and neither did Gabriel. You were on the Pill. Don't blame me for *your* decision.'

'But that was because I thought I had for ever,' I said. 'If I'd known Gabriel was going to die –'

'Well, hindsight's easy, isn't it? We'd both have done things differently if we'd known.'

'But I've missed my chance,' I said. 'I've missed my chance for ever.' I couldn't stop myself. It was as if ten years' – or a lifetime's – pent-up feelings were forcing their way out. There were all these things I had to say, and Sallie was the only one I could say them to. Gabriel was dead; he could never hear me or give me an answer, but Sallie could.

'What are you talking about?' Sallie asked. 'You're still young – you've got plenty of time to have a baby.'

'But not Gabriel's baby.'

She stared at me. 'My God,' she said slowly. 'And I thought it was Gabriel who was so hung up on tragic romance. I thought you were more sensible – cooler, anyway. Do you want another drink?'

I nodded. Below the bar, out of sight, I opened my fists in my lap, striving for calm.

'You don't still believe in all that stuff, do you?' Sallie asked. 'All that one and only, fated to be together, we met in another lifetime stuff?'

'I'm not sure I ever did. You were the one who remembered a past life.'

'Remembered,' she said sarcastically. 'Yeah, Gabriel could make me remember anything he wanted. Anyway, I was just a little hippie then, what did I know? We all believed in all that stuff: reincarnation, karma, working out the mistakes of your past lives in this one.'

'And you don't believe it any more?'

'I don't think about it much. I don't think about Gabriel much. Ben's *my* son, not his. What did Gabriel ever contribute? Some sperm. I could have got that from any passing stranger, or even a sperm bank. OK, I can see Gabe in him physically, but that's all. Ben never had a father.'

'Don't you ever talk to him about Gabriel?'

She sighed and looked away from me. 'Oh, he knows. I've told him. But the present's more important than the past. Why dwell on something that's over?' She looked straight at me then, meeting my eyes. 'Why did you come back to New Orleans? Why now?'

'I told you – I got a job.'

'Uh huh.' Her voice was flatly disbelieving. 'You got a job here so you could come look for Gabriel.'

I swallowed about half of the fresh drink before I spoke. 'I haven't spent the last ten years just mourning Gabriel, you know. After I went back with my parents, it took me a while to get back on my feet, but I did. I went to college for a while. I fell in love with somebody else. And then somebody else. I was with John for almost four years. I lived in Mexico with him. That was more like a marriage than what I had with Gabriel. And then I got involved with somebody else ... well, that was just craziness. What I'm trying to say is: I thought I might stop living when Gabriel died, but I didn't. I went on and made my own life. There's a lot more to my past than just one year of marriage in New Orleans.'

'If that's true, why did you come back here, then? Why not Mexico, or someplace new? Why didn't you stay in Chicago?'

'I made my own life, but it's not good enough. I've just been drifting. I'll be thirty next year – thirty! Unmarried, childless, no career, no skills ... a failure.'

'You're not even thirty yet,' said Sallie. 'You're too young to be having a baby-panic.'

'Well, it's a fine line between too young and too late,' I said. I heard my voice come out in Sallie's Southern drawl – 'fahn lahn' – and knew I was drunk. 'Anyway, it isn't just the baby. It's everything. My best friend just got married. She's pregnant, and she's got a successful business, and she and her husband bought their own house. It made me think. I'm tired of being a waitress – I don't want to be a waitress for ever. So when I got offered this job as a manager ... the job was in

New Orleans, and that was even better. If I could come back and make a fresh start here –'

'Hold that thought,' said Sallie. 'I've got to go serve some customers.'

She was fairly busy for the next half-hour, and I had another drink or two. Then her shift ended, and we went to a tiny, dark little bar on Conti Street which she said was never full but never closed. There we talked about the past – but not our shared past. We filled each other in on our lives up to date and so, although neither of us mentioned Gabriel again, Sallie often spoke of Ben. Every mention of him was both a pleasure and a pain to me.

Sallie had changed, and it seemed clear to me that it was Ben who had changed her. The experience of having a child, the responsibility of being a mother, meant that she was no longer a careless, silly girl. She had a centre and an anchor to her life, and I envied her. Once she must have envied me, for being Gabriel's wife – now our positions were reversed.

At some point, in drunken anguish I must have told her how I envied her, because although I don't remember what I said, I remember her response.

'You don't know what it's like,' she said. 'You have this fantasy, like a little girl about somebody else's doll. Having a child doesn't change everything – well, I'm wrong. I mean, it *does* change everything, in some ways, because you always have to think about somebody else, you can never just be a single person any more. But you don't become a totally different person – you still have the same old needs, the same personality. You're not a mother, not *just* a mother, all the time. It makes things more difficult, having a kid. Like work. Like men.'

'Oh, men, who needs 'em? They're a habit, they pass the time. You've got Ben.'

'Yeah, sure, and I love him, and I wouldn't give him up, but . . . I don't always feel like being a mother. Sometimes I just want to be *me*. Kids don't understand that. They can't, I guess. He resents the time I spend away from him, especially with men. I love Angus – I really do, and I think it's serious between us. Ben can't stand that. He's so jealous . . . he's taken against Angus something fierce. So what do I do? What do I do if Ben won't come around and accept him? Why should I have to choose? Why should I have to feel guilty all the time, or sacrifice my own happiness?'

'*I* would,' I said. 'I'd do anything to make him happy, if he were mine.'

I expected a furious, defensive attack, but she just looked at me. 'Yeah,' she said. 'I bet you would. And it wouldn't make any difference, because he'd grow up and leave you in the end. And he'd probably resent you for making it harder, for sacrificing yourself and making him feel guilty. It never works. You have to look out for yourself, in the end. You can't get Gabriel back. You did everything for him. You did everything he asked, and you still couldn't make him happy. You couldn't stop him from killing himself.'

I got up and walked out of the bar.

Max had a house in Jefferson Parrish, not far from the shores of Lake Pontchartrain. It was a three-bedroomed brick bungalow built sometime in the sixties, with a tree-shaded, fenced backyard. It looked a lot like the houses on either side of it, and a lot like many other houses in similar residential developments all over the country. There wasn't anything wrong with it, but I didn't like it. It had no character.

Instead it had comforts: central air-conditioning and heating, clean white-painted walls and dark wooden floors, and furniture that still smelt new.

The pale brown leather couch didn't squeak as I expected: it yielded, like flesh, when I sat on it. I looked at the palm tree in a clay tub, and at the glass-topped coffee table, and at the patterned Indian rug on the floor, and then at Max, watching me anxiously.

'Where are *you*?' I asked.

'In the back room, I guess.'

'Show me.'

One bedroom was totally empty. Another one held a

computer console and display unit, an office chair, a worktable of stripped pine, bookshelves. I went across to see what they held: books about computers and sailboats; a few fat, worn paperbacks, one-time best-sellers; and a shelf of science fiction. There was a calendar on one wall with a colour photograph of a sailboat against the setting sun.

The third bedroom was his, and like the rest of the house it felt under-furnished to me, although there was nothing obvious missing.

A big bed with a gold spread. A thick, furry, dark brown rug on the floor. A chest of drawers. A bedside table with lamp, clock-radio and remote control for the big television and video recorder nestled in a wall unit opposite the bed.

There was also a kitchen, two bathrooms, a dining room, and a hot, narrow laundry room connecting the kitchen to the garage. It could have been a nice home, but it didn't feel like one to me. It felt anonymous, almost unoccupied. Max had managed to live there for nearly two years without impressing his personality on the place. He had obviously spent money furnishing it, and it wasn't that I disagreed with his taste. But to me everything put together looked like a model apartment or a suite of rooms in a hotel.

'It just doesn't look like you spend much time here,' I said, finding it hard to explain my feelings.

'You mean because I'm so tidy? You thought all men alone lived like pigs?'

'Oh, I'm being sexist now. Yeah, I guess that might be part of it.' We were back in the living room, on the warm, soft leather sofa, with glasses of brandy.

'I don't spend much time here,' he said suddenly. 'It's true. And when I am in, I'm usually either in bed or in the back room with the computer. I only come in here when I've got company, and I've used the dining room exactly once. A two-room apartment, furnished, would probably make more sense for me, and one in the centre of town. This neighbourhood is all families. I'm the oddball. "Don't go talk to that funny man, Junior." ' He made a face.

'So why did you come here?'

'Oh, it was a good investment.' He hesitated, staring at the brandy in his glass, swirling it around a little, while I waited. 'And, there was this woman. It was all pretty new between us, but I fell hard. I started making plans – just in my own mind, nothing was said. I bought this place, which was much too big for me, and not my sort of thing in a whole lot of ways, because *she* seemed to like it. She came with me when I was house-hunting. Because I was with her I kept responding to her, and trying to see things through her eyes. And when she liked something, I thought it meant more than it did. I really thought that within a couple of months we'd be living together. Or married. And by the time I realized that wasn't going to happen, it was too late. I'd signed. The house was mine.'

'What happened?'

'I moved in – what d' you think?'

'No, I mean with her. Why did you break up?'

'I don't think there was anything to break up. Except my fantasy. We got to know each other better and discovered we didn't like each other all that much.'

I felt a pang of unease at the words. Was he warning me?

He finished his brandy and put his arms round me. 'Let's not sit out here. Let's go to bed.'

In bed everything was fine. It had been good from the first, and it went on getting better. But somehow I took that for granted. Gabriel had set the pattern for me. In my relationships with men sex was always there, always important and, at least at the beginning, good enough to overwhelm me, to make me blind to all the obvious reasons why it wasn't really love and wouldn't last. Max, in striking contrast to other men I'd known, had no obvious faults. He wasn't married, he was employed, he'd shown no signs of violence, drug addiction or instability, he was reliable, truthful, and he liked me.

It was this last – his feelings about me – that made me uneasy. Polly said I was being perverse.

I phoned Polly one night – one of the few nights I didn't spend with Max – to talk to her about him.

'He's unmarried, he's not gay, and he doesn't have any deep-rooted objections to marriage – do you realize how rare men like that *are*? Rarer than golden eagles. Or is there something horrible you haven't told me about?' she demanded.

'No, nothing horrible. If there is, I haven't discovered it yet.'

'How does he feel about kids?'

'He would like to have children.'

'And he's good-looking, and you like him in bed, and you can talk to him . . . Really, Dinah, if the only objection you can come up with is that he *likes* you too much – what does that mean? How can somebody like you too much? You think that means he's got bad taste?'

She made me laugh. I felt comfortable, at home, talking to her. Really, I hadn't gone so far away as long as we could talk like this, as we'd been doing for more than fifteen years. I leaned back on my bed and stared at the picture I'd put on the wall: a Pre-Raphaelite lady in a rich blue dress.

'Anybody who likes me has good taste,' I said. 'I just don't know if it's going to last, or what he means by it. He's smitten by me now – that's the word he uses, by the way, "smitten" – but is he going to be bored in two weeks?'

'Are you?'

'Maybe.'

'Oh, Dinah, don't worry about it! Go with the flow. You're looking for things to worry about. You're making problems where there aren't any.'

'He'd like to see me every night. He'd probably spend all his spare time with me, if I let him.'

'He's not there now.'

'No. I told him I wanted some time to myself.'

'And he didn't have a nervous breakdown, did he? He didn't throw a hissy fit?'

I grinned at the lady in blue. 'No. He thought it was a reasonable request. He thinks I'm very reasonable.'

'Little does he know. I thought you said he was bright.'

'When I'm in love, I'm not reasonable.'

'And when you're reasonable you're not in love? So he's

smitten and you're not. So why are you worrying if he'll still be smitten in a week? Just enjoy it, and if you don't, don't see him. Why am I giving you advice?'

'You're paying me back. Am I boring you?'

'Oh, no! I wish I could meet him. Tell me better what he looks like.'

So I went on, continuing the conversation we'd been having ever since we discovered boys – an endless, intimate, detailed picking-over of feelings, of things thought, said, done, imagined, hoped-for, feared. Endlessly fascinating, the sound of our own voices repeating the same words, reaffirming our lives.

I said hardly anything about my job, although it took a lot more of my time, thoughts and energy than Max did. It was more demanding, more boring, and less fulfilling than I had thought it would be. I skipped over it lightly when Polly asked, telling her I was still settling in.

That was what I told myself, too, but it felt more like sinking than settling; a constant struggle to keep my head above water. There was so much to do and yet, at the same time, there was so little. Long hours passed in which no one came in, and I hated sitting in my tiny office all alone, answering the telephone, writing out cheques, waiting for something to happen. I was afraid that as soon as I left something *would* happen – I would be needed and unavailable. I felt as guilty as a kid playing truant whenever I left early or came in late or took a long lunch break, but there were times when I needed the break, needed to escape.

I wondered if my expectations of a job – any job – were unrealistic – like my expectations of a lover. Was I sabotaging myself?

In addition to Rick and Faith I now had two college students, Dawn and Lisa, working part-time. I told myself it was part of the job of a manager to delegate responsibility, but it was a new and unaccustomed strain to keep track of everyone.

I hated getting up early. I would never, by choice, have taken a job that made me get up before eight, but now, three days a week, I had to be at the spa by seven to open up. Rick went early the other three days at my request, but by asking him I felt I'd lost points in the silent, undeclared war between us. He hadn't changed his mind about me. I could tell he thought I was hopeless as a manager, and that he despised me for having the job that should have been his.

One afternoon, when Faith and I were alone together, she told me that the problem wasn't personal, but one of human nature.

'Men don't like taking orders from women,' she said.

I stared at her. 'But I'm not giving orders!'

'You're his boss. It comes to the same thing.' She looked so placid and self-assured. 'I don't mean you're doing anything wrong. It's just the way men are.'

'You think he would have coped better if Mr O had hired another man over him?'

'Yes. Oh, he would have been upset and hurt at first, but I think he'd find it easier to cope after the first disappointment wore off.'

'Well, he'll just have to learn to get along with me,' I said.

'Oh, for sure. For sure he will,' she said, but I knew it was only a polite agreement. She didn't believe it, and neither did I. But in that case, I thought, if Rick really wasn't going to give me his best, I must fire him. I shyed away from the thought. What reason could I give? That he didn't like me? Why not leave it to him? Within a few months he would either have adjusted to working for me or have found himself a better job. And, like it or not, I needed his help. I needed more confidence in myself before I could let him go.

As the days and weeks passed, the ads I'd put in the local paper, and all the promises of 'special introductory offers', began to bear fruit. People phoned, people came in, people joined and paid their money. Not many – not as many as I had hoped – but enough to make a start, enough to make me hope I'd be a success.

Max came in one day, MasterCard in hand, presenting himself as a new member.

'But you don't even work downtown!' I protested, pleased and touched by his offer but also embarrassed by it.

'So? *You* do. I can drive down, work out, shower, change and take you out to dinner. The perfect excuse.'

I accepted it – I could hardly refuse to add another membership to our tiny list – and hoped this wouldn't be a smaller-scale version of the story of his house. I admired his generous impulses and didn't want him to regret them.

Sallie also came in and signed up, which surprised and pleased me. It was her way of saying we were still friends, and it was a way for her to meet me on my ground. We now had another context in which to see each other – regularly if we wanted, not just in the small and smoky interstices between jobs and men. And we were meeting of our own accord, not pushed together by Gabriel.

But although Gabriel no longer came between us, Ben did. I kept my jealousy to myself, trying to deny it, but it still had life, causing me to pass silent judgement on whatever Sallie did, making me reflect that I would have made Ben a better mother than she did. I deliberately did not ask Sallie about Ben, and I made no effort to see him. What was the point? I didn't want to be reminded of what I didn't have. I preferred to concentrate on my real life. Some day I would have a child of my own.

One day near the end of August, when I had been in New Orleans for almost a month, I was wandering around the Quarter during my self-awarded late lunch break. I'd had a tub of yoghurt and an orange on the grass in Jackson Square and now, feeling hot, sticky and fed-up, I loitered outside the windows of an antique shop, looking in without seeing. The heat was really getting to me, and I tried to think of somewhere cool I could go that was neither a restaurant nor a bar. Maybe I should just go back. The spa was air-conditioned, and I could cool down with a dip in the empty pool. The novelty of the French Quarter had worn off. It was too hot for aimless wandering, and I'd already done too much shopping. I couldn't afford anything more than necessities for at least another month.

My eyes slipped from the chairs and vases inside to focus on the window itself, and I saw a face reflected there; not my own, but someone behind me, watching me.

I whirled round, and there was Ben. There was a hesitant, hopeful glow on his face which quickly faded. I don't know what my expression was – anger? annoyance? fear? – but it came back to me in the guileless mirror of his face as apprehension. I felt a rush of concern: I didn't want him to be frightened of me.

'Hello, Ben,' I said as warmly as I could. 'I didn't know you were there. You startled me a little. You should have said something.'

He hesitated, eyes searching my face, and then said, 'You're not going to run away from me?'

'Of course I'm not! Didn't I tell you the last time I saw you that I wouldn't run away any more?'

He nodded, but his lower lip stuck out sullenly.

'What's wrong?'

'You said you'd come see me, and you didn't. I waited. You *know* where I live and you said you'd come and you didn't.'

'I'm sorry. I've been very busy – the days just slipped away.' Looking at that unhappy, pouting face, I felt it very important to make him smile. 'But I'm here now,' I said in a coaxing voice. 'We're together, and I've got a little free time . . . What would you like to do? Shall we go somewhere for ice cream? Would you like to go to the Café du Monde again? We can do whatever you want.'

Hope sparked in his eyes. 'Take me to your house.'

'My house!' I laughed, shaking my head. 'Oh, no –' The sullen mask came down over his face again, and I struggled to push it off, to make contact, make him understand. 'It's just that it's so far away. It would take ages to walk there – it's not even in the Quarter. And I do have to get back to work eventually. I thought maybe we could go to an ice-cream parlour, or walk down by the river for twenty minutes or so . . . isn't there something else?'

Shrugging, he shook his head. 'You asked me what I wanted to do. You said we could do what I wanted. I want to see your house. That's all.'

'But why? There's really nothing wonderful about it. It's just a boring old apartment inside an old house, full of stupid rented furniture – nothing to do there, not even anything good to eat.' I was exaggerating my voice and gestures and I realized, as he gazed up at me unimpressed and ungiving, that our roles were reversed. I was the wheedling child, he the implacable adult. I felt ashamed of myself.

'Look, Ben –'

'Why do you call me that? Why don't you call me Gabriel any more?'

'Is that your name?'

He shrugged, no longer meeting my eyes. 'I like it when you call me Gabriel.'

I didn't ask him why. I was remembering his earlier outburst when we had spoken about Gabriel, and I didn't want to stir that up again. The subject lay between us, beautiful and dangerous as a snake, and I stepped round it. 'Would you like an ice cream?'

'Oh, all right.' Wearily, as if he was doing me a great favour.

We walked in silence to Jackson Square, where I bought two of the sweet ices from a stand: cantaloup for myself, chocolate mint for Ben. I remembered Gabriel's fondness for chocolate, and as I looked down at the boy's dark head I felt a pang of sorrow. But this time it wasn't for what I had lost, but pity for Gabriel, who had died without knowing his son.

Ben looked up and caught my eye. 'Why can't we go to your house? Why don't you want me to know where you live?'

'Of course it's not that – don't be silly!' I paused to marshal my arguments: the time, the distance, my need to get back to work, and then quite suddenly I gave up. If it meant so much to him, why not?

'We'll take a bus,' I said. 'And we can't stay long.'

The look of pure joy on his face made it all worth while.

The day was overcast, but I hadn't realized how heavily the dark clouds were massing until we got off the bus. The light was strange, subaqueous, and there was a charged stillness to the air that didn't register with me until too late – we were walking up Esplanade, away from the bus stop, when the skies opened and began pouring rain.

I yelped and Ben laughed. The raindrops were huge and came down in a steady stream as if poured from a bucket. It was a fierce, hard, sudden tropical shower – common in New Orleans – and it was too late to take shelter. I felt I was already soaked to the skin.

I began to run. I could hear Ben laughing and calling behind me. I knew it was silly to try to outrun the raindrops, but I would have felt even sillier lingering when the house was only a block away.

Gaining the shelter of the porch, I turned round and saw Ben at the bottom of the steps. He made no effort to come up – he was rejoicing in the rain, hopping around with his arms outstretched, splashing in the puddles, eyes squinting and mouth wide open to drink. His hair was sleeked against his skull like wet fur. He could have been some young animal, a seal or an otter pup, playing so unselfconsciously, and if I startled him I thought he might slip into the wet and be gone.

Then he looked up, grinned, and galloped up the steps to me.

'You're soaking!' I cried.

'So are you.' He put his hand on my bare arm and I looked down at myself, seeing how my cotton shirt clung, showing my nipples, and aware of the unpleasant, damp heaviness of my denim skirt. I pulled away from him, digging in my purse for the key. 'Let's go in and dry off.'

'Is this whole house yours?'

'No, I've got an apartment on the top floor. In.' I pulled the screen door wide and shooed him up the stairs.

Inside, I said, 'I want to get out of these wet clothes first thing. I'll get you a towel.'

My beach-robe – a long, slinky dress of green terry-cloth – was hanging on the back of the bathroom door, so after I'd peeled off my sodden clothes I slipped into that, and took a bath towel out to Ben.

He was standing naked by the window, staring out at the pounding rain as if hypnotized. I had turned on a lamp, and the light from it burnished his skin, made it look so smooth and warm that I longed to stroke it. A drop of water formed, like a tear, at one of the dark points of his hair and slid down the gentle slope of his neck, down the furrow of his spine.

'Here,' I said softly, hating to spoil the moment. 'You'd better dry yourself. I don't want you to catch cold.' I held the towel out at arm's length, not moving towards him.

He turned round. 'It isn't cold. It's warm,' he said, his voice dreamy. He took the towel as if he didn't know what to do with it.

'At least dry your hair. What did you do with your clothes?' As I asked I saw them in a sodden heap on the floor. 'They'll never dry like that. I'd better go hang them up.' I kept my eyes away from him and talked to cover my nervousness. I knew I shouldn't be embarrassed. He was only a little boy, and if he was comfortable being naked, that was good. I didn't want to weigh him down with my old-fashioned hang-ups.

That was Gabriel's thought, I realized. I could almost hear it in his voice. How many times had I heard him talk about the difficulties, and necessity, of breaking free of old restraints, of his parents' antiquated hang-ups and religion? I remembered Gabriel stalking around our little apartment in the nude, glorying in his body and making fun of me for being prudish. But I was only shy and inexperienced. I had braved the idea of strangers seeing when I let him paint my portrait nude.

I lit the gas fire in the bathroom and hung Ben's sodden clothes on the towel-rail behind the bathtub. When I turned to go I nearly collided with Ben, who was standing in the doorway wrapped in the bath towel.

'What do you want?'

'What can I wear?'

'Oh. I'm afraid I don't have anything in your size . . . maybe one of my T-shirts would do, just until your things dry.'

He followed me across the bedroom to the chest of drawers

and I pulled out the few picture and slogan T-shirts I still owned. I'd once had quite a collection, but clean-outs before moves had reduced it drastically. There was one in bright yellow advertising a Chicago pizza parlour, a white one with a blue picture of Amelia Earhart; a black T-shirt with eyes for 'Cats' – I hadn't seen the show, but Polly had brought it back from New York for me – and another black one for 'Equus', which I *had* seen; a blue one with a red heart and the words 'New Mexico is for Lovers', and a red one –

'That one,' said Ben, taking it from my hands and unfolding it himself. It was soft and faded, the oldest of the lot, and across the front the white letters of the Coca-Cola logo were peeling away, chipped by time and many washings. I hadn't worn it for years, and only a half-sentimental, half-superstitious reluctance had kept me from throwing it away long before. It had been Gabriel's – one morning, when we'd been married less than a week, I realized I had run out of clean tops, and Gabriel had tossed me one of his, a bright red Coca-Cola T-shirt. We shared clothes regularly after that, being much the same size. I didn't have many clothes of my own, so most of the time I dressed just as Gabriel did, in jeans and T-shirts, sweaters added on in the winter.

'Look at me!'

Ben twirled round, arms outstretched. The shirt, tight on me, fitted him loosely, like a sack dress. It was almost long enough for modesty, but when he raised his arms above his head I caught a glimpse of childish genitals. I wanted to laugh and I wanted to hug him: he was so vulnerable, so easily pleased, so young and beautiful. But I bit back a smile and said, 'Very nice. Very attractive. It's positively *you*.'

He dropped his arms and beamed, pleased with himself. 'Now take me on a guided tour,' he said.

'A tour?'

'Show me everything. Start at the beginning, at the front door. Make believe I just came in.' He waited for my nod of understanding and scampered out.

The rain stopped long before the end of my guided tour,

and I was uneasily aware of the passage of time. But Ben would not let me skip: he had to be shown inside the kitchen cupboards and under the sink, and although the furniture had come with the apartment, the pictures on the walls were mine, and he had to be told what each one meant to me.

'Who's the lady reading the letter?'

'Somebody who lived in Holland about three hundred years ago. The artist's name was Vermeer.'

'So why do you have it?'

'It's just a reproduction, you know. I was in a poster shop looking through their pictures for something to put on that blank wall, and when I saw this one I knew it was right. I've always loved Vermeer. I love the light and the colours. His rooms are so cool and peaceful-looking, and so real. They make me wish I could go back in time.'

Ben raised his eyebrows sceptically. 'They didn't have air-conditioning then.'

I laughed. 'In Holland they probably don't need it.'

'Or cars. Or television.' He moved away and discovered a stack of smaller pictures on top of a rickety table. Most of them needed frames, and I wasn't sure yet what to do with them. On top was a print of an Escher drawing which I'd bought in the place where I found the Vermeer.

'Who are they?'

He had bypassed the Escher to go for the photographs underneath. I looked at the old-fashioned sepia-toned portrait he held up. I had never known the young woman with the gentle face and slightly drooping eyes beneath a soft cloud of hair, but the man standing beside her, so stiff and handsome, was very familiar.

'My father's parents,' I said. 'Their engagement photo. They're both dead now.'

'And these?'

'My parents.' It was a colour photograph taken in a studio twelve years back, at the same time as my graduation portrait. Ben stared – trying, I supposed, to see some fragments of me in their middle-aged faces. The last picture made him catch his breath. My heart beat faster. He didn't ask me about it – he didn't have to. After a long moment he touched the matt black and white surface as gently as if he touched a living face.

'It's the only picture I have of him,' I said. 'We didn't have a camera, and he didn't like pictures of himself. That one – some friend took it, I don't remember who – was taken a couple of months before he died. He didn't know there was a camera aimed at him. He was sketching, I don't know if you can see there –'

'He's holding a pencil, I can see that. Was he drawing a picture of you?'

'I don't know. I can't remember.'

'Where are you going to hang it?'

'I'm not sure I will.'

'You have to! So you'll see it every day! Put it over your bed, like –'

'Oh, I don't know. I used to keep it tucked away in a drawer. I never looked at it. I didn't forget him, so I didn't need to see what he looked like. The problem with photographs is that they force the past into just one shape; they tend to cancel out other memories, because they claim to be the truth. When I think about Gabriel I can remember him in so many different ways. I remember him as he was, changeable. But if I saw that photograph in front of me all the time it would dominate, until all I'd have would be the picture, which is like the memory of a memory.' I saw by his face that he didn't understand, and shook my head. 'It doesn't matter.'

'It *does* matter. This is what Gabriel looked like. If you saw it every day you'd have to think about him, you couldn't forget. Just like I think about you every time I see your picture over my bed.'

His eyes on mine were fierce and blue but not, I thought now, exactly the blue of Gabriel's.

'But that's a painting,' I said. 'A painting is different. It's art, and it doesn't claim to be an exact record. It's about colour and form and feeling more than facts, and it will probably tell you as much about the painter as about the subject. That's what Gabriel used to say.' As I spoke I remembered that it was Gabriel who had distrusted photographs, claiming they destroyed memory. I said we hadn't had a camera, but I had had one. My parents had given me a little Instamatic especially for my trip to New Orleans, and Gabriel would not let me use it. Not only would the pictures take the place of genuine memories, he said, but the very act of taking them would force me to look at people and things as potential images, and so distance me from the reality. As long as I was a tourist taking pictures I'd be isolated from experience, he said, and I had been so impressed by his philosophy that years later I was spouting it as my own. But did I believe it? Had I ever thought it through for myself? I felt as confused as I would have discovering that some cherished memory was only a dream.

I looked at my watch and saw that it was almost five o'clock.

'Hey, kiddo, you're going to have to get dressed and go, because I've got to get dressed and go.'

'Go where?'

'Back to work.' In the bathroom I found his T-shirt was nearly dry, but not the jeans.

'Ugh, these are wet!'

'Well, I'm sorry, but you'll have to put them on. You can't go home without them.'

'I might catch cold,' he said in a plaintive little voice, by luck or cleverness hitting a nerve of guilt. I could imagine my mother's horrified face at the very idea of sending a child out in wet clothes, especially after I'd shown enough sense to get him in out of the rain and dried off. How many times in my childhood had she warned me of the colds, and worse than colds – pneumonia, rheumatic fever – which would result if I went outside in damp clothes or with a wet head . . .

But that had been Massachusetts; this was New Orleans and summertime. Reason struggled valiantly, and I said, 'Don't be silly. You know how hot it is. You'll be dry by the time you get home.'

'Couldn't I just stay here, and leave when they're dry?'

'No.'

'But why? Why couldn't I? I wouldn't do anything wrong. Why couldn't I?'

'I'm not going to argue,' I said sharply. 'I have to go to work and you can't stay here by yourself and that's all. Get your clothes on right now. We're leaving in five minutes.'

I shut him inside the bathroom, feeling like a monster. It was so easy to bully a child, and I had always meant to be above such tactics, to exercise sweet reason when I had children of my own. It wasn't even as if Ben was asking something outrageous. If he'd been an adult friend, if Max had asked to stay on after I went to work, I could hardly have refused, but if I had I would have explained and apologized, not given orders.

But Ben was not an adult. He was a child, and he wasn't mine, and he couldn't stay here . . . why? I felt a spring inside winding tighter. I went to the wardrobe and stared at it blindly.

The bathroom door opened and Ben came out, dressed, solemn-faced.

'I'm sorry,' he said. 'I didn't mean to make you mad.'

'You didn't –'

'But could I still come over some other time, some time when you don't have to go to work?'

'Oh, Ben, of course you can!' The anxiety on his face twisted the spring so tight I thought it would snap, and I had to go to him. Before I'd even thought about it I was on my knees and my arms were round him. The pressure of his embrace eased me, brought me close to tears. Not my child. But how I wished . . .

'I'm sorry,' I whispered, feeling his soft, sweet neck against my lips. 'You can come over any time you want.'

'I'm glad,' he whispered back. The soft words buzzed against my ear and made me shiver. 'I don't ever want to make you mad at me.'

I swallowed hard, drawing back. As I stood up I felt awkward and could not look at him. I grabbed something from the wardrobe and hurried to lock myself in the bathroom. The words still ran through my head: his words, Gabriel's words when we made up after our first, tiny quarrel. They were common words, everybody's words, just like 'I love you'.

Had I imagined it, or had Ben said that, too, before I pulled away from him?

chapter eight

In Illinois there was a difference between August and September: September was the beginning of autumn. But in New Orleans one slipped imperceptibly into the other – it was only more of the same, endless summer.

I shut down the spa for the Labor Day weekend and went out camping with Max on the shore of Lake Pontchartrain, where we sailed, fished and burned in the sun.

Max and I were spending nearly every night together by that time – when he was in New Orleans. And when he was out of town on business, he phoned. I didn't miss him too much when he was away, but when he came back I was always happy and relieved. He told me he loved me, and I believed it. I was less certain of my own feelings, and the cynical observation, ' "I love you" in bed doesn't count', haunted me. I didn't want to hurt him – I cared about him that much.

I hadn't told him about Ben. What could I tell him? Here's your rival, this little boy whose face and gestures and tricks of speech remind me of my dead husband; he stirs profound and basic emotions in me that you never will – not you or any other man. Because he isn't a man, and you can't compete with him. He's a child, and he could so easily have been mine.

Because he wasn't, did that mean I had no right to my feelings? It was easier, and seemed saner, just to keep quiet about the whole thing. I had told Max a lot about Gabriel, but not everything – Sallie was just a name.

My life was divided into three parts: work and Max and Ben. September meant school for Ben, so he had to stop hanging around the Quarter all day in the hope of seeing me.

But he called me sometimes, and we would meet for a late-afternoon snack at the Café du Monde, and a couple of times Sallie brought him along to the spa. I offered her my services as a babysitter and once, when Max was out of town, Ben and I went out to dinner and to see a movie. Of the parts of my life, only work was unsatisfactory. I had to spend more hours at it than I'd imagined, more than I had ever worked before, and they were hours which I longed to spend with Max or Ben or even just sleeping. Still, I was gaining confidence, and the membership list was growing, however slowly. I thought I could be pretty proud of myself.

The second week in September, Max and I went to dinner with his friends Nick and Tessa. They were his best and oldest friends, so I couldn't take the invitation casually. I knew it was symbolic, almost as if he was taking me home to meet his mother. But his mother lived far away, in another state, and there were only his friends to pass judgement on me.

I left the spa at a quarter to five that day, to give myself plenty of time to dress. Not that I was wearing anything elaborate, but because of my nervousness I needed to be able to put things on and take them off again, trying nearly everything in my wardrobe in search of the perfect 'look'.

It wasn't vanity, although if Max or anyone else had seen me staring at myself in the mirror, then changing shoes or shirt or jewellery and staring again, it would have looked that way. I knew that by the end of the evening it wouldn't matter: they would like me or they wouldn't and my clothes wouldn't change their feelings. But the first impression was important. I didn't want them to think I had dressed up too much, that I was trying too hard to impress them, but neither did I want them to think that I didn't care, that I was a mess, that I had no taste . . .

If they'd been Max's parents it would have been easier. I might have been just as nervous, but I would have known what to do. For parents you dressed neatly, smiled a lot, were polite, and didn't swear. Parents didn't have to like you; it was enough if they didn't disapprove too much.

I remembered how nervous I had been of meeting Gabriel's parents, and how he had mocked my fears. We had been married a month before he suggested taking me to meet them. 'Of course they'll like you,' he said. 'But so what if they don't? We don't need their approval. You're my wife.'

Ray and Jeannie Archer lived in a heavily forested area near the Texas border, in a little town called St Cloud. Ray Archer had worked at the paper mill – St Cloud's main employer and reason for existence – until an accident crippled him. The acrid stench from the mill was always in the air. Gabriel said he'd never noticed the smell until after he moved away, it was such an accepted part of his surroundings.

Physically, Gabriel was very like his father, and the two men had a similar intensity of character. Gabriel's mother was a quiet, dark, handsome woman. I was a little intimidated by Jeannie, feeling she was waiting for me to prove myself before she really accepted me into the family. Not that she was in the least unkind, but when she looked at me with her steady brown eyes I felt she was trying to look past my appearance, to find out what I had to offer beyond a young, pretty face, to see if I could possibly be good enough for her only child.

Ray was much friendlier – openly approving of me. He made teasing, flattering remarks about his son not deserving such a beauty, and I responded with relief to what I saw as welcome, unimportant flirtation. It never occurred to me that Mr Archer meant anything more than kindness by his words, and I never imagined that Gabriel, or anyone, could see anything wrong in it. Also, Gabriel was more interested in talking to Jeannie than to Ray. I thought I was being useful, winning over his father. I thought Gabriel would be pleased. Really, I suppose, I hardly thought at all. I responded to Ray's flattery as I had responded to Gabriel's love: simply, directly, immediately, without any thought for the future. And I still knew so little about Gabriel.

He never talked about his parents. He had answered my questions, but I hadn't known what to ask beyond the bare details. I didn't know (later I told myself I should have guessed) about the fierce rivalry he felt with Ray; I didn't know they were always in competition and that Gabriel would see my friendliness as a betrayal of him, a defection to the enemy camp.

I should have known; I should have felt it, behind all the things he didn't say. But I didn't know, and couldn't guess, how he would react. It was the first and only time I ever saw him in a rage.

Dinner was over and we were all still sitting round the kitchen table when Ray touched me. He only patted my hand: a friendly, harmless gesture. It was a response to something I'd said, like a smile or a word of encouragement, and I wouldn't have thought anything of it except for Gabriel's reaction.

He stood up so suddenly the table jarred.

'We're going,' he said in a harsh, angry voice I'd never heard before.

'What are you talking about?' said Jeannie. 'You're going to stay the night.'

I stared at Gabriel, my smile dying before his incomprehensible anger.

'She doesn't want to go,' said Ray. His hand closed over mine on the table. 'Settle down, son. Just sit down and drink your coffee.'

'Are you coming with me?' Gabriel asked, glaring at me.

'What's wrong? I thought we were staying until tomorrow.'

'You are,' said Ray.

Gabriel shoved the table violently, knocking it into Ray, whose half-smile never wavered.

'I'm going,' said Gabriel. 'You can do what you want.'

The table was wedged against my chair, making it difficult for me to move. I struggled, feeling trapped.

'Stay,' said Ray in an undertone. 'Don't give in to him when he's like that! Somebody has to be sensible.'

'I'll go talk to him,' said Jeannie. She gave Ray a sharp look. 'I'll try to settle him down.'

I broke loose just as she got up, and ran after her. Gabriel was in his old bedroom, where we were supposed to stay, and his battered brown suitcase was open on one of the twin beds. He flung my nightgown to the floor just as I came in.

'Gabriel, don't. What's wrong? What happened?' I ran to him, trying to hold him, but he jerked viciously away.

'Stay if you want! You're so happy with him –' T-shirt, shoes, a bright cotton skirt joined my nightgown on the floor.

I would have wept if I hadn't been so completely bewildered. I touched his arm. 'Please tell me –'

He pulled away, his hand coming out of the suitcase with my perfume. He swung away from me with all his force and threw the little bottle to the floor.

The bottle glass was thick and heavy. I had dropped it once before without harming it. I realized the force behind Gabriel's anger, the sheer power of his fury, when the bottle smashed. I cried out as the glass shattered, feeling it as if he had struck me. The piercingly sweet fragrance filled the air, cloying within seconds.

'I thought you'd outgrown your little tantrums,' said Jeannie from the doorway.

I looked at Gabriel, certain his mother's words would trigger some new explosion. But he was staring at the broken glass. He looked at me then, and began to shake.

'I'm sorry,' he whispered. 'I'm so sorry.'

I was relieved to have him back again, the Gabriel I knew and loved. I put my arms round him and held him tight.

We left a few minutes later to return to New Orleans. Gabriel kissed his mother goodbye and said nothing to his father. The only apologies came from me – embarrassed, whispered, half-coherent words to both Jeannie and Ray.

We never spoke about it afterwards, but I often thought about that moment when I'd seen a stranger, like a wild beast caged inside the familiar body of my husband. It was that animal which had carved the scars on his hand, years before I knew him. And it was, just possibly, that same jealous beast who flung him, in his agony, off the roof of an apartment building to his death . . .

Amid a jumble of beads and ceramics, chains and stones,

silver, gold and brass, the tarnished silver hoop of my wedding ring gleamed up at me. It had always been a symbol more than a piece of jewellery, and it was out of place among all the other decorations, a piece I could never wear again but couldn't bring myself to discard. Telling myself that I must get a real jewellery box with compartments instead of throwing everything in one small box, I pulled out a long strand of dark blue beads and fastened them round my neck. Cool, blue stones: I couldn't remember their name. They came from Mexico, like the box. I closed it. Painted in red on the black varnished lid was 'Recuerdo de Mexico'.

I looked at myself in the mirror, having finally settled on my cream-coloured linen suit. I liked the way I looked in it. I touched the beads. I had bought them for myself, and no dangerous emotions, no powerful memories, clung to their smooth surfaces.

Max's knock at the door drew me away from my reflection, and I went with him to be shown off to his oldest, dearest friends.

They were even more than that: Tessa had been Max's girlfriend before taking up with his good friend Nick. There must have been tensions, I thought, but whatever trouble had once existed had long been buried. Max spoke about them both with untroubled affection. They were his family – his family by choice, better than the relatives chance might have foisted on him. They had even been the deciding factor in his move to New Orleans, since they had come first and Nick, a computer programmer, had suggested Max try to get a job with his company.

My hands were cold and my mind a blank as Max drove through the Garden District to the slightly shabby but still expensive neighbourhood near Tulane where they owned a house. I was the outsider now, I thought. Tessa would look at me with critical eyes. Maybe I should have worn jeans, or a dress. And what was Nick like? Would he flirt with me? Would he try to take me away from Max as he had taken Tessa?

But my nervousness didn't last through the first five minutes. Nick and Tessa were too friendly, casual and genuinely warm for that. They accepted me. And Max was pleased. Of course he was. He beamed at us all, so happy to have his favourite people gathered together. I felt relieved and a little ashamed of myself. I'd created a problem that didn't exist. I'd been confusing Max with Gabriel, and I should have known better.

I had imagined – on no evidence but her name – that Tessa would be dark, voluptuous, beautiful and very sophisticated. Instead, she was rather like me, at least physically – which made sense, since Max had been attracted to us both, but I hadn't expected it. She was blonde and blue-eyed, my height, similarly slim, and she moved like a dancer. She was very pale, with short hair in fine, wispy curls, her eyes dark-lashed and enormous. She had an appealing, waifish look which she emphasized. I was a little wary of her – perhaps jealous? – but I knew I could like her.

Nick was small and scruffy, no taller than Tessa. His green plaid shirt was mis-buttoned, gaping at the midriff, and his leather belt had been mended with plastic tape, but on his feet were pristine white sneakers. He had sharp blue-green eyes gleaming out of a mass of curling brown hair. His brown beard was turning grey in patches.

Max hugged both his friends, then put one arm round me and pulled me into the front room. It was small but high-ceilinged, with a thick, dark red oriental rug on the floor, cream-coloured walls decked with ornately framed pictures. A scarlet dragon-kite floated above an overstuffed bookcase, and most of the flat surfaces had books on them. It was a crowded, comfortable room.

'Red or white?' asked Nick, putting a glass in my hand.

'White, if it's open, but –'

'Sit down,' said Tessa. 'Max, I'll get you a beer.'

'That's all right. I'll have wine. Red.'

'My man,' said Nick, pouring.

Gold chrysanthemums glowed in a pot in the cold fireplace.

Above the cluttered mantelpiece was a pastel portrait of a young boy sitting in a large chair, holding a flute.

'Tessa did that,' said Max.

'And everything else on the walls in here,' said Nick. '*Galerie Tessa*, we call it.'

'Sit down,' said Tessa again. 'Please.' She collapsed gracefully on the brown velvet couch. I wanted to look at the other pictures, but obediently I took a seat.

'You're an artist?' I said.

'*Quod erat demonstrandum*,' said Nick.

'You're such a show-off,' said Max. 'Everybody knows Latin is a dead language.'

'QED' said Nick, and handed Tessa a glass of white wine.

'I'm an art teacher,' Tessa said to me. 'I draw and paint for my own pleasure, but I've never had a show, and I don't sell much . . . does that make me an artist?'

'Where do you teach? Tulane? Sophie Newcomb?'

'God, no. I wish I could, wish I had the credentials. No, I teach elementary art classes to little kids. You know, finger paints and watercolours and mosaics out of dried beans and macaroni.'

'You like it?'

'I like working with kids.' She had a sweet smile.

'Speaking of which,' said Max. 'Where are yours?'

'Upstairs, watching TV. They've had their dinner. I thought it would be nicer if we weren't bothered.'

'Bothered!' said Max sounding outraged. 'You think I came all the way over here just to see you guys?'

Tessa shrugged. 'I told them they could come down and say hello before they went to bed. I have to tuck Angel in, anyway.'

'I think I'll just go up and say hello, so they don't think I've had anything to do with their being banished,' said Max. 'I'll be right back.' He patted me on the shoulder as he left, but I still felt abandoned.

I looked at Tessa. 'How old are they?'

'Dominic is eight, Angel is five. She started kindergarten two weeks ago.'

Tessa was, at most, four years older than me, possibly no more than two. Yet the gap between us was the gap between an adult and an adolescent, I thought. What she had was so simple and ordinary, yet so far removed from my world.

Nick asked me questions about the spa. He probably meant them sincerely, but I felt he was humouring me, and I found it hard to answer as if my job meant anything serious.

It was even worse later when the children came downstairs. They were beautiful, blond, blue-eyed angel-children. Angel – it couldn't be her real name, I thought, but it fitted her perfectly – was breathtaking, a tiny, perfect, golden doll, shining on her father's lap. But it was Dominic my heart ached for. I realized when I saw him that the faun-eyed boy with flute above the fireplace was his portrait, but it didn't do him justice. I would have sold my soul just then to be his mother, to have the right to put out my arms and draw him to me possessively, as Tessa did; to stroke his burnished, untidy hair and kiss his soft cheek while he sat quietly, a half-smile lighting his beautiful face.

I drank a lot of wine that evening, but it didn't help. After dinner, Tessa asked me to go into the kitchen with her while she made the coffee.

'Are you always so quiet, or are you just shy tonight?' she asked. 'Do we intimidate you?'

'I was feeling a little shy,' I said. 'You've all known each other so long, it's a little hard to get into the conversation.'

'Don't let it be hard.'

'Really, I'm enjoying myself. It's all right.'

'You're good for Max,' she said. 'I haven't seen him looking so happy in a long time. We were getting kind of worried about him – well . . . I was, Nick never noticed. But he was going out with the most unlikely women. Anyway, I just wanted to say: I'm glad. We're both glad. Here, take the cheesecake. I'll bring the coffee and everything else on the tray.'

So I had passed the inspection.

'They liked you,' Max said in the car, going home. 'They really, really liked you.'

'I know.'

'Didn't you like them?'

'Of course I did.'

In the shadowy light of the car I saw that he was worried, blinking rapidly. 'Did I do something wrong? Say something wrong?'

'No. Oh, no. Nothing wrong.' I tried to make my voice warm and loving. I reached out to press his hand on the wheel.

'But something is wrong.'

I knew that if I spoke I might start crying.

'Dinah, please. Can you tell me about it?'

'When we get home. It's not about you, I promise.'

Home meant my place. We rarely spent the night at his house – not only because I didn't like it, but because without a car it would have been too complicated for me to get to work in the mornings.

'Tell me,' he said when we were settled at last in my living room, on the navy blue couch, one of my hands held comfortingly in his.

I drew a deep breath. 'I guess I'm jealous.'

'Darling! Of Tessa? But that was ages ago – we were kids. It's been over for years, I promise!'

'Not that!' It almost made me laugh, his egotism. At least it pushed the tears away. 'I'm not talking about you and Tessa. I mean . . . I guess envious would be a better word than jealous, except that it sounds so sinful – "Thou shalt not covet" and that's just what I do. I covet her *life*. She has everything I wish I had: a job that means something and that she likes, artistic talent, a happy marriage, a nice house, some money – I know what a rug like that costs – and those perfect, beautiful children. The children most of all.' Then I shrugged, trying, too late, to make light of it. 'I get like that sometimes, just depressed about my own life, feeling that it's too late. It's probably just my period coming.'

'It's not too late,' he said softly, giving my hand a shake. 'How could it be too late? You're young. You're younger than me, and I don't feel washed-up yet. You can have everything you want. Why not?'

'I know. I know. But I haven't.'

'Dinah, you can. We can.' He looked at me and I couldn't look away. His lips quivered slightly before he spoke. 'I can't promise you artistic talent, but just about everything else, I'll do my best to give you.'

'Oh, Max,' I said uneasily, shaking my head slightly.

'I see. Thanks but no thanks.'

'Oh, Max!' I couldn't bear the pain in his eyes, and flung myself at him, hiding my face against his chest.

'I mean it,' he said. 'I want to marry you.'

I couldn't speak. I was finding it hard to breathe.

He said, 'So you want to be married, but not to me.'

'I love you,' I said, almost angrily, wondering if he was aware, as I was, that it was the first time I'd said it out of bed.

'But.'

I looked up at him. 'I don't think we've known each other long enough, that's all.'

'When is long enough? I know how I feel. You said yes to Gabriel when you'd known him about two days.'

'That has nothing to do with this. That was completely different.'

'Oh, different, yes, you knew how you felt about him.'

'I didn't know anything. I was eighteen. I thought I *had* to marry him, or else give him up and go back with my parents. It was a different situation.'

'He was a different man,' Max said, and twisted round to look at the wall where I had hung the photograph of Gabriel along with the one of my grandparents and the black and white Escher print. 'He wasn't me.' He turned to me again. 'You've never got over him. You can't accept that he's gone for ever.'

'If the picture bothers you, I'll take it down.'

'Oh, no, we're not talking about me. It's not jealousy. It's that I can't live up to your teenage fantasy of romantic love. Even Gabriel couldn't, but you don't realize that – you're still looking for Gabriel, or someone just like him. You're looking for a fantasy.'

'You're wrong,' I said, shaking slightly with the need to make him understand. 'I'm trying to change, trying to grow up, trying *not* to make the same mistake again, and here you are, like Gabriel, offering to rescue me, as if marriage were the fairy-tale answer, and all I had to do was say yes!'

We stared at each other, hurting and baffled by the pain we'd so innocently caused.

I said softly, 'I do love you.'

He groaned and fell on me, and then, blessedly, we were past the need for words, eager to let our bodies do the talking.

After that night, Max seemed happier. There was no more talk about marriage, but somehow there was a feeling that a commitment had been made. I knew it was time for me to draw the different parts of my life together, to introduce Max and Ben, to be as honest with him as Max thought I was, but when I was offered the perfect chance, I refused it, and didn't even let myself think about why.

The chance came from Sallie, who wanted to meet Max and wanted me to meet Angus, and so invited us for dinner. We agreed upon a day. I chose one when I knew Max would be out of town, said nothing to him about it, and phoned Sallie the night before to say that Max had been unexpectedly called away.

'Aw, that's too bad,' she said. 'Still, we can do it another night. You come over tomorrow anyway. I've already bought the food, and I want you to meet Angus . . . I guess I'll just have to wait to have my curiosity about Max satisfied.'

I felt guilty for lying, but the relief was greater than the guilt. I felt reprieved. I'd managed to buy a little more time.

Ben answered the door when I arrived, and I hugged him and kissed his soft cheek before I entered. It was the first time I had been inside the apartment: Ben always came to see me, and Sallie and I met at the spa or the bar. It was dark inside, and I stood still for a moment to get my bearings. I could smell curry, and Linda Ronstadt was singing 'Blue Bayou'.

'Sallie's changing,' Ben said. 'Can I fix you a drink? We have Coke, or milk, or beer, or wine, or orange juice or vodka. I can make you anything you want.'

'Studying to be a bartender?' I smiled. 'I guess they would teach that in New Orleans schools, huh? I'll have some wine, please. I brought a bottle, but it should be chilled.'

'I know about that,' he said. 'We've got a bottle of leeb-fraw-milk. Do you like that?'

I had to restrain myself from giving him another hug. 'Yes, that would be wonderful,' I said, and watched him bustle away importantly.

The curtains were closed, and the only light came from the kitchenette and from a couple of candles flickering in stained-glass holders on the low coffee table. It felt like a bar, and I remembered Sallie saying she hated bright lights, including sunshine. She'd been born to live at night, she said, a natural bar-fly.

The surface of the low table gleamed and cast back reflections of the flames, and I had a sudden image of Ben dusting and polishing carefully in preparation for my arrival.

'Here's your drink.' He handed me a long-stemmed glass full of cold white wine, and the record clicked off. 'What do you want to hear?' he asked. 'The other side? Do you like Linda Ronstadt?'

'Yes, that's fine.'

'I'll turn it over. You sit down. There, on the couch, that's best. I can sit next to you.'

It was a lumpy old couch, draped with Mexican blankets, and I sat down carefully, suspicious, but it was comfortable enough. Ben had just scrambled to sit beside me when Sallie came into the room, vivid as a flame in a long red cotton dress.

'Have you got a drink?' she asked. 'Oh, good.'

'Ben is the perfect host,' I said.

'I'll just check the curry and then I'll join you. I'm so sorry Max had to leave town. If I'd known sooner I could have changed it to another night.'

'I'm glad you didn't, or I'd be all alone tonight.'

'The two of us could have gotten together. I thought this was going to be a real dinner party, you know, with y'all and Angus and me . . .'

I felt Ben tense beside me and I put an arm round him. 'It'll still be a party. Ben will be my date.'

'You and Max can come over another time soon. I'm dying to meet him, after hearing so much about him.'

I felt uncomfortable, wondering what Ben was thinking. I had never spoken of Max to Ben, and I didn't want him to think his mother and I had secrets from him, even though it was true.

There was a knock at the door and Sallie's face lit up. 'Angus,' she said, almost prayerfully.

I looked at Ben. His face was fixed in a cold, miserable mask, and my hopes for a pleasant evening wilted. Knowing Ben's vehement dislike of the man, and remembering Sallie's former bad luck with men, I didn't expect to like Angus Purdy. My first sight of him did nothing to dispel my preconceptions.

He was a big man with wiry reddish hair and slightly protruding pale blue eyes beneath peaked eyebrows which gave him an air of perpetual surprise. His face was round and rather soft – one of those faces which you could imagine on the body of a child. Some men seem never to have been babies, while some look like babies grown huge, and he was one of the latter.

He was perfectly friendly, perfectly polite, well-spoken and soft-voiced, but there was something underneath his manner, a steely core reflected in his pale eyes, that kept me on guard. If he'd come into a bar where I was working I would have kept my eye on him as a potentially mean drunk, I thought. Or was I being unfair?

Certainly he wasn't the loser I had expected to find sponging off Sallie. Not only was he employed, but he owned his own bar and was in the process of buying another. He had a degree in history, it seemed, although he shrugged it away when Sallie brought it up: no money in it, and he found academics stuffy. But history itself was interesting, and people's attitudes towards it and the methodologies of studying the past . . . someday he might write a book, he said, but only *after* he'd made his fortune.

Sallie obviously adored him, and he was easily, openly affectionate with her, touching her and teasing her from time to time throughout the evening. He was friendly with me without overdoing it – he let me establish the boundaries. As for Ben, Angus made no effort to woo him, but he didn't seem unkind. I had the impression that the boy's existence barely registered on him. Given Ben's sullen, scowling silence through dinner, though, Angus might have been right to ignore Ben. I felt more comfortable myself when Ben left us after dinner – I hadn't realized what a burden his unhappy presence had been until it was removed. As adults together, we talked more freely, and I decided I approved of Angus after all. He was good for Sallie, he made her happy. I would invite them – just the two of them – to dinner with Max and myself very soon.

chapter nine

Ben was in love. It was the most wonderful feeling, the most important fact, in the whole universe. Dinah was never out of his thoughts. Every night before going to sleep he clambered up on to the wooden bedstead, risking a precarious perch in order to plant a kiss on her portrait, and every morning he woke wondering how soon he could see her. His whole life shrank to those moments when he was actually in her presence – the rest of the time he was dreaming about her, thinking about her, plotting how to spend more time with her.

His favourite fantasy was to live with her. When things were particularly bad or boring at school, he would pretend that it was already true, and look ahead to the end of the day when they would be together in their home, eating the dinner she had cooked, and then sitting together on the couch, watching television, until it was time for bed. Sometimes in his daydreams he was a grown-up like Gabriel, and sometimes he was his own age, but always his imaginary Dinah let him hold her hand, and hugged and kissed him often.

At night he sent himself to sleep by pretending that she was in bed beside him, and he could curl up in her arms, make himself as small as a baby to be snugly protected, enveloped in her welcoming body.

The dreams were nice, but they weren't enough. He wanted them to come true. He was only really happy when he was with Dinah, and those times were too few. If they lived together, school and her job wouldn't matter because he could be sure of seeing her every day, waking up with her in the morning and going to bed with her at night.

It could be so simple, he knew. Sallie wanted to live with Angus, and there was no room for Ben in Angus's apartment – he'd heard them talk about it. Maybe Sallie would tell Dinah, and Dinah would say, 'Oh, that's no problem – Ben can come live with me!'

The thought made him shiver with happiness. And it would be so easy . . . One day he tried the idea out on Dinah.

She didn't respond as he had hoped. Instead, she was quiet for a little while, and then she told him how much his mother loved him, and that he should never worry about Sallie wanting to get rid of him.

'Wherever she goes, she'll have room for you. She loves you, Ben, you're the most important person in the world to her.'

'No I'm not. She loves Angus.'

'But she still loves you, and she'd never send you away.'

'Not even if I asked her to? Not even if you and Angus said it was a good idea? Everybody would be happy, then.'

'Sallie wouldn't be happy if you were living somewhere else.'

'Why not? I could still see her – I could see her as much as I see you – I could see her every day if she wanted. I could see her as much as I see her now. And there isn't room for me at Angus's place.'

'Oh, Ben.' She smiled at him tenderly. 'Don't worry so much! If Sallie decided to live with Angus I know she'd get an apartment big enough for the three of you. Why do you think she'd move in with him? Why shouldn't he move in to your place?'

'Because I don't want him to! He makes me sick,' Ben said fiercely. 'I hate him! I won't live with him – if he tries to move in, I'll run away.'

She shook her head. 'I hope not. I'd miss you.'

'Can I live with you, then?'

'I don't think so. Look, I haven't got room for anybody to live with me. You know I've only got one bedroom, and one bed.'

'I don't care.'

'Well, I do.'

'I could sleep on the couch – I don't mind.' He was getting desperate, feeling his dream slipping away. He had to convince her.

'It's not going to happen. Angus or no Angus, you belong with Sallie. Now, can we talk about something else, please?'

'Does that mean you don't want me? You wouldn't let me live with you no matter what? Not even if I didn't have any place else to go? Not even if Sallie died?' As soon as he said the words he was horrified. He wanted to call them back, afraid that by speaking of Sallie's death aloud he might cause it. But he couldn't say anything else. It was as if he was frozen, waiting for Dinah's words to release him.

This time, she didn't let him down.

'Oh, Ben. Is that what's worrying you, sweetheart? Look, it's not going to happen. But if it does, if *anything* happened and you were left alone, why of course I'd take you. And I'd love to have you. Don't you know I love you?'

He was in heaven. She had given him so much more than he had dared to hope. And when she put her arms round him and hugged him close, he had his heart's desire. He only wanted that moment to last for ever.

Aware that he would be guilty if she died, Ben did not imagine Sallie's death for his fantasies. But something else had to happen to allow him to live with Dinah, since she didn't find Angus reason enough. Maybe Sallie would have to go into the hospital. Not for anything too terrible, not for anything painful, but there must be some disease or operation which wouldn't hurt but would keep her there a long time. Maybe she would have something catching, and he wouldn't be allowed to be near her. He'd have to be sent to stay somewhere else – Dinah would take him in. She had said so; she had promised. They would live together in her apartment, they would share her bed. At that thought, a feeling as warm and delicious as melted butter flowed through him, making him shiver with desire. If only. If only it would happen. If only Sallie would go away and leave him with Dinah, for any reason at all.

He no longer cared what his mother did or thought, or how often she was out. He no longer minded about Angus. Only Dinah was important.

When he was near her he felt alive in a new way, as if all his skin bristled with tiny feelers, little antennae all tuned to her and quivering with the signals they received. He was aware of her every change in mood, even though he didn't always understand them, and he tried hard to please her, to make her always happy, to keep her attention focused on him.

She had said that she loved him, and that was what he wanted to know. He loved her; she loved him. But he didn't understand: if she really loved him, why weren't they together more? Ben knew that if he was a grown-up, he would let nothing stand in his way. He would make sure of seeing Dinah every day. Things like school and jobs got in the way, but he wanted to spend all his free time with her, and couldn't understand why she didn't feel the same – love demanded it.

But he couldn't count on her. Although she always seemed glad to see him, she obviously did not share his hunger for constant, regular contact. He couldn't pin her down. One day she would agree to meet him at 4.30 for *beignets*, but the next she would say it was impossible, she was much too busy to see him even for five minutes.

Sometimes pleading worked – he could coax and wheedle her into giving in – but sometimes it had the opposite effect, and she would grow impatient and snap at him not to whine, and then he would be afraid of pushing her too far and making her stop loving him. Over the phone he never knew where he stood with her. He couldn't predict her reactions or influence her. Only when he was actually with her, when he could touch her and watch the expressions flickering across her face, did he feel connected, and as sure of her love as he was of his own.

Always before he left her, Ben tried to make Dinah promise another meeting the next day. But she was tricky and would rarely give him a definite answer. Probably she knew that if she said no to him then he would be able to change her decision, while over the phone, later, she would be safe and he could not move her.

He rarely understood her excuses. He only wanted to be with her, it didn't matter what they did. *Beignets*, ice creams, walks along the river were all OK, but he would be as happy just sitting in her apartment, watching while she did whatever it was that kept her from going out with him. Even if she was too busy to talk, it didn't matter – he wouldn't disturb her, he promised. If it was housework, he would help. He wouldn't get in the way. If she loved him, why didn't she want him around?

There was someone called Max, he knew that much. And without ever seeing the man, Ben hated him. Dinah rarely mentioned him except to call him 'a friend', but Ben knew from his mother what that meant. He imagined another Angus – bigger, meaner and uglier – and then tried not to think about him. Maybe one day Max would just disappear.

This was one of her busy days, Dinah said, and she wouldn't have time to see Ben. Not didn't want to, but wouldn't. Ben imagined a stern-looking boss, like a teacher, pointing at a stack of papers and barring the door. He knew that her hours at work weren't the same from day to day – sometimes she could leave early to meet him in the later afternoon, and sometimes she had to stay at work until past his bedtime.

This was apparently one of the latter, and at first Ben thought he'd have to accept it. But then he had a great idea. Why not go see her at work? He knew where she was – he'd been there once with Sallie – and because it was a health spa where people came and went all the time, he wouldn't seem out of place or cause any trouble.

Dinah might be annoyed to see him, but she might be glad, too. And once she understood that she didn't have to look after or entertain him, she would surely let him sit in a corner of her office while she worked. He had his schoolbooks and his sketch pad to keep him busy. He came straight from school, on the bus. There was a bus stop just across the street from the bank tower.

Ben stood on the corner and stared up at the building, shading his eyes against the sun. She was up there. He saw a swimming pool, and people leaping off diving boards into the high, blue sky, then plunging down, down into the water. The thought made him dizzy. He closed his eyes and held his breath, remembering. Dinah was inside, safe. Not on the roof, but inside a room safely enclosed by the building. It was safe to go up. He would always have a floor beneath his feet and a ceiling over his head – he was being silly, forgetting what the spa looked like.

His heart still hammered with guilt, anticipation and a residue of fear as he crossed the street and entered the bank. He hoped Dinah would be pleased to see him. He hoped she wouldn't send him away.

But when he emerged at the top from the elevator, a lady behind the desk asked what he wanted, and then told him that 'Miss Whelan' had gone home for the day.

Home! It was only four-thirty-five according to the clock downstairs. If she had known she was going home so early, why had she told him she had too much work to see him? Did she mean housework? But he could help her do the cleaning – he loved to vacuum and to clean windows, and he was also good at dusting. For Dinah, he would even do dishes. Didn't she know? Did she think he would get in the way?

Indignation sent him to the bus stop, and he caught the bus that would take him down Esplanade Avenue. Then he started feeling uneasy, as if by going to her house uninvited he was doing something forbidden. But he was on his way now and he wouldn't turn back. He had to see her, even if just for a minute.

He ran from the bus stop, up to the porch, then inside, all the way to the top of the stairs. But although he pounded at the door and called her name, there was no response. Going back down, at last, he clung to the railing and took each step as cautiously as a crippled old man. He was afraid of becoming afraid: he tried not to think of falling.

'Hey, you, what do you want?'

A woman in faded jeans and a baggy red sweatshirt was waiting for him at the bottom of the stairs. She didn't look friendly. He stopped.

'I was looking for Dinah,' he said.

'She's not here. She's at work.'

'They told me she'd gone home.'

'Well, who are you? What do you want Dinah for?'

'She's my mother.' He hadn't planned to say it, but once they were out he liked the sound of the words, and wasn't sorry.

'Your mother! She didn't say anything to me about having a kid. If she's your mother, how come you don't live with her?'

'I have to live with my stepmother. But Dinah's talking about getting a bigger place so that we could live together, just the two of us, for ever.'

'Mmm.' She no longer looked hostile, only bemused.

Ben came cautiously down another step. 'Do you know where she is? Or when she'll be back?'

'No, I haven't seen her today,' the woman said. 'She comes and goes, so there's no telling when she'll be in. Was she expecting you?'

'Not exactly. Not today. But she's always glad to see me.'

The front door opened. From where he was standing, Ben couldn't see who it was, but he knew when the woman said, 'Hey, there's a kid looking for you. He says he's your son.'

Ben's fingers tightened on the railing. He wondered if he should run.

'Ben?' Dinah came in sight, her arms full of a big brown paper bag. 'What are you doing here?'

He couldn't tell what she was thinking. She was frowning slightly, but he thought it was in puzzlement rather than anger.

'He doesn't look anything like you,' said the woman. 'I wouldn't have believed it.'

Dinah flashed a quick, false smile and said, 'No, he takes after his father.'

Within him a knot of nerves dissolved. She hadn't betrayed him. She wouldn't.

'I can't talk now, Morgan,' Dinah said. 'I've got to get these groceries put away. Ben, open the door for me, would you, sweetie?' She tossed him a ring of keys and, to his great delight, he caught it without fumbling, so then he was able to run up the stairs without looking down, without the slightest qualm.

Only after they were inside and Dinah had deposited her bag in the kitchen did she ask, 'Why did you tell Morgan I was your mother?'

'Well . . . you could have been.'

She caught her hair in the splayed fingers of one hand and raked it back. 'Could have been . . . You're as bad as me with your could have beens!'

'Should have been.'

'Why?'

His skin prickled under the chill of her steady blue gaze, but he told her what he had worked out for himself.

'Gabriel was my father.'

'Yes.'

'Gabriel was married to you.'

'Yes.'

'Mothers and fathers are married to each other . . .'

'Usually.'

'So you should have been my mother.'

'But I'm not,' she said gently. 'You know that.'

He ran and flung his arms round her and held her tight, feeling her tension ease as she gradually relaxed in his embrace. 'It's better that you're not, though,' he said.

'Why is it better?'

'Because if you were my mother, I couldn't marry you.' He kept his face pressed against her, aware of the soft swell of her breasts. He felt her catch her breath and then expel it in a little laugh.

'Oh, Ben. Was that a proposal?'

His heart thudded painfully. He closed his eyes. 'Yes.'

'I'm very flattered. But aren't you kind of young to be getting yourself engaged?'

'I'll grow up.'

'Is that a promise?'

'Don't laugh at me! I'm serious!' He gripped her more fiercely.

'All right. Ask me again a little closer to the time. When you're grown up.'

'I will. You'll see. I'll never change my mind. I'll marry you someday. I'll always love you.'

'All right, Ben. Let go of me now. I have some things to do.'

Reluctantly – because he was aware of her coolness and of the fact that she had promised him nothing – he set her free. She vanished into the kitchen and he could hear the sound of cupboards being opened and closed, and the rustling of the paper bag. He stood where she had left him, feeling restless and sad, dissatisfied in a way he could not explain.

She looked surprised and a little uneasy when she returned to find him standing still in the same spot.

'I thought you'd left,' she said. 'I don't have time for a visit today.'

'I won't get in the way,' he said. 'Can't I stay and do my homework?' He gestured at the stack of books he'd dropped on the floor.

She caught a handful of hair and combed it back with her fingers, and Ben wondered why she was nervous.

'But I'm going out. I mean, I have to get ready to go out, you know, have a bath, change my clothes . . . I don't have any time to waste.'

'That's OK. I'll just stay until you have to go. I'll just sit here with my books.'

Her shoulders slumped and she gave in. 'Oh, all right, if that's what you want.' She went into the bedroom without giving him another look.

Ben felt uneasy, as much guilty as pleased that he had won. He picked his books off the floor and settled with them on the couch. But he didn't feel like reading his homework – he couldn't concentrate. He stared at the bedroom door, waiting for Dinah to return.

But she didn't come. Instead, he heard the distant, steady roar of water thundering into the bath, and realized he would have a long wait. Mentally, he relaxed a little, and began to leaf through his sketch book. Pictures of Dinah predominated, most of them copies of the portrait in his bedroom, although a few of the more recent ones were attempts to draw her from life. It was time to try that again, he thought, to draw Dinah not from memory but from the reality, with her sitting in front of him. It would be the best thing he'd ever done. Although that wouldn't be hard. Most of the sketches looked bad to him, crude or stiff. Only a few, near the beginning of the book, had Gabriel's touch which made them live on the page. He stared down at the very best one, trying to understand it. He stared until the lines stopped showing a face and became meaningless marks, black against white. He stared until his vision blurred, stared and tried to feel the pencil in his hand, tried to remember what it felt like to draw that way.

'Studying hard?'

Her voice pulled him back. She was standing in the doorway, smiling across at him, dressed in a long blue and white kimono, her hair turbaned in dark blue towelling, her feet bare. He gazed at her as if she was a vision. Where had he been? Where was he now?

Dinah sank down on the couch. She held a red and white dress in her hands, and a needle and thread. 'I have to sew this button back on before I can wear it,' she explained. 'It won't bother you if I sit here? Go on studying if you like.'

He found his voice at last. 'Let me sketch you.'

'Sketch me! Not like this.'

He nodded. 'But let your hair down.'

'It's all wet. It'll look awful. Oh, all right, don't give me that look! Is this for your art class?'

'It's for me.'

Drawing depended chiefly on looking. He had to look at her in a different way from usual, a special way, in order to see what he had to draw. If he could see the truth, see it properly, then he could put it on paper. But it was hard to do.

'Put your hand up to the side of your head – tilt your head a little – comb your fingers in your hair.'

'I can't do all that and sew at the same time.'

'Please. It's important.'

She hesitated. He stared hard at her until she put down her needle and did as he asked. 'But not for long,' she warned. 'I can't spend all evening posing for you.'

He didn't answer. He was drawing. His hand moved the pencil across the page beyond his control, outside his conscious intent. He scarcely glanced at Dinah after the first, long look – he didn't have to. He no longer needed his eyes to tell him what his hand knew. He saw her through memory, through the tips of his fingers, through his sense of smell and his ears.

Around them the room altered. There was a heavy, musky, seashore smell in the air, the smell of sex. Dinah curled naked on the bed and smiled her innocent, seductive smile. He could taste her still on his lips, and the sleek, warm softness of her skin clothed his nakedness as he sketched furiously trying to capture it all, struggling to depict the moment and the eternity of his love for her in a few dark lines on the page. She stretched like a cat on the bed, teasing him with her body.

'Hold still,' he muttered.

'I am still – I couldn't be stiller!'

He was getting it right. At last, he felt that wonderful sense of power and freedom, the knowledge that everything was moving exactly as it should, that he was in harmony with the rest of the universe, all of it coming together, coming to a point at the tip of his pencil.

'Ben?'

The intrusion of her voice made him frown and hunch over his pad. He didn't want to be distracted – not now, not when he was finally getting somewhere. He probably wouldn't be satisfied with the picture when it was finished – he never was – but for the moment something was happening, he was a part of something else, something greater, and that was all that mattered.

'Ben, why are you holding your pencil like that? Ben?'

Words tore at the fragile link but he clung grimly, refusing to hear her, not letting her reach him.

'Ben!'

He screamed. She caught hold of him and the pencil slashed across the page, ruining it. She pulled him back to her reality.

They stared at each other in shaken silence. Still clutching his arms, she looked hard into his face. Her kimono had fallen open and he could see her breasts. The sight gave him a hot, prickling sensation from his chest all the way down to the bottom of his stomach, an almost painful feeling. He closed his eyes, but the feeling remained. He could feel the heat coming off her naked skin, and smell the tang of her shampoo. He imagined himself pushing the kimono down her arms and pressing his face against her soft, warm scented flesh. Her breasts.

'What is it? What's wrong?'

He shook his head, wanting and not daring. He wanted her so much. If only she could feel it, if he didn't have to do anything, if she would pull him close, enfold him in her arms . . .

She let go, and he heard the rustle of cloth as she wrapped her kimono more tightly, and then he opened his eyes.

'You ruined it,' he said bleakly.

'Don't be silly.' She bent down to pick up the discarded pad. There was a dark lead line, a disfiguring scar, across the sketched face. 'Oh. I'm sorry.'

'See, it's ruined.'

'You can do another. I'll pose again.'

'Not like that.'

She sighed. 'Well, I'm sorry I spoiled it. But you scared me when you wouldn't answer.'

'I was concentrating! I can't always be talking to you!'

She bit her lip. 'Do you want to start over? Do you want to try again now?'

But the moment was gone. He felt too jangled up inside. He was too confused and he knew he wouldn't be able to let go and concentrate in the same way, he wouldn't be able to relax. He felt angry, although he wasn't sure exactly why. He shook his head. 'Not now.'

'Another time, then. I promise I'll pose again, however you want me.'

– naked on the bed –

He stood up suddenly, feeling sick. Gabriel. Gabriel was back. He had called him back, and that was what he had wanted. He should be pleased. He didn't know why he felt so frightened all of a sudden.

'Ben?' Her hand closed about his wrist. 'Are you all right?'

'Yeah.'

'I'll tell you what worried me, and why I broke your concentration. When you were drawing you started to hold the pencil in a funny way. Do you know why?'

'Funny?' he asked blankly.

She turned his hand over, and her thumb traced a pattern on the smooth skin of his palm. 'There's nothing wrong with your hand. No scar, no damage. You were holding the pencil as if you couldn't bend your middle finger. It was jutting up as if at some time a tendon had been cut and never properly healed. But I've seen you bend it before. There's nothing wrong with your hand.' She flexed his fingers back and forth while he stared, uncomprehending. 'It must have been awkward to hold the pencil like that. Why were you doing it?'

'I don't know.'

'Did you know you were holding it differently? You didn't answer when I called your name, but I think you heard me.'

He shook his head, but he knew. Gabriel had made him, for Gabriel's own reasons. But why now, when he hadn't called him – why had Gabriel come back when he no longer wanted him?

There were footsteps outside on the stairs. Someone approaching the door. Ben broke away from Dinah and ran. Not to the front door – someone was knocking, there was no escape there – but back into the bedroom, and then into the bathroom.

Like all the doors in the apartment, the one to the bathroom was thick and sturdy and equipped with a big, old-fashioned lock and key. Safe behind it, he turned the key in the lock, knowing that no one could get in unless he let them. No one except Gabriel.

Ben sat gingerly on the smooth, curving lip of the bathtub. His legs were trembling. He was aware of Gabriel's presence as a confused, inward turmoil. Not a good feeling; not a friendly presence. He had almost forgotten about Gabriel – he had certainly forgotten this part of him. But he recognized it well enough now, remembering Gabriel's wild, impatient anger, and the times in the past it had burst free. But he didn't need Gabriel, now, and he didn't want him. He had Dinah, and he didn't want to share her with anyone, not even Gabriel.

After a moment he stood up. It was stupid to stay here, locked in a bathroom. He was hungry and, although he didn't have a watch, he guessed he was late for dinner. He unlocked the door and went out.

Dinah wasn't alone. There was a man with her, kissing her. And his hands were inside her kimono. He had pushed the kimono open, or she had opened it for him, and his hands touched her naked body, just as Ben had longed to do. She was letting the man touch her. She liked it. She didn't even know Ben was there.

He had to run past them to get out of the apartment. He went as fast as he could, not even pausing to pick up his books. Burning with shame and anger, he could think only of escape. He hardly noticed the stairs, tumbling away beneath his feet. He could hardly breathe. He was stifling. He needed the open air. Running was clumsy and slow – if only he could fly, as he did in his dreams.

He was halfway home before he felt much more than the panic urge to escape. Only then did he feel the pain, the dreadful shock, as if he had been shot in the stomach. He felt weak, too, as if he had already bled half to death.

Why did she let it happen? Why did she have to be like that? Why couldn't she just love him? She was like Sallie, no better than Sallie. She didn't care for him any more than Sallie did. She would be glad if he died, if he just went away and left her to that man.

Max. Hatred bloomed with the name. That man was Max. Her 'friend'. If Max was her friend what was Ben? Not her friend, not her son, not her husband, not anything. Ben was nothing to her.

Anger and loathing mingled, unfocused but powerful, ready to be aimed. It churned inside him, a force demanding release. It was so overwhelming that he could think of nothing else.

'Where've you been? Your dinner's probably cold by now, but I couldn't wait for ever. I have to work tonight, you know. Hey, I'm talking to you – look at me when I'm talking – where are you going?'

Sallie's voice as he came in was just a background sound, hardly more meaningful than a mosquito buzzing past his ear. He wasn't thinking at all. Emotional forces drove him on, back to his room.

Where Dinah watched from the wall, her face blank, smug, unreachable. Sallie's face was a painting, too, although it moved. It moved like a mask, sending meaningless words into the air.

He was trapped and stifling. Painted faces mocked him, and he turned round and round, seeking escape from his lonely rage. Someone took hold of his arm, tried to stop him, and that made him fight harder. He wouldn't be held. She didn't love him. No one loved him. He hated himself. He despised his weak, puny body, and he slapped and scratched at it ineffectually, wanting out but having no idea how to get there, how to escape the pain.

He twisted and turned helplessly, furiously, and all the while felt Dinah's dead, painted eyes on him. His flailing arms knocked something, and warm Coca-Cola splashed him, the glass rolling on its side. He caught it before it fell to the floor, glass smooth and hard and solid in his hand, the only reality, anchoring him to the world. He stopped and looked up at Dinah.

But she wouldn't look back. Her eyes looked over his head, beyond his face. She was always looking at someone else. She wasn't his, and she never would be.

Gabriel's rage tore through Ben's body, to emerge as an incoherent snarl, and the hand with the glass hurled it as hard as he could at Dinah's indifferent face.

chapter ten

I heard about Ben's temper tantrum the next day, when Sallie came by the spa to pick up his books, and stayed on for a while to chat.

'Luckily the glass didn't shatter, it broke into three pieces,' she said. 'And luckily he threw it and didn't punch it into the painting, like –'

She stopped, not invoking Gabriel, but of course I knew what she meant.

'Then what happened?'

'He stood there for a minute like he was stunned, and then he started crying. After that he was himself again. After he finished crying I scolded him a little, made him eat some dinner and put him to bed. I was late for work.' She shrugged.

'Does he get like that often?'

'Not a lot . . . sometimes. He hasn't had a tantrum like that for years – well, a year, I guess. I thought he'd finally outgrown it.' She frowned at me. 'What set him off? Any idea? What was he like when he left your place?'

'He left suddenly. He just ran out,' I said, and hesitated. I had thought of my relationship with Ben as private and special. I hadn't even shared it with Max, and it seemed unfair to tell Sallie. But maybe it wasn't such a harmless secret – maybe Sallie should know.

'I'm still not sure exactly what happened,' I said. 'Ben and I were alone together, and he seemed different somehow . . . he was in the bathroom when Max came over, and when he came out, Max and I were kissing. Ben ran out without a word. I don't know whether he was embarrassed, or maybe jealous.'

Sallie nodded. 'He does have a big crush on you.'

Her awareness shook me off balance. 'A crush! Oh, come on. He's not old enough for anything like that.'

'How old were you the first time you fell in love? I was six, and let me tell you, it was pretty heavy.'

'Nothing like that for me – not until after puberty, when the old hormones were working.'

'Oh yeah? What about your father?'

'What d'you mean?'

'You were crazy about him, from what you told me.'

'That's not a crush! My god, Sallie, my own father – I certainly didn't have a crush on him. If you mean Ben loves me the way I loved my father, you may be right. He thinks of me as his mother.'

'He's already got a mother,' she said, and the sharpness in her tone reminded me of the jealousy that had simmered just below the surface early in our friendship.

'He's so much like Gabriel, it's uncanny sometimes,' I said. 'I can't believe it's all genetic – not things like his rages, and his drawing, his personality . . .'

We looked at each other, and I was sure she must be following my thoughts. 'Do you ever think about it?'

'What?'

'Reincarnation.'

She shook her head hard. 'No way. No way. You mean, like, Gabriel jumps out the window and dies and his soul flies straight into my womb? Come on, Dinah. I know Gabriel used to like to talk about having lived before – maybe he even believed in it. I don't.'

'You did once.'

'We all believed different things once. No, I don't believe in old souls in new bodies. Sometimes Ben does seem a lot like Gabriel, and I guess all that can't be explained by genetics. But it could be explained by other things.'

'Does Ben ever *say* he's Gabriel?'

She frowned, and I thought she might be remembering something, or trying to. But she shook her head. 'No . . . but he used to talk about him a lot. Not like he was his father, but like he was his friend, somebody who visited him sometimes. He was a kind of lonely kid, and I guess he took Gabe's name for his imaginary playmate. He knew a lot about Gabriel, but that's not too surprising. I used to talk about him, talk to Ben when I thought he was too young to understand, just because I was lonely. Kids pick up a lot more than we realize. And Angus told me about this theory –'

'You've talked to Angus about this?'

'Sure.'

I felt betrayed. Not for myself, but for Gabriel . . . for Ben. 'And what does Angus say?'

'Well . . . I did kind of think just what you were saying, that maybe reincarnation could be true. Gabriel believed it – and Gabriel always got his way, didn't he? If anybody could come back and live again, he's the one. And when you die violently, before your time – well, it almost makes a kind of sense.'

'But what did Angus say?'

'He told me about a book which investigates a lot of cases where people remember past lives. They're not lying – under hypnosis they start talking in other languages they don't even know when they're awake. But according to this book, people can learn things they don't even know they know. Like, if you had a Polish grandmother who used to take care of you, you might find out under hypnosis that you could speak Polish – you would have learned words when you were two years old and then consciously forgotten them . . . but unconsciously it's still there. Or you might have the memory of something you saw on television when you were three, and now it feels like the memory of a past life. Ben heard all sorts of stuff about Gabriel when he was a tiny baby. And it's normal for little boys to want to imitate their fathers. His wanting to be like Gabriel is a phase, I'm sure. It'll pass. I thought it *had* passed, until you turned up.'

'Oh, so it's my fault?'

'I didn't mean that. God, Dinah, why are you so sensitive –'

Staring into my face, her clear grey eyes clouded. 'You think he *is* Gabriel?'

'Haven't you ever looked at his drawings?' I asked. 'Haven't you ever *watched* him drawing? You know he's got Gabriel's temper –'

'So he's got his father's temper – he *knows* about that –'

The telephone rang and I snatched it up, dealt much too briskly with someone enquiring about membership and then buzzed Dawn and asked her to handle all calls.

'You haven't been talking to Ben about this, have you?' she asked.

'No, of course not.'

'Good. Don't. Don't encourage him. He's got to be himself – he can't be anyone else. He's Ben, that's all. He's not Gabriel.'

'But if there's a chance – don't you see, there might be a chance that Gabriel isn't really dead, that he's been reborn –'

'If there's a chance – what are you talking about? Two people can't be in the same place at the same time. If Gabriel isn't dead, then Ben has to be. Forget Gabriel, Dinah! He's dead. Even if – all right, *even if* Gabriel was right and souls are reincarnated, and Gabriel's soul came back as Ben – he's Ben now. He's somebody new. If reincarnation happens, that must be the point of it, surely – new lives, new chances. There's no point in trying to relive an old life; the thing is to forget and start again. Ben has his own life, and it started the minute he was born. He isn't your husband, he's my son, and he isn't going to die when he's twenty-three, and he isn't going to marry you. If it makes you feel better to think that something inside him, his soul, used to be part of Gabriel, then, fine. But don't impose it on him. Just leave him alone.'

She began stowing away Ben's books into her large straw carry-all. I felt a pang of regret as the sketch pad vanished, wishing for another chance to look at it.

'I wouldn't do anything to hurt Ben,' I said. 'The only time Gabriel has been mentioned it's come from him, I promise you. I love him, you know that, don't you? I love him like he was my own son.'

She nodded, but she didn't look at me. 'Because he *should* have been yours?' she asked quietly. 'Because you think he's Gabriel?'

'Because he's Ben. I wish I hadn't said anything – Sallie, you're taking all this too seriously! It was just an idea, just speculation. I haven't said anything to Ben about it, and I won't. But I thought I could talk to *you*.'

'I'm not blaming you,' Sallie said. 'But it's got to stop. It's not good for him, he's too old to be so hung up on Gabriel. At his age he should have real, live friends, and he shouldn't go around measuring everybody up against this image he has in his mind of Gabriel. It doesn't seem to matter what Angus does – Ben made his mind up to hate him long before he met him. Angus thinks maybe we should send Ben away to military school.'

'Military school! For Ben? It would kill him!'

'Angus says it would toughen him up. I didn't like the idea at first, but we've got to do something. Ben's been playing hookey from school, and not doing his homework. He lives in his own private world most of the time. And if he's not going to be happy living with us, he'd better go somewhere else.'

'You and Angus . . .?'

'He's asked me to marry him.' She almost blushed. For one crazy moment I wanted to hit her.

I said, 'Have you told Ben?'

'No, because I haven't decided yet. If it was just me, I'd be married now. But I have to work out what would be best for Ben.' She looked at her watch. 'I've got to go talk to Ben's teacher. Maybe she'll have some ideas. I'll see you, Dinah.'

She didn't hug me when she left. I wondered if she would send Ben to military school just to keep him away from me.

I hoped, when I got home from work, to find Ben waiting for me on the porch, but he wasn't there. I hoped he would soon get over his disappointment and jealousy, stop sulking and come back to me. Probably it would take a few days – and yet I kept hoping he would show up, and I couldn't settle to anything else. I kept walking to the window and lingering there, gazing up and down the long, wide avenue below in the endlessly frustrated hope of glimpsing a small dark-haired boy.

What I finally saw instead was Max's car. After waiting and hoping for Ben, that was a let-down. I tried to change the mood of my thoughts from brooding about Ben to pleasure at the thought of Max.

Max wasn't as quick up the stairs as usual. I had two drinks poured and was beginning to wonder if I had mistaken his car when I finally heard his knock. When I kissed him I sensed some tension, a slight holding-back.

'What's wrong?'

He shook his head.

'Beer?'

'Thanks.' Then as I turned away for his glass, the question came. 'Who was that kid here yesterday?'

'I told you. Sallie's little boy, Ben.'

'Yeah, you told me.' He looked away, at the picture of Gabriel that still hung on the wall, and I felt a premonition of danger like a chill wind on the back of my neck. 'I saw Morgan on the porch. She said something odd. She thinks he's your kid. Said she asked you. Said you told her he was yours.'

'He's not mine.'

He looked at me. I said flatly, 'I've never had a baby. You've seen my body – what do you think? He's Sallie's.'

'What did you say to Morgan?'

I wanted to lie. But if I couldn't tell Max the truth now, I might as well forget our relationship. I said, 'I let her think that he was mine, because I wish he was.'

'Oh, Dinah.' I saw him melt. For a moment I thought he might cry. Then he came and embraced me.

'Marry me,' he said, hugging me hard. 'Let's have a baby.'

'Oh, Max.'

'You want to, right? So do I. We'll have our own little baby.' He rubbed the base of my spine, still holding me tight, grinning. But it was a tremulous grin – he was terrified I would refuse.

I felt a rush of love, pity and desire. 'Yes. Yes, Max. I want you. I want your baby.'

He laughed, and squeezed me so hard I couldn't breathe. 'Oh, great, great, great. Let's start now.'

'What?'

His hands fumbled at the fastening of my jeans. 'Start the baby. We can get married after. Next week, tomorrow, whenever you want. You don't think we ought to wait until the wedding night, do you? You didn't want to wear white, did you?'

He was getting absolutely nowhere with my jeans, so I undid them for him. 'But will you still want to marry me after I let you have your wicked way? Why buy the cow when you can get free milk? Isn't that what you men say?'

'My darling, I've wanted to marry you since I first saw you. I'm selfish and possessive and I want you all to myself.'

'You'll have to share me with the baby.'

'That's OK. As long as I'm first.'

I pressed my hand to his lips. 'Let's go to bed.'

Much later, the room grown dark around us, I needed to talk. Not about the when, how and where of our marriage as Max wanted, but some unfinished business.

'You know you were asking me about Ben – Sallie's little boy,' I began.

'Doesn't matter. I was just jealous. I thought you were keeping something from me,' Max said comfortably, moving his head closer to mine on the pillow.

'I was. I didn't tell you that Ben's father was Gabriel.'

'So why are you telling me now?'

'Because I want you to know. I don't want any secrets to come between us. Maybe I should have told you sooner, when I found out, but I felt so strange, so angry and jealous and –'

'You didn't know before?'

'Oh, no. I left New Orleans right after Gabriel died, and I didn't stay in touch with anybody. Ben was conceived the night Gabriel died. He was the last thing Gabriel ever did,' I said, and smiled self-mockingly.

'So he should have been your son.'

They might have been my own words. But as Max said it, for the first time I saw how wrong it was.

'No, he shouldn't have been. I was just a kid – I could barely look after myself. I don't know what kind of mother I would have been, but I wasn't ready. I didn't want a baby then – that's why I was on the Pill.'

Lying there, still warm in afterglow, I knew I had changed. I was content with my life. I took Max's hand and pressed it low down against my flat stomach. 'This is the baby I want.'

'Do you think?'

'I know.'

'It wouldn't hurt to do it again, just to make sure.'

Days passed without word or sign of Ben. I was sorry to think of him sad, lonely, possibly hating me, but he didn't come to mind very often. I was too occupied with Max and with thoughts of the baby I was sure we had started.

We planned to get married the week before Christmas, and then go up to Lake Bluff so I could show him off to my parents.

I phoned Polly to tell her my news and invite her to the wedding – Nick and Tessa were the only other guests we planned to ask.

But Polly was far too pregnant, she told me. 'I'm hoping I'll have a two-week old baby by that time, and I just don't think I could manage! But I'll be thinking about you.'

'I'll be thinking about you, too,' I said, and I was smiling at the thought of Polly with her baby, and not feeling any envy. It was on the tip of my tongue to tell her that I was pregnant, too, but I held back. It might be bad luck, so soon. I didn't know for certain anyway – if there was a baby it couldn't be measured yet; it was no bigger than a feeling.

I wanted to tell Sallie about my engagement, but she didn't come in to the spa, and I didn't want to call. She and Ben had both vanished from my life, and in a way it was a relief.

A northerly blew in one night in November, bringing the first cold weather of the season. From an afternoon high of eighty-six degrees, by late evening it was forty-five degrees.

The winds that blew cool through the streets of the city changed more than just the temperature; spirits were altered, too. There was a bubbling sense of anticipation, as if for a holiday. There was a little of the same excitement that always built up before Mardi Gras. Strangers grinned at each other, the weather a secret they shared, and everybody had the same topic of conversation: how strong were the winds, how low would the mercury drop. Even people who swore the fiercest hatred for winter and cold weather pulled on their coats and sweaters with extra energy, as if arming themselves for a fight they secretly enjoyed.

I was elated, of course. Walking home from the spa, buffeted by the wind, I was happy to shiver, to have my summer clothes finally unsuitable. After so much heat for so long I had stopped believing in winter, had grown to believe it was something, like really good pizza, which couldn't be found this far south of Chicago.

At last I could get my sweaters out! Wear some different clothes! The sound of dead leaves ticking on the pavement was music to my ears, and it was hard to keep myself from breaking into a run, I was so eager to be home with a hot drink, appreciating my warm sanctuary all the more for the cold, dark night outside.

And when I was home, music playing softly and a steaming cup of tea in my hands, the electric heater plugged in and dragged near the couch to beam its unnecessary but welcome heat at me, there was only one thing which kept me from being completely happy: the absence of Max. He had left early that morning to Chicago on business. I expected him to call after eleven and tell me it was snowing there, but his voice on the phone wasn't what I longed for. I wanted his body to heat mine beneath the blankets. Cold weather was for cuddling. Still, the whole winter – erratically warm as it would be in New Orleans – stretched ahead; our whole lives, filled with possibilities, and I was happier than I'd been in years.

The very next day – crisp, cold and beautiful though it was – sent me tumbling down again.

Mr Opacek was waiting for me at work.

I remembered his face, like an expensive wood carving, sleek, brown and polished, and how his teeth had seemed to glow against his tan. They weren't glowing now because he wasn't showing them. It was the first time I'd ever seen him look unfriendly.

Despite the falling-elevator feeling in my stomach, I smiled and strained to project warmth and enthusiasm.

'How nice to see you again! But I had no idea you were going to be in New Orleans – you should have called.'

'I tried calling. Several times. You were never in,' he said. 'Shall we go in the office? We can talk more privately there.'

Not 'your office' but 'the office'. I think I knew then what he'd come to say, but I followed him meekly back to listen to it. I had no choice. I couldn't even defend myself when he told me how disappointed he was. That's what adults say to children, and I felt like a child at school, caught evading work. There was no defence. I didn't know what to say. I hardly even knew him, for there was no trace in his manner of the old flirtatiousness, the friendliness I'd always had from him.

'I don't know whether you just couldn't cope, or whether you haven't bothered to try, but the result is the same. Well, we all make mistakes. I made one when I hired you. I knew you didn't have any experience, but I thought your enthusiasm would make up for it. I thought you'd work twice as hard if I gave you a chance. Well, I gave you a chance, and it backfired.'

It was an immense effort to speak, to find something I could say. It was like being trapped in a nightmare. 'If you could give me another chance . . . more time . . . more suggestions about what I should do? I'll try, I'm willing to try, and work harder, if –'

'But you haven't tried,' he said flatly. 'You haven't worked hard, you haven't done a damn thing, just the minimum to keep this place going. Where are all the new customers you should have had by now? In a very little while, do you realize, I'll be making an active loss on this place. And that's no way to do business. You've been in charge here more than three months – we'll say four months. I'll pay you for the whole of this month. I'm not vindictive. I blame myself as much as I blame you. But I can't afford to give you a second chance. No free rides.'

I tried to think of some explanation or excuse, but there were none. I knew he was right to fire me – that was why he was a success and I was not. He was always working. It was his life. And I hadn't made it mine. I'd done what felt like a lot of work – but never too much. It hadn't obsessed me. My real life had always been outside the spa, apart from business, and I wasn't sure, even now, that I could have done it any differently, that I could have made myself fall in love with the job to the exclusion of all others.

'I'll make out your pay cheque now,' he said. 'Why don't you clear your things out of the desk? No sense hanging around. Let's make it a clean break. No hard feelings on either side.'

But his eyes were as hard as stones – as hard as his feelings. And he had every right to despise me. I despised myself. No excuses. I'd blown it. I'd thought I was someone I wasn't. I felt I'd just been caught out in a four-month lie. I was a waitress in disguise.

I left feeling dazed, my shoulder bag weighing me down. It was heavy with all the personal items that had accumulated in my desk over the past weeks. I felt homeless, cut adrift with all my worldly possessions in one bag. Where could I go? What could I do? Somehow, through all my varied, speckled career, I had never before been fired. It seemed monstrously unfair that this, the first time, should be from the job that most mattered. But I knew it wasn't unfair. I hadn't deserved the job. That was what hurt the most.

Going through the heavy glass doors to the street, I saw Ben waiting for me on the far corner.

I began to cry as I crossed the street, and by the time I reached Ben I couldn't see him for the blur of tears; I couldn't even speak. He put his arms round me and held on tight: small as he was, I felt he was protecting me. My self-esteem was so low I felt I needed someone to take care of me, and even this child could make a better job of it than I had.

All this time, of course, people were passing us. And not all of them just passed: because this was New Orleans and not Chicago, some people stopped to ask the problem.

'It's all right,' said Ben. 'She's all right. She thought I was lost, and she's glad because she found me. She's crying because she's happy.'

His smooth explanation – did he believe it? – made me laugh, which choked off the tears.

'I'm all right now,' I said. 'At least . . . I will be. I'd like a drink of water, and some place to sit down.'

He took me by the hand and led me into the nearest grill and sandwich shop. It reeked of hot fat, onions and milky coffee, but there was an empty booth and they served us free ice water. I wet a paper napkin and pressed it to my closed eyes. Around me I could hear the clink of forks against plates, the sounds of people eating their solitary breakfasts before going in to work. They had jobs, all of them, and the thought almost started me crying again. Then I heard Ben ask the waitress for a banana split, and something about his unaffected, childish greed comforted me. I realized that what he had said on the street was true: I had thought him lost, and I was glad to have found him again.

I opened my eyes to look at him, and he was looking back, self-contained and inscrutable in his silence. So like his father.

I frowned, and looked at my watch to escape his eyes. 'Hey, shouldn't you be in school?'

He shrugged. 'It doesn't matter.'

'How can you say that?'

'I just did. It doesn't matter. See? It's easy to say.'

'Don't be so cute. How are you going to learn anything if you don't go to school?'

'I don't learn anything when I'm there. It's a big waste of time, mostly, sitting around reading stupid books, listening to stupid teachers . . .'

The waitress brought the banana split and set it down in front of me.

'No,' I said. 'This –'

'Yeah, I ordered it for you,' Ben said. 'Go on, it'll make you feel better.'

I stared down at the mounds of artificial cream, the bright red cherries on top, and couldn't imagine eating. Even the bananas looked false.

'It's too early in the morning for this kind of thing,' I said. 'Thanks, but . . . no thanks.' I pushed the chilly silver dish to one side and saw Ben follow it with his eyes. 'Do you want it?'

'Well . . . only if you're sure you don't.'

'Pity to waste it,' I said, and pushed it across the table, enjoying the way his eyes lit up and his tongue appeared briefly between his lips. How nice to be so easily pleased, to find ice cream a cause for joy.

'What would you have done if I hadn't come out of the building so soon?' I asked. 'Would you have waited on that corner all day?'

'I don't know. Anyway, you *did* come out.'

'I did.'

'Why were you crying? Because of me?'

I shook my head. 'I was happy to see you, though. Especially then. I'd just lost my job. I was fired.'

He stared at me. 'I thought you were the boss?'

'I was. But there was a bigger boss over me, the owner, the man who hired me in the first place. He decided he'd made a mistake, so today he came and fired me.'

'I wish they'd fire me from school.'

I laughed. 'It's not the same thing.'

'Did you like your job?'

I hesitated. 'Well . . . I don't know. I guess I didn't really.'

'Then it's OK. It's good you got fired. Now you can get a better job. You can find something you like.'

'I don't know about that. I thought I'd like this one. It was supposed to be my big break . . . Oh, you're right. I'll find something. I always do.'

'Now that you don't have a job, you don't have to stay in New Orleans, right?'

'Oh, I'm not going to leave. Don't worry about that. You being here is good enough reason for me to stay.' I leaned across the table with my napkin in my hand to wipe away his ice-cream moustache.

He hunched his shoulders up, eyes burning brightly and fixed on my face. 'But together. We could leave together. We could go somewhere else, just jump in the car and go!'

The breath caught in my throat. I shook my head.

'Why not?'

'Well . . . I don't have a car, for one thing.' As I spoke I saw Max's car parked in front of my house. He'd left it in case I wanted to use it.

'We could go in Sallie's car.'

'Go where?'

'Anywhere.' He waved his hands to encompass the world. It was crazy, but I was feeling some of his excitement. My heart beat oddly, as if it were possible.

'But why? For how long? When would we come back?'

'Whenever we wanted. Maybe never.'

'I think Sallie might mind.'

'No she wouldn't. She never uses it, and Angus has a car. Angus takes her most places.'

'I didn't mean about the car. I mean she'd mind about you. Don't you think she'd miss you?'

He looked sullen and shook his head. 'She'd be glad. She wants to have a baby. I heard her say so to Angus. She wants to marry Angus and then send me away to boarding school or something. So I'd be gone anyway, and she wouldn't care. Why can't I go with you? Don't you want me?'

'Oh, Ben, of course I want you! But you don't honestly think I can take you? That we can make this big escape just by stealing a car and going?'

'Why not?' He stared as if I were the one being unreasonable. 'You're a grown-up. You can do whatever you want.'

The challenge seemed to echo down the years – it reminded

me of Gabriel's argument when I had said I would have to leave him and go back to my parents.

'If you loved me you would.'

'You don't know what you're talking about,' I snapped. 'I might be a grown-up, but you're not. I can't take you off somewhere without telling your mother – that's kidnapping.'

'Kidnapping! It's not – I want to go! I'd tell them – I'd tell the police you weren't kidnapping me.'

'I'm afraid it wouldn't make any difference. Look, I know you don't like it, and I know it's not fair, but you'll just have to do what your mother decides. I'll talk to her – I'll try to get her to change her mind about sending you off to boarding school.' I felt pretty hopeless as I offered, and I saw by Ben's scowl that it wasn't enough. I wanted to kiss him and I wanted to shake him at the same time. Life was so horribly unfair. It would be so easy to make Ben happy, if only I had the right. If only I were his mother.

'Look,' I said. 'I'm tired of sitting around this place, and you've finished your ice cream . . . if I can't talk you into going to school, why don't you spend the day with me? We can go home, or someplace else. We'll find something to do.'

With that I allied myself to him, to his side and the forces of anarchy, against the parents, teachers, police and other adults of the world with their unfair, unpleasant rules. His suggestion – that magical 'just get in the car and go' – had stirred me more than I felt it safe to show. It was exactly what I longed to do; it was what I needed. To get out of New Orleans, to shake off my failure, to be a free spirit and yet anchored to reality by Ben.

Of course it wasn't possible. Not the way he imagined. Not for ever.

But why not for a day? Why shouldn't we have a childish, selfish adventure, and forget school and work and laws and duties, just the two of us? That was another aspect of my relationship with Ben that I enjoyed, although I usually tried to deny it. He resurrected the child in me. He not only reminded me of what childhood had been like, he brought my childishness back to life. He was a kindred spirit, my best friend, my brother, as well as being the son I longed for.

'I've got my sketch book,' he said as we walked along Esplanade, hurrying a little because the wind had a bite to it. 'I can draw you again.'

I remembered the last time, how he had changed while drawing me. Had he changed? Or had I imagined it? I felt an almost sick eagerness to know, alternating with dizzying speed between repulsion and attraction. How much of Gabriel was there in him? How much did he remember? If I asked him –

But I couldn't ask him. Gabriel was dead, and Ben was alive, and I loved Ben for himself, not for his father's sake.

There was Max's car. 'Use it to go wherever you want,' he had said.

'Why don't we just get in the car and go?' I asked aloud.

It was a beautiful day for it, bright and crisp and clear. A day for getting out of the city and rolling along country roads under the open sky, the sky as vividly blue as Gabriel's eyes. I remembered . . . and suddenly I knew what I wanted to do.

chapter eleven

Ben didn't ask about the car: maybe he thought I'd stolen it. He did ask where we were going, but I wouldn't tell him.

'You said you wanted to get in the car and go – well, that's what we're doing!' I started singing: 'The horse knows the way to carry the sleigh...'

I was happy and so was he – it was a buoyant, intoxicating madness. We were children together, sharing an adventure. I was eager to get away from the city – New Orleans seemed to have more than her fair share of eccentric drivers, and it had been several years since I'd done much driving. I was getting by on nerves and luck rather than skill, and felt a great easing of tension by the time I was safely on Highway 61.

The air smelled faintly of wood-smoke, and the hard, bright sky was all around us and seemed, like the road, to go on for ever.

'How far could we go if we just kept going?' asked Ben.

'Today?'

'On this road.'

'Well, we're driving north – towards Yankee-land, where this weather comes from. If we kept going in this direction we'd come to Canada in about three days, I guess.'

'Are we going to Canada?'

'Oh, no, before long we'll start heading west.'

'And what's at the end of that road?'

'The Pacific Ocean – don't they teach you geography at that school of yours? Or do you skip those days? I'll show you on the map when we stop.'

'I don't want to stop,' he said. 'I want to keep on driving for ever.'

I knew exactly how he felt. I wanted that free, gleaming day to go on for ever.

But we had to stop to fill the tank, and then we had lunch at a redwood barbecue shack by the side of the road. There was just the service station and the barbecue hut, and at some distance further back from the road, amid the pine trees, a small wooden house with a car up on blocks beside it. Nothing else, and we hadn't been through anything remotely like a town for at least thirty miles. This was real country, real backwoods territory, I thought, filling my lungs with the smells of pine and barbecued beef.

'We could buy a tent and camp out all the way to the Pacific Ocean,' said Ben.

'You're reading my mind.'

We ate our sandwiches at one of the two long trestle tables in front of the shack. We were the only customers. Ben had the road atlas opened to the Arkansas-Louisiana-Mississippi page and was tracing our route with a sauce-stained finger.

'Show me where we are,' he demanded. 'I can't find it.'

I showed him.

'Is that all? Is that all we've come?'

'Afraid so. It's a big country.'

'How long will it take to get to California?'

'Three or four days – but we're not going to California, Ben. That's too far away.'

'Where *are* we going? When are you going to tell me?'

He fixed me with his eyes, and I felt suddenly nervous. It had been a stupid idea; worse than stupid, it was bad. What kind of game was I playing? What was I trying to prove? Fortunately I hadn't said anything yet, and our destination could be changed.

'Where would you like to go?' I asked. 'You choose some place.'

I expected a request for California or the North Pole, but he fooled me. He knew what was possible and what wasn't.

He looked down at the map, moving his finger along the red line of road. He seemed to be concentrating, as if

170

estimating distances, and then his finger stopped.

'St Cloud,' he said. 'There.'

I felt frozen with disbelief. Then I thought it was a coincidence – he had seen the name and liked it. Or maybe I'd even let the name slip in my mindless singing in the car.

'OK?' he said. 'It won't take us long to get to St Cloud.'

'But why? Why there? Why St Cloud?'

'You know.'

I wouldn't admit it. 'Tell me.'

'That's where Gabriel comes from.'

'And you'd like to see it?'

'I've seen it.' He cocked his head and gave me a very adult look, smiling a little. 'Why are you pretending? We've been going there all the time.'

I stopped pretending. 'It was a dumb idea.'

'No, it wasn't.'

'Oh, yes. I don't know why I –'

'I know why. You wanted to find Gabriel. You wanted to bring him out, like I do when I draw you.'

His eyes were Gabriel's, his certainty, his power over me. I closed my eyes. 'What do you mean?'

'Gabriel isn't dead. He's real. He's still around. And sometimes he comes out.'

'What do you mean, "around"? Where is he, if he's not dead? Where does he come out?' I stared at him. I was trembling slightly, but I could see that he was perfectly calm.

'He's in me,' Ben said, pressing one hand flat against his chest. 'I'm Gabriel, sometimes.'

'Like when you threw a glass at my picture?'

'She told you about that?'

'I think she blames me for it. She thought you were over those kinds of outburst, until I came along.'

He nodded agreement, and I said sharply, 'If that's what Gabriel does for you, you're better off without him!'

'That's *not* all. That's just the bad side. The good parts – oh, all the memories! He lets me feel things and see things – I'm not a dumb kid any more, and it's great!' His face was glowing, his voice rich with remembered pleasure.

'What's wrong with being a kid? There are times I wish I was a kid again.'

'You wouldn't like it. Kids have to do what other people say. They can't do what *they* want. Can we go to St Cloud?'

I felt he'd manœuvred me into a position where I had to agree, and yet – wasn't this what I had planned all along? I felt uneasy, but I said, 'If that's what you really want.'

And he glowed again.

I looked at my watch. 'I'd better call Sallie and tell her you're safe with me, or she'll worry when you don't turn up. But she thinks you're in school, doesn't she?'

'Tell her they let us out of school early, for a teacher's meeting.'

There was a pay-phone at the service station next door. I fed in quarters and called Sallie at the bar, to tell her one lie after another: that Max was with us, taking us on a plantation tour, and we wouldn't be back until very late, so if she didn't mind I would keep Ben overnight. Sallie was understandably surprised, but seemed perfectly agreeable.

'So Ben and Max are getting along now?'

'Ben's a little wary, still, but Max is winning him over with his famous charm.'

'I wish Angus could. Oh, well. Have a good time.'

I was surprised at how easy it was. As I hung up I remembered the contempt I had once felt for the overheard, lying phone calls of a married lover. I had thought then that I would never stoop so low. This was different, of course. This was not adultery, but something worse.

Back on the highway there was no traffic. I put my foot down, enjoying the sensation of freedom and effortless power as the car ate up miles of sun-striped road. We were less than an hour away from St Cloud, and the day was still crisp and clear and bright.

'Do you know the last time Gabriel was in St Cloud?' I asked.

'With you,' he said, unhesitating.

'What happened then?'

'I don't remember now. I will later.'

I twitched my shoulders, uneasy because he was so calm, because he took the impossible so much for granted. And then I said, 'Does Gabriel know where we're going?' It was an odd question, and I didn't know why I asked it – was I playing a game, trying to enter into Ben's fantasy, or did I believe Gabriel's spirit really was hovering around us, somehow in touch with Ben?

'Probably,' said Ben. 'I can't feel him now, but I think he probably knows everything that I know.'

Like God or Santa Claus or some other omniscient figure from childhood's pantheon. Ben might believe, but I should know better. Feeling ashamed of myself, I asked him no more questions. But I didn't turn the car round; we kept on driving to St Cloud.

I hadn't seen Jeannie or Ray Archer since Gabriel's funeral. Jeannie had written me a letter a few weeks later – she must have got my address from one of my parents, for I certainly hadn't given it to her – and for several years after sent me Christmas cards. I answered none of them. I had cut them out of my life, and for all I knew Jeannie or Ray or both of them might be dead by now.

The car seemed hot, although my window was wound down a couple of inches to let in a stream of chilly air. My hands were sweating on the wheel, and I could smell the familiar acrid tinge of the paper mill.

I had turned my back on Jeannie at the funeral. She said something about God. I know she meant to be comforting – I knew it even then. But all I could think of was how contemptuous Gabriel had been of his parents' god, and how little use I had for any deity who would let my husband die, and so I turned my back without a word and walked away.

How could I face them now? And why should I? They had never known me – they wouldn't want to see me. My appearance would only stir up bitter memories and old pain. Better to let them rest.

A sign on the side of the road promised St Cloud in four miles; a minute later Ben bounced on the seat. 'There! There's the Gulf station! Turn there!'

I clenched my teeth on a shudder. From down the years it came back to me: Gabriel turning the car just here, off the highway on to the narrow, rutted, dusty road by the Gulf station, saying that this way was faster, the back road into town.

The road was still there – I wouldn't think now of how Ben had known – but at some time over the past ten years it had been surfaced. The heavy forest I remembered had vanished: the trees were thinner, and the town began sooner than I expected with some ugly, boxy little houses in a row. And then the white, wooden, steepled church where Gabriel's parents worshipped. A green sign-board on wheels spelled out JOIN GOD'S TEAM AND WIN ETERNAL LIFE.

'Turn here! Here!'

I slowed the car to a crawl. 'But the main part of town is straight ahead, I'm sure.'

'But we turn here to get to Mama and Papa's.'

My scalp prickled. 'I'm not sure . . .'

'*I* am. Turn.'

So I turned. But I wished I hadn't come so far.

Down another blacktop road, past old wooden frame houses and some newer ones, some with aluminium cladding; all of them, although small, well cared-for with neatly trimmed lawns and cars of the latest model parked on the driveways.

'Turn!'

The car bumped off the surfaced road as I followed his instructions. So not all of St Cloud was equally prosperous – some roads were still unpaved.

'There it is! There it is!' He was trembling like a puppy on a leash, and his eagerness, his knowledge, seared me. How could he know? How much did he know? Was he Gabriel now? I looked sideways, almost afraid of him.

'There's Papa's car – they're home!'

A dusty white Ford was parked on the driveway – probably

174

the same car they'd had ten years ago, and for nearly ten years before that. The house was, now as always, a faded green wooden box with a tar-paper roof, built high off the ground. Solid concrete steps led up to a screened veranda. I could see a large hole in the bottom half of the screen door.

I stopped the car in front of the house and, before I'd even switched off the engine, before I could question or advise him, Ben was out, flying free across the patchy, weedy lawn towards the front steps. As he reached them, the screen door opened and a grey-haired woman in a blue dress appeared.

For a moment it was as if they were both frozen. Then Ben's glad, ecstatic cry 'Mama!' split the air. She rushed down, he rushed up – they met, anyway, and she held him in her arms.

She knew him, no doubt about that. I considered driving away, leaving them to each other while I disappeared in the distance. Who was that masked woman? But I couldn't turn my back a second time. I went to join them.

'Sallie, why didn't you call us –' Her voice faded as she focused on me, and surprise silenced her.

Ten years had greyed Jeannie's hair, but her face was as smooth and firm as ever, her eyes as bright. Maybe she had put on a little weight, but she carried it well. She was still a handsome woman, and not at all my idea of someone approaching sixty.

'Dinah?' She sounded disbelieving.

'Hello, Jeannie. I didn't call, because I didn't know how welcome I would be, and I didn't know what to say.' I shrugged. 'I'm sorry.'

'Don't be silly. Of course you're welcome.' She looked down at Ben and pushed him towards the house. 'Go surprise your Papa. He'll be so happy! Dinah and I will be right in.'

He flashed me a questioning look, grinned, and vanished inside.

'I am glad to see you,' Jeannie said, and stretched out her arms. Feeling awkward and fraudulent, I went into them and we hugged each other. As we separated I saw all the questions she hadn't yet asked in her eyes. 'Let's go inside,' she said. 'I know Ray will be pleased. You can tell us everything. How did you come to –'

'I came back to New Orleans about three months ago, looked up Sallie, and was very surprised to find out about Ben . . .' I shrugged, making light of it, looking away from whatever sympathy or pity she might have to offer, and mounted the steps to the house.

One day spent here nearly eleven years earlier had left me with only the most fragmentary images. I didn't know this house, and that was just as well. I couldn't have coped with any more memories and confusion. The realization that the Archers knew all about Ben and Sallie – and that Ben hadn't told me – turned my reincarnation theory not just to nonsense, but to a bad joke – Ben's joke on me.

Inside the house was much nicer than the exterior seemed to promise; Jeannie was house-proud. The long hall which ran from the front door straight through to the back had a pale green runner down the centre of highly polished floorboards, and white wallpaper with a pattern of tiny green fleurs-de-lis. At the end of the hall was the main room, the heart of the house: the kitchen.

Flower-sprigged curtains drawn back from the wide windows, red and white linoleum tiles, a big, round, wooden table and, next to the back door, Ray stiffly upright in a big rocking-chair, Ben leaning at ease against his knee, clinging confidently and talking into Ray's receptive silence.

The sight of Ray shocked me. He had changed so much that in another place I wouldn't have recognized him. I wasn't prepared, after Jeannie's vigour, to find such an old man.

His hair was completely white and had receded, giving him a high forehead. The blue of his eyes was still vivid, but all round them were deep lines of pain and age. And he looked so small in that big chair, as if the years had shrivelled him.

But when he saw me he smiled, and the old intensity was there, reminding me again of his son.

'You're a sight for sore eyes,' he said. 'Come give me a kiss. You won't be jealous, will you, Ben?'

Did he still brood about my last visit here with Gabriel? Did he feel guilty? Hesitantly I went forward to give him an obedient kiss on the cheek.

'Nothing to be jealous of there,' he sighed as I backed away. 'Sit down, sit down. Pull up a chair. Makes me uncomfortable having people looming over me, even beautiful women. Reminds me of being flat-out in a hospital bed.'

'How are you?'

'Not dead yet. Can't complain, but I do.'

'Coffee or tea?' asked Jeannie, filling a kettle.

'Tea, thank you.' I looked at Ben, so relaxed as he leaned against his grandfather's knee. The old man stroked the boy's sleek, dark head. I thought of the antagonism between Ray and Gabriel, how they couldn't come close without sparks flying. Was it always like that between them? There might have been a time when they simply loved each other, when it was as easy for them as it was for these two. Would Ray live long enough for his grandson to learn to hate him?

'Here's your tea. Ray, honey, it's time for your pills. Here's some apple juice to swallow them.' She looked at me while Ray, grimacing, gulped down the tablets. 'How long can y'all stay?'

'For ever,' said Ben.

Jeannie's eyes were doting as they rested on him, but she shook her head. 'You'd miss your mother. And she'd miss you.'

'She doesn't want me.' He moved away from the rocker, tense again. I wished he would look at me.

'Now, Ben . . .'

'She doesn't! She wants to marry Angus, and he wants to send me away.'

'I'm sure that's not so. But Sallie knows – she's always known – that if she ever feels she can't manage, you are welcome to come to us for however long she needs.'

Ben moved closer to Jeannie and put his arms round her

waist. As always, when words didn't work, he tried to persuade with his physical self. 'Call her now and ask if you can keep me,' he coaxed. 'She'd say yes if you asked her. Please?'

But Jeannie obviously had a steely core which I lacked. She was fond of him, but he could not move her. She shook her head. 'Don't cry for the moon, honey. You can't stay here. A boy belongs with his mother, and Sallie loves you just as much as we do. No, don't pout at me. You're here now, and we're happy to see you. Make the most of it. Nothing lasts for ever.'

For all the attention they paid me I might as well not have been there. I said, 'Wouldn't you miss me if you came to live here?'

With his head pressed against Jeannie's midriff, Ben gave me a sidelong look, calculating. 'Would you miss me?'

'Of course I would.'

'Well, you could stay here, too. Nobody's making you go back to New Orleans.'

I wondered how he saw me: a child like himself, a playmate and sister to be adopted by Ray and Jeannie? It would not occur to him that I might be jealous of Jeannie's place in his life and that there was no room for me in this house, no role for me to play.

'All right, honey, don't cling to me, there's a good boy,' said Jeannie, detaching herself. 'I've got too much to do. If y'all are staying for supper, I've got to get some groceries in. Dinah, you sit down and chat with Ray; Ben, why don't you come along and keep me company?'

How easily, how firmly she managed things! I watched Ben trot happily after her, leaving me behind with Gabriel's father, this man who was little more than a stranger to me. But I would make the best of it, I decided.

'How long has it been since you've seen Ben?' I asked.

'Oh, a couple of years, at least. Sallie left him with us for about a month one summer while she drove with some friends to California. Before that . . . well, they came for Christmas a few years running. Of course, it's a long way to come – Sallie has her job, Ben's in school now. We're too far away for regular babysitting, and we never get to New Orleans ourselves. It seems like, lately, she's just forgotten us, but I guess we can't really blame her.'

'When did she first – I mean, how long have you known about Ben?'

'Oh, she didn't tell you?'

'I didn't ask her.'

'No, I don't guess you'd want to talk to her much after what she did . . .'

'When did she tell you?'

'Oh, before he was born. Well, she didn't have anybody else to turn to. We offered to adopt him, but she didn't want that. She came to live with us after he was born; stayed with us, off and on, for a couple of years. Well, you know what Sallie's like . . . She didn't like living out in the sticks, away from her friends and the kind of life she was used to, but she couldn't really manage a little baby all on her own. Sometimes she'd leave him with us, come to visit every couple of weeks. We were as much his parents, in a way, as she was.'

I felt wounded and betrayed, almost as badly as when I'd first discovered Ben's existence. Why hadn't he told me? Why hadn't she? Why had I been so gullible, believing that Gabriel wasn't really dead, that Gabriel could speak to me still through Ben?

'Did you talk a lot about Gabriel to Ben when he was younger?' I asked. 'Did you tell him a lot of things about his father?'

Ray frowned. 'Not especially, not that I recall. Mostly, he was too young to understand, and then again, what could we say? You don't want to tell a boy that his father wasn't married to his mother and killed himself while high on LSD, now, do you? It seemed better to put all that behind us. Ben was like a second chance. Sallie wanted to call him Gabriel, even, but we talked her out of it. Dead man's shoes, you know. It didn't seem like a good idea. If it really was a second chance, Ben was going to have to be his own person, and that starts with the name.'

I believed him, but it was only natural that they should have let things slip. Even if they didn't want to talk about Ben's father, they would have been bound to remember their own son, the sweet little boy before he grew up and went wrong. Surrounded by Gabriel's past, Ben would naturally hear stories. And – thirsty little sponge – would soak them up.

'We wanted to do the best for him,' Ray said. 'We wanted to give him everything, teach him right from wrong, help him to know God and accept Jesus as his personal saviour. Well, it wasn't any different from what we wanted for Gabriel, and what we tried to do for him. We did our best for Gabriel, and he just turned his back on it, on everything that was important to us. I've never understood it, why Gabriel went wrong. I don't know how we could possibly have done any more, Jeannie and I. He just turned his back on all morals and decency.

'I thought there was some hope when I saw you, when I knew he was married to you. I thought maybe he'd straighten up, forget his crazy ideas, get a decent job, start raising a family. Well, you must have thought the same. It must have been a terrible shock to you – not married even a year! – to find out he was, uh, looking elsewhere for his . . .'

At that moment I started to hate him. I felt as if Gabriel's inarticulate rage was boiling inside me, and I had to let it out. It was *his* fault, this narrow-minded old man: he had forced Gabriel to rebel, he had driven Gabriel over the edge. Gabriel's sort of outburst wasn't my way, but I couldn't sit quietly, accepting what he said in silence. I had to let him know that I was on the other side; that, like Gabriel, I stood for the things he despised.

'It wasn't a shock,' I said. 'Not the kind of shock you mean. Gabriel didn't cheat on me – we didn't have that kind of marriage. I knew about Sallie – I knew she loved him as much as I did. And I loved them both. There was no sneaking around. They had my blessing.'

He looked at me from somewhere far away – he wasn't

going to let me have the satisfaction of seeing him shaken – and then he smiled, the same tight smile he'd worn when goading his son.

'Well, well,' he said softly. 'Aren't you the liberated lady. I guess you and Gabriel were just right for each other, after all.'

'I always thought so.' I stood up and made a big production of making myself another cup of tea, not offering him anything.

Fortunately we weren't left alone together for much longer. When Jeannie came back in with Ben, I said, 'I think we'd better start back. It's a long drive, and –'

'Nonsense,' said Jeannie, setting a bag of groceries down on the big oak table. 'You certainly didn't come all this way to have a cup of tea and leave.'

'If they want to go, Jeannie, just let them,' said Ray.

She gave him a sharp look, sensed our quarrel and then dismissed it. 'They're staying for dinner.' She looked at me, cool and straightforward. 'I've already bought the fixings. The least you can do is stay and help us eat.'

There wasn't any use in arguing. I realized I could leave only by repeating a scene like Gabriel's of eleven years earlier and, angry though I was with Ray, I had no heart for that. Besides, Ben didn't want to go. He was so happy, so much at home, as he busily helped his grandmother put things away. He knew everything in this kitchen. He belonged here. I had the bleak feeling that I'd been used. Ben didn't care about me – wouldn't care if I walked out. I had been just the means of getting him back here.

Then he looked across the room and our eyes met. It was a connection as solid as if we'd clasped hands.

'Can I show Dinah around?'

'May I,' Jeannie corrected. 'Yes, you may. Your old things are still in your room, where you left them.' As he went by, she reached out and rested her hand very briefly on the top of his head, like a blessing.

Ben's room – naturally, in this two-bedroom house – had been Gabriel's formerly. I remembered my first sight of the narrow twin beds, and how I'd felt sad, realizing we would sleep apart for the first time since our marriage, but also relieved that his parents wouldn't have to think of us in bed together. I had used my left hand more than usual that day, fluttering it and flaunting the wedding ring as if my right to be with Gabriel was in question. He had told me, on the way, how conservative and conventional his parents were. He had been so scornful of them and their fixation on marriage – 'a piece of paper', he said. And yet he had married me.

While I stood musing, Ben was diving into his own past. Down on his knees on the floor, he had the deep bottom drawer of the old-fashioned tallboy open to reveal a treasure trove of games and toys.

At first he was excited, pulling things out and exclaiming over them: plastic dinosaurs, movable robots, coloured blocks and puzzles, board games, stuffed animals, an Etch-a-Sketch. Then his interest flagged. Dismissing them scornfully as 'baby toys', he crammed them all back and found he couldn't close the drawer.

'Don't force it,' I said. 'We just need to put the things back carefully. They'll all fit. Here, let me help you.'

I liked that, sitting beside him on the floor, doing something so simple yet useful, working together towards a common goal. I liked his nearness, his warmth. We needed no words to communicate. His smooth, soft arms brushed mine now and then, and our hands sometimes collided. It was as good as the drive down had been, but in a different way. It was so ordinary. I wished it could go on for ever.

Ben wanted that closeness, too, I knew, because when the toys had all been put away, he took me into the parlour to show me the photograph albums.

The parlour was 'the good room', used only for company. It was obvious from the stale, cool air, the feeling of emptiness, the way that the furniture, which was certainly not new, looked as if it had been taken out of plastic wrappings only recently.

There was a small Hammond organ beside the front window, and there was a bookcase containing only a Bible, a hymnal, a home encyclopaedia and five fat photograph albums. Ben took them all at once and staggered to the sofa to drop them into my lap. Then he scrambled up beside me and opened the top album.

'There I am,' he said, pointing. 'That's me when I was a baby.'

It was a black-and-white picture, a baby I didn't know. My eyes slid away down the page, alighting on a more familiar face: Jeannie, younger than I'd ever seen her, hair long and straight on either side of her smiling face as she held the dark-haired baby up to the camera.

'That's not you, that's Gabriel,' I said.

Ben smiled to himself. 'Same thing.' He turned the page and there was a toddler staggering across the floor in drooping rubber pants, pushing away from his mother, staring at a cat.

Page after page of Gabriel as he was long before I knew him: baby, child and sullen adolescent. The snapshots fascinated me – I wanted to examine every one – but they made my heart ache with the knowledge that he was gone, out of my reach for ever. I could never hold that baby, never smile at that little boy. They were as dead as the man I had loved.

Then, in colour this time, came more baby pictures. They sent me scrabbling for the first book, to compare. Were the two babies so much alike, or was it just a generic likeness that all baby photographs share? There was Sallie: a much younger Sallie, smiling self-consciously into the camera, holding her baby with such pride. Jealousy, hot and bitter as nausea, made me close my eyes, and I clenched the edge of the album, waiting for the feeling to pass. Why couldn't I get over my stupid resentment, my feelings of loss? What did it matter who had given birth to Ben? He was here now, and I was glad of that. He wouldn't even be the person I had come to know and love if I had given birth to him. And I would have a child of my own one day soon – why begrudge Sallie hers?

Ben's hand closed round mind and squeezed it gently. 'I'm here,' he said.

I smiled at him. 'Of course you are. Let's not look at these old pictures any more. We've been sitting around all day. Why don't we go out for a little walk? I'll just ask Jeannie how long until dinner.'

I knew I was being selfish. I should have suggested we help in the kitchen, or at least sent Ben in to his grandparents. They hadn't seen him in two years and didn't know when they'd have another chance. But they didn't matter to me, and Ben did. I wanted every moment of him to myself. It was worth everything, I thought, worth any later reproaches, worth the Archers' loneliness, just to be alone with Ben in the open air, walking down a quiet country road, talking or not talking as we chose. Even the acrid tang from the paper mill was not unpleasant because it was special to this place. And Ben was as relaxed and happy as I had ever known him. It was a magical day, a day I would never forget.

At dinner, this time, Ray didn't flirt with me. He hardly spoke at all, and never once caught my eye. I had shocked him deeply and deliberately, and even though I regretted it now, there was no changing that, no taking back the truth.

I had thought we would leave directly after dinner, to reach New Orleans before midnight, but Jeannie wouldn't hear of it. Of course we would spend the night, she said. It was silly to think of going back now – the morning would be better and safer. I felt out of place in that house, but I did prefer the thought of driving in daylight, and when Ben made it seem a favour to him that we should stay, I couldn't refuse him. It seemed a small enough thing, and I wanted to prolong our day together just as much as he did.

When bedtime came, Jeannie gave me one of her night-gowns, unwanted but impossible to refuse. For Ben there was a pair of pyjamas striped red and white, faded from years of washing. They must have belonged to Gabriel, I thought, although my Gabriel, grown-up, had never bothered with pyjamas, rarely even with underwear. Of course we had known different Gabriels, Jeannie and I, and we had met very different needs in him. But there was only one Ben, and how many mothers did he need?

Jeannie was better at mothering than Sallie, I thought, and certainly better than I was. I felt an awkward intruder, almost a spy, as I watched Jeannie watch him saying a prayer for her, kneeling beside the bed, hands folded, eyes closed, clean and shining and innocent as he called upon God's blessing. And I closed my eyes and offered my own wordless, unbelieving prayer.

chapter twelve

He had everything he wanted. He was in his favourite house, snugly tucked into bed, his grandparents were safe and close at hand in the next room, and the love of his life, his beautiful Dinah, would stay with him all night long. He should have been perfectly happy. He would have been, except that Dinah was not.

Dinah stood there, still dressed in her daytime clothes, arms crossed over her chest, holding herself, looking miserable. Her unhappiness snared and grounded him, and he couldn't understand it. What more, what else, did she want?

'Aren't you coming to bed?' he asked.

'I'm not sleepy. It's too early for me.'

'You don't have to,' he said eagerly. 'We can stay up and talk – or play a game.'

She shook her head. 'You go to sleep. I'll – maybe I'll read.' Then her mouth twisted in a pained smile. 'If I can find a book in this house that's not the Bible.'

'Look in the closet. All Gabriel's books are there.'

'The closet. For books. They just saved them because they were *his*, like his clothes. They could have put them on the shelves in the parlour – but then somebody might see and think they actually read them.'

He didn't understand her bitterness. Why was she getting so upset about books? He explained: 'They were Gabriel's, so they belong in here. That's why. Find one for me, too, and we can both read.'

But she turned away from the closet with an impatient shake of her head. 'I'll take a bath. That might relax me.'

Ben was content to lie still and watch her move about the room. He could pretend that this was ordinary, that life was always like this, the two of them sharing this room every night. But he didn't want her to leave him.

'Don't be long,' he said. 'I might fall asleep.'

She laughed, looking more relaxed. 'Why shouldn't you fall asleep? You're in bed and it's night, what more do you want?'

'I want you to be falling asleep, too. I want us to go to sleep together.'

'I'll follow you,' she said gently. 'I promise.' Her hand was on the door.

'Wait,' he said urgently.

'What is it?'

'Kiss me good-night before you go. Just in case I'm not awake when you get back.'

He loved watching her come to him, the way her body moved, the way she smiled, the fact that all her attention was on him, the anticipation of her kiss.

She would have kissed him lightly, but he wrapped his arms round her neck and hung on, making it impossible for her to pull away.

'Aren't you glad you're here?' he asked.

'Since you are.'

'But for yourself?'

'I wouldn't be here for myself,' she said gently. She made no effort to escape. 'I don't belong here.'

'Yes you do – you belong with *me*.'

'But not in this house.'

He suddenly butted his head up and pressed his lips, firmly closed, against hers, kissing her hard.

She broke it off after a moment and pulled away. 'I love you, too,' she said. 'Now go to sleep. I won't be long.'

He lay in a haze of bliss, scarcely aware of her leaving. She loved him . . . she loved him . . .

Yes, it was true she didn't belong here – they couldn't stay in St Cloud. But that didn't matter. The important thing was that they belonged together, and they must stay together, wherever they went.

He knew it – she knew it – but he wanted to hear her say it. Because he had a nagging suspicion that no matter how she felt (and she had told him she loved him!) she would cling to her stupid, adult 'reasons' for doing what neither of them wanted. She would say something about the law, about police, about school, about his mother – as if any of that mattered to them! Everything was perfect now. He didn't want anything to change. He thought he couldn't stand it if all they had together was this one night, and then a few hours in the car the next morning before she returned him to Sallie and returned herself to Max.

It wasn't fair! Grown-ups could do whatever they wanted. Dinah could, only she made up reasons not to because she was scared. And, like everybody else, she told Ben what to do and never listened to what he wanted.

Yet she had listened to Gabriel. She had done what Gabriel said.

If only Gabriel could be here now, to make her understand, Ben thought. If only he could be Gabriel. Then no one would have any right to separate them. Ben and Dinah would be Gabriel and Dinah, together for ever.

They were together now, in this house. Gabriel was here, if he was anywhere. Ben could feel Gabriel's presence all around him – it was why he felt whole and happy in this house as he never did so completely anywhere else. Here he was in Gabriel's room, in Gabriel's bed –

And suddenly Ben knew. Suddenly it seemed so obvious that he didn't know why he hadn't always known.

Of course. *He was Gabriel* – he was all of Gabriel that was left. Gabriel wasn't an invisible friend who came and went – Gabriel was always present, inside him, a part of himself.

Understanding filled him with a soft, glowing peace. It would have been so easy to slip into sleep, but Ben clung to wakefulness. He had to wait for Dinah to come back; he had to tell her. Once she knew about Gabriel she would realize it didn't matter what anybody else said – she would know that they must stay together.

The sound of the door made him open his eyes. 'Dinah?'

'Are you still awake?' She was whispering. She came to the foot of his bed, wearing one of Mama's pink nightgowns, her hair pulled back like a little girl's in a pony-tail. 'Go to sleep, honey.'

'I will. I just thought of something I need to tell you. Why are you whispering?'

'Because it's late. Your parents – your grandparents have already gone to bed, and we should too.'

'They won't hear us. You're not sleepy, are you?'

'Yes I am.' She yawned, closing her eyes and stretching her mouth, and before he could stop himself he had yawned too, in sympathy.

'See,' she said. 'You're sleepy too. We ought to get an early start tomorrow. We can talk in the car.'

'Where are we going?'

'You know where we're going, Ben.'

'Don't call me that.' He sat up in bed, doubt and sleepiness vanished.

She shot a nervous glance towards the door. 'Just lie down and try to sleep. We can talk in the morning.'

'You think I'll forget,' he said. 'I won't. You know who I am.'

Her shoulders sagged, and she took a couple of steps and sat on the edge of the other bed. 'Oh, Ben,' she said sadly.

'Don't call me that! I'm Gabriel. Call me Gabriel.'

'Why? What good is that? It won't change anything.'

'I *am* Gabriel.'

She looked at him across the small space that separated the two beds as if across miles or years. She shook her head. 'No good, kiddo. I was married to Gabriel. I knew him – as well as anybody did. I saw him die. You're his son. You're like him in some ways, but you're someone separate. You're Ben. You're not Gabriel.'

'But where did Gabriel go when he died?'

'I don't know. Where does anybody go? To heaven or hell or nothing. It doesn't matter.'

'It *does*; it does matter. Gabriel's here. I always knew that; I could always talk to him and feel him, ever since I was a baby. It's not pretend – he's real. But I used to think he was outside somewhere – hanging around, I don't know how, exactly. But that's not right. I know now – Gabriel is real, and he's inside. He's a part of me. He *is* me.'

He had finally reached her. She met his eyes and looked as she had when she said she loved him. 'All right,' she said. 'He's a part of you, and as long as you're alive he'll never die. It's a nice idea. I'm glad you feel that.'

'I didn't make it up – it's true!'

'Hush. Yes, I know it's true. It's true. There's a lot of Gabriel in you – I've known that since I first saw you.'

He could no longer stand being physically apart. He had to touch her; he had to feel that she believed him, and be reassured of her love for him. Words were not enough. He scrambled out of bed and across the short gap before she could stop him, flung his arms round her and clung tightly, like a baby monkey.

'Hey! Hey, what's wrong?' She stroked his hair.

She smelled of Dial soap – like Mama, and like himself. For a moment it seemed strange, as if she wasn't really Dinah.

'Come on, Ben. Time to go to bed. We're both tired –'

'Promise you won't leave me.'

'Of course I won't! Did you think I was going to sneak out in the night?'

'Not just tonight. Ever. Promise you won't ever leave me.'

'What, not even to go to the bathroom?'

Her joking made him cling more tightly. He almost hated her. Close as he was to her, it wasn't enough. He wanted to be closer and didn't know how. He wanted her to want him just as fiercely and forget about jokes and bedtime and the long drive back to New Orleans . . .

'Let go of me, Ben.'

'I'm Gabriel.'

'Oh God, not that again. If you're Gabriel, what's happened to my friend Ben? I'd really miss him if he wasn't around any more.'

He slackened his hold slightly in order to pull back, to be able to see her face. She looked serious, a little sad.

'Why would you miss Ben, if you had Gabriel?'

'Because I love Ben. Not just for having parts of Gabriel in him, but for himself. You're not just a pint-sized version, a little carbon copy, of Gabriel, you know. I wouldn't like you so much if you were.'

'You loved Gabriel. He was your husband.'

'Yes, he was. Ten years ago. Then he died. I had ten years to get over him, and stop missing him so much.'

'But don't you want him back?'

'Not if it means losing Ben.'

He didn't know what to say. While he hesitated, Dinah stood up, forcing him to stand up too. 'Come on, let me tuck you into bed,' she said.

As she bent over him, when he was back in bed, Ben caught her round the neck and said urgently, 'Do you love me?'

'Yes, I do. How many times do I have to tell you?'

'But you love other people, too.'

'Everyone loves more than just one person. You love Jeannie and Ray and Sallie, not just me.'

'But I love you best of all. Do you love me best?'

She smiled and said, too easily, 'Yes. I love you the best of all.' She kissed him on the cheek and tried to pull away, but he wouldn't let her.

'Will you marry me, then?' He demanded. 'As soon as I'm old enough?'

She twisted adroitly out of his grasp, still smiling. 'Ask me then, if you still want me. I'll seem like an old lady to you when you're nineteen.'

'I'll still love you. I'll always love you. Promise me you won't marry anybody else. Promise you'll wait for me.' He managed to catch hold of her wrist. She looked down to where he held her as if she had not heard his question and said only, 'Let go of me, Ben.'

'Promise, first. Promise you'll never marry anybody but me.'

Her hand clenched into a fist, and he tightened his hold, expecting her to jerk away, but she did not move.

'Promise,' he said again.

'No.'

Her voice had never been so cold, and it frightened him. Even his fingers couldn't warm her now. Although he clutched her wrist, there was no contact between them. She had withdrawn, and he knew that she could be every bit as stubborn as he was. She was letting him hold her, deliberately not using her strength to hurt him. She had won.

Abruptly he let go of her, and pulled his hand beneath the blankets as if to warm it. She walked away from his bed.

Ben closed his eyes. She was going to marry Max. That was why she wouldn't promise. He clenched his teeth to keep from shaking. He didn't want to start crying, not now. There had to be a way to change her mind. There had to be a way to make her *see*.

The light clicked off, and he heard the rustle of sheets and the creaking of the mattress as Dinah settled. Then he heard her sigh. She sounded so close, as if she was in bed with him. But she wasn't. He couldn't touch her. He should have been happy to be spending the night with Dinah, but he was miserable.

What should he have done differently? What should he have said? Gabriel would know, he thought. Only Gabriel could change her mind. If only she had believed him, if he could have made her understand that Gabriel wasn't dead.

She couldn't marry Max. She had a husband already. She said she didn't want to lose Ben, but that was silly. That was a lie. If she really loved Ben she wouldn't want anyone else. If she had Gabriel, she wouldn't marry anyone else. She couldn't.

He needed Gabriel. Gabriel was the only power he had over Dinah, the only reason she loved him. He tried to call Gabriel, to will him to come, even though he knew that never worked. Somehow he had to relax, to relax and concentrate at the same time, the way he did when he was drawing, and then Gabriel might appear. He tried to think of nothing, to make himself still and empty as if he was nothing but a suit of clothes for Gabriel to slip into. Clothes weren't nervous, they didn't wait, they expected nothing. Only when he wanted nothing, knew nothing, would he have what he needed.

But trying to keep his mind empty was a strain worse than holding his breath. Maybe he could think about Dinah instead. If he concentrated on her face, imagined himself drawing her, that might help him fall into that suspended, floating state of mind when Gabriel came. He would imagine himself looking at the picture above his bed –

The room changed shape around him in the darkness. Where was he? He felt dizzy. Who was he?

He opened his eyes. Despite the darkness he had no difficulty seeing. He was high, floating in the air near the ceiling and looking down. Below him he saw a little boy tucked into a single bed and apparently fast asleep. That was Ben.

And next to Ben – no, it wasn't a single bed after all, he saw. There was another mattress, a double mattress, adjoining the one in which Ben slept. On it, Gabriel lay sleeping beside Dinah.

Then he saw that a fine, gauzy veil separated Ben from Gabriel, the single bed from the double. It fell like a fine rain, and would keep them from ever touching, although from his overview the two figures slept side by side. He was somehow above the curtain.

He was floating free, but he couldn't remain where he was for ever. He would have to return to earth, and he had a choice to make. He had to decide which body to inhabit.

It was no choice at all. He knew; he had always known what he wanted. Like a stone, he let himself fall.

And opened Gabriel's eyes.

It was good to be awake at last, good to feel his body's unused strength, to flex his hands and remember their skill as he felt the tug of stiffness in the injured one. It would be good to paint again, to hold a brush or a pencil. And it would be even better to hold Dinah.

He reached out a hand to stroke her, and was surprised to

feel the edge of the bed. He had thought they were sleeping together, on the old double mattress at home. But it didn't matter. She was close by. The gap between the two beds was a small one, and in a moment as quick as thought, he had crossed it and slipped beneath the covers beside her.

She wore a nightgown, and that was another oddity, for he had been so certain of meeting her familiar nakedness. He didn't stop to think about it. The nightgown had tiny buttons all up the front, and he began at once to undo them. She stirred slightly at his touch but did not wake.

Her bare flesh was as soft and smooth as he remembered, and the sweet, beloved smell of her made him tremble. To stop the trembling, he put his arms round her and held on tight, pressing his face against her breasts.

She sighed in her sleep and her hips moved as she pressed against him in unconscious response. His tongue wet his dry lips and then he tasted her fragrant skin. At first he was almost shy as he rediscovered her body, but then he began licking and kissing her breasts more demandingly, rubbing his face against them. He was still trembling, but no longer aware of it. She was all that mattered: the warmth of her, the taste, the smell. Something pounded in his head and in his stomach as well as in his chest – it was as if he had multiple hearts. Every part of him that touched her was newly alive, throbbing and glowing. His skin was singing. He was hot and golden, close to melting as he clutched her more tightly, rubbing and licking and doing his best to become a part of her, no longer separate, no longer alone.

Low in her throat she groaned, and he felt her hand on the back of his head, fingers weaving in his hair. She guided his head with her hand, turning it, pushing it, until he felt a hard, erect nipple against his lips. His mouth opened and fastened on it. Gently at first, then more hungrily, more certain, his eyes tightly shut, he began to suck.

Now she was shuddering, and she wrapped her arms round him and they rocked together, one creature. Now, he knew, she would never let him go.

chapter thirteen

How long was I dreaming? How long, after I realized, did I let him continue?

I was dreaming of Gabriel, but his name on my lips burst the dream and woke me to a nightmare. Not Gabriel, but Ben: too old to be my baby, too young to be my lover.

Shaking, terrified that I would burst into tears or start screaming at him, I shifted my grasp and rolled over and away from him, pretending to be asleep. I wanted to pretend that we both were sleeping. I wanted to believe it had never happened, that by morning we could both have forgotten.

And maybe he was asleep; maybe he didn't know. I wanted to protect him from the knowledge, as well as to forget my own responsibility. In silence and sleep the memory might fade. I told myself that he had nuzzled against me in all innocence, seeking comfort and suckling instinctively, like a baby.

Except that he wasn't a baby, and in the light of morning I saw him looking at me through Gabriel's eyes.

I was terrified that Ben would say something, or that Jeannie, with a mother's sixth sense, would somehow discern what had happened. To my mind, everything had changed: the way he looked at me, the way he moved, his very silences. I thought she was bound to notice. And if she questioned me, despite my desire to deny what had happened, I knew I would break down and confess, wanting absolution.

Fortunately, Ben said nothing, and she noticed nothing. I was able to get us out and away quickly after a breakfast of only cold cereal and coffee.

It was a long way back to New Orleans, even though I drove too fast, and we passed most of the journey in silence. There was nothing I could say, and whatever Ben thought or remembered he was keeping to himself. His silence made me more nervous than any words; it could be interpreted in too many ways. I thought how self-possessed he seemed, how certain, like Gabriel.

Only after we'd reached the outskirts of the city, when the traffic was giving me something else to worry about, did Ben say, 'I'm hungry. What are we going to have for lunch?'

'Don't ask me,' I said, not taking my eyes off the road. 'That's up to Sallie.'

'What?'

'I'm not hungry.'

'Oh.' He was silent. Then: 'I guess I can wait. Maybe we could go somewhere and I could eat and you could just have a Coke or something?'

'I don't want to stop. I'll just drop you off and head back home.'

'Drop me off where? Why?'

'I'm going to take you home. Sallie must be worried –' I stopped, remembering the lies. 'Oh, hell. She's probably been trying to call me, wondering where you are. I guess we'd better tell her where we really were or she might hear . . .' I couldn't face her, I knew that. I needed time to recover and construct a mask. 'You'd better just tell her . . . tell her I'll call her. And apologize if she's worried, and if not –'

'I'm not going to tell Sallie anything,' he said crossly. 'I don't care what she thinks, and I don't want to see her. I'm going home with you.'

'Don't be ridiculous.' I felt sick with dread. It was starting again; he was starting the Gabriel argument, and I didn't know how it would end.

'It's not ridiculous,' he said. 'Forget about Sallie and everything else. I'm going to live with you, now. We're together again.'

'We've been through this before,' I said. 'Nothing has

changed. You can't live with me. You're not Gabriel. I told you last night –'

'I told *you* last night,' he said, and reached across and touched my breast.

Jerking away from him, I lost control of the car for a moment. There was a loud, unmelodious chorus of horns, but I didn't hit anything and it was all right again. I pulled the car to the kerb and stopped. Then I turned in my seat to look at Ben, who was smirking. I wanted to slap his face, but I knew I mustn't let him know how much he had affected me. I had to stay cool. I was the adult.

'Get out,' I said. 'You can find your way back from here. Tell Sallie I'll call her.'

He looked as if I had slapped him. 'I'm not going.'

'Oh, yes you are. And if you don't get out of this car by yourself, I'll pull you out. I'm bigger than you.'

'But I'm Gabriel,' he said. 'Don't you love me any more? I'm your husband.'

'You're nine years old, which is too young to be married to anybody, and old enough to know your own name, which is Ben. I'm giving you one more chance –'

'You knew me last night.'

'Don't touch me.'

We stared at each other, frozen, his hand upraised to caress, mine to slap.

'Nothing happened last night,' I said. 'Except maybe in your dreams. I'm not responsible for your dreams.'

He went on staring, hoping for some reprieve. I kept my face icy and blank. Finally his shoulders slumped and he turned away and got out of the car without another word.

I watched him walk away and vanish down a side street. He didn't look back. I concentrated on my breathing until I felt numb, and then I drove myself home.

Max was due back that evening – luckily I had left a note for myself on the pad by the phone. I drove out to the airport to pick him up.

On my way, I glanced at the mileage indicator and wondered if Max would notice how far I'd taken his car. Would he ask? Would I tell him? I was afraid of saying too much. I wanted to forget what had happened, not make more of it. Did Max really need to know?

Just to see him made me feel better, because he was the way I remembered him, the way he always was: warm, happy to see me, easy to be with. Ben's madness and my own faded like a bad dream.

We had a good meal with lots of wine at a seafood restaurant on the shore of the lake, and after that, because I'd made sure I packed a few things with me, we went straight to his house. When we tried to make love, though, things went wrong. I flinched when he bent his head to my breast, jerked away so violently that there could be no pretending I hadn't meant it.

'Sore?'

'Yes,' I lied. 'I'm sorry –'

'Don't be sorry. I'll be more gentle.'

'No – just not my breasts. Not tonight. Try something else.'

But it didn't matter what he tried. I was trying, too, and what should have been effortless became a competition, and impossible. Whenever I began to be aroused I remembered Ben, and self-loathing iced my feelings. My lack of response cooled Max's interest, too. Fortunately, he didn't take it as an insult. He didn't even take it seriously, or so it seemed to me. I wanted him to shout at me, blame me, interrogate me so that I could break down, cry and confess, and his almost indifferent acceptance wouldn't allow that.

'Are you sure you still want to marry me?' I asked.

'Are you trying to scare me off?'

'No. Only, I want you to be sure.'

'I was sure the first time I asked you. How about you? Changed your mind?'

I hid my face against his chest. 'I haven't changed my mind. As long as you want me.'

'I want you. God, do I want you.' He held me tightly, then

released me and sat up in bed. 'Let's fix a date right now. Let me think where I've got a calendar . . .'

'Don't get up. Just hold me for a while.'

'What's wrong? Want to talk to me about it? Bridal nerves? Dem ole cosmic blues again, Mama? Could it be your period? Isn't that about due?'

Of course it was. Things clicked into place. I couldn't be sure without checking my calendar, but if my period wasn't due that day it was the next or the one after that.

'It is,' I said. 'If I'm going to get it this month. Would you mind if I didn't?' I realized from the way he was looking at me that he didn't understand. 'I might be pregnant,' I explained. 'What would you think about that?'

'You know what I think.' He put his hand gently on my stomach, just the fingertips – as if to feel the difference. 'I think that would be great. And if you're not pregnant now, you will be soon. Maybe we should get married tomorrow.'

I laughed, safe in his arms, feeling our child anchored and growing within me. New beginnings were possible. I could forget the past now, this was the life I had always wanted.

'Don't worry, we have plenty of time before I start to show . . . nobody will know it was a shotgun wedding. I'll tell you what I will do tomorrow, though, to show you how shameless I am – I'll move in with you.'

'Great! I was hoping that would happen.'

'I'll probably still have to pay a month's rent, but I'll phone Morgan tomorrow and she can start looking for somebody else. There's no reason why I should stay there when I could be with you.'

'You'll even put up with my unhome-like home?'

'I'll start redecorating right away. You won't know the old place.'

'We'll get you a car soon,' he said. 'Until then, you'll have to take the bus in, but I'll pick you up in the evenings, and when I'm out of town you can have my car.'

'I'll try to find a job on this side of town,' I said, although the thought of job-hunting made my heart sink.

'Oh, no, don't quit your job –'

'Quit?' I laughed. 'Oh, it's too late to quit. Mr O fired me.'

He stared, disbelieving, and I remembered it had happened only the previous day. It seemed that weeks had passed. I told him the details, coolly, as if they didn't concern me. In truth, I hardly felt they did. The job didn't matter any more.

But Max took the news seriously. 'I knew something was wrong,' he said, more than once. 'From the moment I saw you waiting for me, I could tell you were unhappy. You should have said something. Why didn't you tell me sooner?'

I shrugged. 'It doesn't matter. I didn't want to worry you. You know now, anyway. It's not important, not compared to other things, like us. It really doesn't matter to me.'

Although I phoned Morgan in the morning, I let the days pass without making any attempt to return to my apartment and pack. I had a few clothes and other necessities with me and was in no hurry for the rest. I felt safe at Max's house. There were no bad memories lurking in the under-furnished rooms, and Ben couldn't find me. I could forget the past and live in the future as I spent my days planning for Christmas, for our wedding, for redecorating the house, for our baby . . .

I knew it was too soon for an accurate pregnancy test, and Max said 'if', but I was convinced I was pregnant. My period had been up to a week late before, but this time felt different. Every day that passed without a show of blood reinforced my belief and made me happier. Max told me that I looked pregnant – I glowed.

The following Monday, Max had to go away again. It was only a short hop to Houston and he would be back the following night, but as I clung to him at the airport I felt terrible premonitions, and had to fight a ridiculous urge to burst into tears.

'You look like Ingrid Bergman saying goodbye to Humphrey Bogart,' he said, holding my chin. 'Cheer up, schweetheart. We've still got Paris.'

He made me laugh and realize all over again how much I

loved him and how lucky I was to have found him, but even that seemed like cause for tears as I walked slowly and alone out to his car. The weather was warm and sticky again, the cold front gone as if it had never been. I didn't feel like going back to the house. It would be the first time I had stayed there while Max was out of town, and I would be too painfully aware of his absence. It seemed a good time, low though I felt, to go back to my old apartment and pack my things. It would be useful activity after a week of dreaming.

As I turned off the freeway, my stomach started to hurt. I tried to remember what we'd had for dinner the night before. Or was it hunger I was feeling? As usual, I'd had nothing but coffee for breakfast. There probably wasn't anything edible at my place – I imagined curdled milk and a loaf of bread turning to penicillin, and laughed. Then gasped, clenching the steering wheel more tightly, and involuntarily hunched forwards as my insides cramped with pain.

The pain increased, and I felt a wave of nausea. Hang on, I thought, hang on. It wasn't far now. I wondered if Max was feeling it, too. Food poisoning? Had the milk in the coffee been bad?

Waves of pain came and went. There was a sour taste at the back of my throat, and my head started to pound with the effort of maintaining control, but at least I was driving down broad, familiar Esplanade, and within a couple of minutes I was outside the house and had the car parked.

As I got out of the car another kicking spasm of pain made me double over, and then I felt the blood. The familiar, downward tug, the wetness between my legs, astonished me. The pain was explained, although it was worse than any cramps I'd had before. I understood, but I didn't believe.

I had been so certain there was a baby. But there wasn't. There was only the slow, heavy blood, and the pain. Climbing the stairs, I grew dizzy, and my vision was starred with strange lights. I managed to get my door unlocked and stumbled through to the bathroom just in time to throw up into the toilet.

No baby. Only this . . . mess. It seemed like a punishment.

I shook so hard I dropped the aspirin bottle twice before I managed to get some out and down my throat. I forced them down dry, unable to cope with the difficulties of tap and glass.

Then another savage twist of pain made me press my back against the wall, close my eyes and slide to the floor. I was too weak even to cry. I just sat there, praying for the pain to go.

I'd had cramps before, and I knew I must relax and give the aspirin time to work. I knew that, but I couldn't manage to do it. I'd always thought of period cramps as an ordinary discomfort, unpleasant but bearable, like a tension headache or a runny nose. They'd never made me shake like this before, never made me actually sick with pain.

It couldn't just be my period causing this. It must be something else, something more. Earlier I'd thought of food poisoning, and maybe that was it. Or maybe I had the flu or some other illness which just happened to coincide with my belated period. Or maybe it was a miscarriage.

Spontaneous abortion. The words came into my head, as painful, unwanted and undeniable as the cramps in my belly. The very act of thinking it seemed to make it true. The sudden, heavy, painful flow I was suffering now could be no ordinary period.

I *had* been pregnant. Instinctively I had known it. I had been aware of that tiny cluster of cells, too small for the eye to see, which would have developed into a baby, given time. But it had had no time. My baby was gone without ever having been more than potential. My body had expelled it. Why? How could it have happened? What had I done? Why had I been punished? Why had my baby preferred to die rather than grow inside me?

I drew my legs up close to my chest and wrapped my arms tightly round them, holding myself against the pain as if I could become the foetus I had lost, and I wept.

There was no one and nothing to stop my hysteria until I was quite exhausted and physically couldn't cry any more. I lay on the floor, breathing raggedly, my mind blank, so numb

I could hardly remember what had made me cry.

Then I heard something: a small sound that told me I wasn't alone. Someone else was in the apartment.

I struggled to my feet, still too dazed with misery to feel frightened, turned towards the door, and there was Ben.

He looked thinner and dirtier than I'd ever seen him, with greenish shadows beneath his dark eyes. His hair was lank and too long, and his filthy blue jeans had holes in both knees. He looked like an abandoned child from some underdeveloped country, and in spite of everything I felt a powerful tug of sympathy for him that nearly wiped out all other considerations.

'Are you all right?'

He shrugged skinny shoulders beneath a dirty T-shirt. 'Where've you been? I've been looking for you every day and you're never here.'

'Let's go sit down,' I said. For a moment I thought he wouldn't move, that he was going to try to keep me trapped in the bathroom, but then he shrugged again and moved out of the doorway. 'Do you want something to drink? Something to eat?'

'Well . . .'

'I don't know what I've got,' I said. 'Maybe some coke or frozen orange juice. I'll have to check.'

'I'm kind of hungry,' he admitted reluctantly. 'I haven't had anything to eat since yesterday.'

Or longer, I thought. Pity and concern stirred in me. I wanted to put my arms round him and keep him safe, make him well, but the fear of his response stopped me. I wanted things to be simple between us, and they weren't – they could never be simple again.

'Oh, Ben. How long have you – does Sallie know where you are? Have you run away?'

'What do you care?'

'Of course I care.'

'But not about me.' He sneered at me, and I was reminded of the way Gabriel had once looked at his father. It was a look of hatred, but the sort of hatred that can only come from a love betrayed. It wasn't a look or a feeling a child should know.

'Whether or not you believe me, I do care,' I said. 'I want what's best for you. And if you've run away, Sallie must be frantic.'

He thrust his chin out. 'She doesn't care. She's going to marry Angus. They're going to have a baby.'

No child but pain kicked inside me. A drink might help, I thought, and went back to the kitchen, aware that Ben was trailing after me.

There was a can of tomato soup in the cupboard, I noted as I got out the bourbon, and also a can of tuna and a pack of spaghetti.

'Why don't I make you some soup?' I said. 'Would you like that? Is tomato soup OK? Sorry I can't offer you a choice.' As I spoke, I poured myself a healthy slug of bourbon and knocked back half of it before adding ice and Coke to the glass. 'Would you like some of this Coke?'

His silence forced me to look at him. He shook his head, smiling slightly, eyes fixed on mine. 'I just want you.'

If he'd been a man I would have known how to respond. Because he wasn't, my skin prickled and I shuddered.

Like an animal, he seemed able to smell my fear. It made him grin. And the way he looked at me was no child's look.

I moved towards the door but he was closer, and he was expecting me. Swiftly he pulled the door shut and turned the heavy, old-fashioned key in the lock. I heard the tumblers clunk into place and saw him pull the key out and cram it down into the pocket of his jeans.

'You have to listen to me now. You can't throw me out. You can't call Sallie. You can't run away.'

I stopped myself from backing away. I didn't want him to know I was afraid of him. I shrugged and hoped I looked casual. 'Fine. You talk, I'll listen. I hope you don't mind if I go on making you lunch. I'll just heat some soup. You did say you were hungry. How long since you ran away?' I had to be careful, I thought. I had to say the right things. What were the right things to say? What should I do? I had to think clearly. I wished I didn't feel so weak and exhausted; wished my thoughts weren't so scattered. I took down the can of soup and pawed through a drawer of jumbled cutlery, seeking the can-opener.

'I'm not going back,' he said. 'You can't make me. Nobody can make me. Not unless Angus leaves. Anyway, I don't care. I don't want to live with Sallie. I want to be with you, all the time. We belong together. You know we do.'

His voice dropped to a whisper which rubbed against my nerves. Opening the can, I dumped the soup hard into a pot and set it down on the stove. 'I've already told you –'

'Don't say it again! I don't care about the stupid law, the stupid police, my stupid mother! That doesn't matter. It's not important. The only thing that matters is that we should be together. You know we can. If you really want to, you can talk Sallie into it. You could get Angus to talk her into it. She'd do anything for him. She was going to send me to military school. That's what he wanted. So you see, she doesn't want me around. She'd be glad to let you have me. It's just how you ask her, or get Angus to ask her. You know that's true. If you loved me you'd do it.'

I was reminded of Gabriel telling me that if I loved him I would stay with him and forget college, my parents, all my own plans, to marry him. Had I ever said no to Gabriel? Everything I did was a further proof of my love for him, or was meant to be.

And I knew that Ben was right, as Gabriel had been. Yes, I could do it. If I wanted him enough, I could manage something, make some arrangement with Sallie. I didn't have to antagonize her. If I was careful and had Angus on my side, she might come to think it was her own idea. She wouldn't have to feel that her son had chosen me in preference to his own mother, she wouldn't have to know I'd finally won Gabriel back from her.

I struck a match, and the gas burner lit with a sudden ferocity that made me jerk back. I felt I'd been shocked to consciousness out of a seductive dream.

'No, Ben.'

'I'm not Ben! I'm Gabriel!' The husky whisper had grown to

a roar, and he rushed at me, catching hold of my wrists. 'Look at me! Look in my eyes and see who I am! I'm your husband!'

He was only a child, I told myself. He couldn't hurt me. I didn't have to be afraid of him. He wasn't Gabriel. But his hands, his searing grasp on my wrists, made me remember and feel things that I didn't want. His hands unbuttoning my gown. His mouth on my breast. My own treacherous pleasure.

'Gabriel is dead,' I said.

'No. Not now.' His eyes seemed darker. 'I came back for you.' He smiled, let go one wrist and reached up to touch my face. One finger was stiff, jutting above the others as if it wouldn't bend properly, as if the tendon had been damaged.

I jerked free, backing away, desperate. I used too much force. I moved too quickly, and my elbow caught the pot handle and overturned it. Hot red soup spattered everywhere. I cried out in alarm. Flames licked up and then died.

'Are you all right? Dinah, are you OK? Did you hurt yourself? Let me see.'

A spasm of pain in my lower belly caught me unexpectedly. I gasped and bent over, then slipped to the floor, trying to ease it. 'I'm OK,' I gasped. 'Give me a minute. Let me rest.'

He was all over me, pawing at me. I tried to push him away. 'I'm OK – leave me, leave me!'

'I'll never leave you again.'

I wanted to weep: for my pain, for his madness, for the husband I had lost and the child I'd never had. But I couldn't lose control. I dared not let him see my weakness. Although I was older than Ben, and stronger and smarter, his conviction that he was Gabriel seemed to put me at a hopeless disadvantage. Maybe I should give in, give him what he wanted, say whatever I had to to get out of the kitchen and away. It wasn't a question of betrayal. It was survival, for both of us.

'All right,' I said wearily. 'I'll talk to Sallie. I'll talk to Angus. We'll work something out. I'll have to get a bigger apartment, but if they're willing to pay something towards your keep that shouldn't be a problem.'

He stopped breathing for a moment. Then: 'Promise?'

'I promise. I'll do my best. Now would you mind unlocking the door? I'd like to phone Sallie just to tell her you're all right.'

'Not yet.' He was still leaning against me, keeping me pressed down with his weight. Now he shifted slightly so we were face to face. 'Say my name.'

'Gabriel.'

I spoke flatly, without emotion or belief, just giving him what he demanded, and it was enough. Triumph flared in his eyes, and when he smiled he was so very like his father that I almost did believe.

'Now kiss me.'

He brought his face to mine and our lips touched. After the briefest pressure I tried to pull away, but he wouldn't let me. Instead, his arms circled my neck, holding me tightly, and I felt his tongue between my lips.

I twisted convulsively, pushing him off. 'Stop it! Get off me, you nasty little thing.'

'I'm not. I'm Gabriel, remember? I know what you like. Just relax.'

His hands were all over me, touching my face, stroking my breasts, pulling my shirt up to touch my bare skin.

'Stop it – let go of me!' It didn't seem to matter how many times I slapped his hands away, they always returned. And he spoke to me in a hoarse, low voice not his own.

'You like it. I know what you like. Let me . . . Let me love you.'

Finally I managed to get to my feet, but he clung to me like a monkey, pressing his face against my chest, licking and sucking at me through my clothes, pulling at my blouse. I tried without effect to pry him off. I was having a hard time standing under his assault, and a hard time breathing. I felt dizzy and sick.

'Let me go,' I said. 'Oh, please, I feel sick – I need some water – please . . .' As I spoke I knew it was hopeless. He didn't hear me or he didn't care.

Buttons popped off and my blouse fell open. Ben chuckled,

and for a moment his grasp loosened. As I struggled free of him I was aware of an odd smell, and a steady, hissing sound. Something was wrong. It was the stove – the gas was still on, but the flame had died when the soup overturned.

Ben touched me again and I shoved him away, hard, no longer concerned to temper my strength – too worried about the danger to both of us. But as I turned my back on him and stepped towards the stove, Ben threw himself at me, tackling me round the legs and pulling me down. As I fell I cracked my head against the counter, and the pain was so sharp and sudden that I nearly passed out.

I couldn't move or think of anything but the pain. Tears blurred my vision and seeped down my cheeks. Ben – I gradually realized – was sitting on my stomach, tugging ineffectually at my bra and muttering things that made no sense.

'Stove,' I said. 'Gas. Turn off. Dangerous. Please. We'll die. Please, please, please. Turn off. Let me turn it off. Let me, please.'

He stayed where he was but stopped pulling at me. His head was cocked and he seemed to be listening without understanding.

'Gas,' I said again, hopelessly.

'Stay there,' he said. 'I'll fix it.'

He went away. I was too sick and stunned to try to move. I heard the oven door open and the hissing sound grew louder. Then Ben was back. His soft cheek pressed against mine, his lips close to my ear, he whispered, 'It won't hurt, I promise. We'll be together. We'll fall asleep together, just like before, and when we wake up we'll start all over again. We'll find each other and be together again.'

He lay down on the cold linoleum beside me. He was nice now, gentle and loving. He stretched one arm across me, and pressed his face against my hair. I could feel his breath soft and warm on my neck. No more struggling, no more nastiness. He was my baby now, my sweet little boy. I would have been happy, except that the floor was so hard, and my head hurt, and that smell was still in the air, making me feel sick.

I knew that I should lie still as Ben said, but if I could have a glass of water – if I could first turn off the gas – I tried to sit up, but he pulled me back.

'Lie down,' he whispered. 'We'll sleep. It's nice. We're together. It won't hurt. It won't take long. We'll wait.'

But what we waited for was death. And, I finally realized, I didn't want to die.

This time I got to my feet before Ben could stop me. I made it to the stove and turned off first the oven and then the burner.

Ben turned it on again. And while I coughed and fumbled with the knob for the burner, he turned the oven full on, and wrenched off the white plastic control knob and flung it clattering behind the refrigerator.

I almost wept as I struggled, unable to gain purchase on the short metal stump, black and slimy with grease, which controlled the oven gas. Meanwhile, Ben turned on all the burners and pulled off all the knobs.

It was hopeless. There had to be another way.

I lunged at Ben. 'Give me the key!' He wriggled and fought me off. I could feel the key deep in his pocket, but it was impossible to put my hand on it.

I was growing weaker, shorter of breath. How much time did we have? I realized I was wearing myself out and wasting precious time. I ran to the window.

It hadn't been opened for years. The lock was jammed and it might have been painted shut. I struggled, arms trembling, muscles like jelly, and didn't know if I could manage. At any moment my system might overload and I would pass out if I didn't get fresh air. If the window didn't budge on the next heave I decided I would smash it.

With a resentful screech the heavy sash gave an inch. Then another inch, and finally the window was open.

I leaned out, drawing deep breaths of the warm, wet, fresh air. The sky was overcast and the colours looked oddly muted, but everything was so peaceful and ordinary that it seemed another world from the one in the kitchen. Outside was reality, sanity and life. Inside, madness and death. Another deep, lung-swelling breath which made my head throb, and I turned back to deal with it.

Ben was holding the box of kitchen matches in one hand and a single wooden match in the other. He was smiling at me.

I remembered that smile on Gabriel, when he had held out those harmless-looking little squares of paper: one hit for me and one for him.

'No,' I said. I took a step forward.

Ben brought his hands together, match sweeping towards the side of the box, still smiling like an angel.

I didn't wait for it. I couldn't. Let him go if he would, but I would save myself. Already in my mind I could hear the terrifying exhalation and boom of a gas explosion. I whirled round, caught the sides of the window, hauled myself up and threw myself out.

Cool air tore at my skin. Better than burning, I thought, and closed my eyes against the terrible light. I heard Gabriel scream my name, scream the anguish of my betrayal, as he fell.

Then the earth slammed hard against me and I couldn't breathe. I thought I heard Ben crying my name, I thought I felt him grab me, and then I lost it.

chapter fourteen

Something was wrong. Even through the exhaustion, pain and triumph of giving birth I knew something was wrong.

I knew it from the way the nurse looked when I asked to see my baby. But I insisted, and at last they brought it to me.

The baby was so swaddled in blankets it couldn't possibly move, so wrapped round in white it looked like a cocoon. Only the head was visible. And as they put it into my arms I saw that it had Gabriel's head, monstrous on that tiny body.

Gabriel smiled, his blue eyes fixing mine, and said, 'I came back.'

I woke up, then, trying to scream but unable to make a sound.

I told Max about the dream and he asked if I wanted to 'see somebody'. I said no. I didn't need a psychiatrist to explain that dream or tell me what I was afraid of. I thought maybe Max would suggest we should stop trying for a baby, put it off for a while longer, but he didn't.

Except in my dreams, I never thought about Gabriel. Ben I thought about more often – with regret, with guilt and with fear. I knew I could never see him again. I knew that the only thing I could do for him was to get out of his life. Without me around, he would no longer be haunted by Gabriel. He could become himself again. Sallie would send him to a psychiatrist, or away to school. He would grow up, start to forget, and become someone else. I miss him, and I regret that I couldn't have known him under other circumstances, but that's all over now. Ben is only a part of my past.

We were lucky; we both escaped. I might have broken my

neck when I jumped; I might have killed myself. All I did was crack a bone in one arm. It took a long time to heal, but it might have been much worse. Ben was unconscious for nearly two days, but there was no lasting damage.

Max and I got married very soon after that and moved to Austin. We chose Austin because of Max's job – he could be transferred easily enough – and because we had heard it was a nice place to live. He sold his house in Jefferson Parrish, and we bought a one-storey, three-bedroom residence in northeast Austin. The only real drawback to the neighbourhood, and the reason we could afford the house, is the noise from the nearby airport. But because Max still has to travel a lot, it's useful being so close to the airport.

Tessa had a friend called Mae who owned an art gallery in Austin, and I got a job there, working three days a week. The money wasn't much, but I liked the atmosphere, and it inspired me to take some courses in art history from Austin Community College.

Everything began to come together – it was like a dream, I thought. Sometimes it was a shock to wake in the morning and find Max solidly there in bed bedside me. Sometimes I thought that he was the dream, and my real life was going on somewhere else.

Mae's gallery was in an old white house on Nueces, one of those surrounded by ancient, moss-bearing trees and with a Texas historical marker on the front. Inside, the rooms opened one on to another, stripped of furniture, with nothing to distract from the paintings except the gleam of polished floors and the green blur of leaves at every window. Even on the sunniest days the light that filtered through the leaves was pale, subaqueous. From the ceiling, recessed lights compensated. Paintings weren't meant to be seen in sunlight, anyway.

One day when I arrived there was a man inside, standing by a window. His back was to me, but my heart lurched at the sight of him, and I was suddenly afraid that I knew him.

'May I help you?' I said.

He turned round. He was a stranger, a man in his mid-twenties dressed in jeans and a T-shirt, and with the scruffy beginnings of a reddish beard. 'I'm waiting,' he said. He held an artist's portfolio.

The door to Mae's office opened, and she came out. 'I'm sorry to have kept you waiting,' she said to the man, and smiled and nodded at me. They went into her office together, and the door closed.

I sat down at the desk near the front door and began going through the mail. I found it hard to concentrate; I kept trying to hear their voices, and wondering when they would emerge. When the door finally opened, I knew from the way Mae spoke that she had turned him down, and that he wasn't even a borderline case. She hadn't liked his work; maybe he wasn't even a real artist. I pretended to be busy with some papers so he wouldn't realize that I knew, but when he reached the door I looked up, involuntarily, and our eyes met. Neither of us said anything, and he left.

I knew then that he would be back, but he came sooner than I had imagined. When I left that evening he was outside on the street, not even bothering to pretend that he was doing anything other than waiting for me.

'Want to go somewhere for a cup of coffee?' he asked.

'I'm married,' I said.

'I'm Steve,' he said.

That made me laugh.

'How about Old Pecan Street?' he asked. 'They've got great chocolate cake.'

I shook my head and said very firmly, 'I can't.'

'Another time?'

'No. I'm sorry.'

'So am I.'

I could feel him watching me as I walked down the street, and I liked the feeling. I told myself I had handled it well. Nothing had happened and nothing would. It was all right to enjoy his admiration and to let myself think of what might have been. I didn't expect to see him again, unless it was by accident somewhere in town, but the very next week there he was, standing in front of me, leaning across my desk and saying, 'You have to have lunch anyway, so you might as well come have it with me.'

'I don't go out to lunch,' I said. 'I have cottage cheese and carrot sticks and stay at my desk.'

'Can I show you my work?'

His eyes were muddy brown, flecked with yellow. His nearness made me edgy.

'There's no point,' I said. 'Mae's the one who makes the decisions around here. It's her gallery – I just work for her. It doesn't matter what I think of your work –'

'It matters to *me*.'

I couldn't take the intensity of his gaze. To escape his eyes I looked down at the desk, at his hands braced there, at his bare arms – and saw the old, healed scars on his wrists. I shuddered, pushed myself away from the desk, and stood up.

'You'd better leave,' I said. 'You're wasting my time and yours. I'm not going to go out with you, and I can't buy your work.'

'You could look at it,' he said. 'By God, you could at least look at it! I did it for you – I've been dreaming about you, every night since we met. I made a collage, about the dream – it wasn't an ordinary dream!'

The anger in his voice got to me, more than what he said. I looked at the piece he put on the desk.

It was a piece of cardboard, eight by ten inches, decorated with cuttings from magazines and with a grey-green watercolour wash over it all. At the centre was a photograph which might have been taken from one of the glossy architecture magazines I loved to look at: a Louisiana-style house with steps, high porch and shutters. In the lower right-hand corner, attached to the house by a piece of string, was a full-colour photograph of a well-developed foetus. The string was in place of an umbilical cord. In the upper right-hand corner was a tiny figure I thought must have been cut from a reproduction of some medieval religious painting, an angel blowing on a horn. Most of the left-hand side of the picture was filled with the pencilled sketch of a woman's face. It was my face. I recognized the style.

I looked at the man who had done it. I didn't know him. 'What does it mean?' he asked, sounding scared. 'Why do I feel like I know you?'

I gave up. How long can you go on running? In my case, there was no point. Gabriel would find me, he would always find me. I finally understood that he had not been reborn as Ben – he had come from me. I was carrying Gabriel around inside me, and he was looking for a way out.

'Wait for me outside,' I said. 'I may be a little while.'

When Mae came back from lunch I told her I wasn't feeling well. She looked concerned and touched my forehead.

'You're feverish,' she said. 'Better take the rest of the day off.'

I got into Steve's car and we drove out to the lake, finding a secluded place to park. I thought I was going to tell him everything, all about Gabriel, and Ben, and me, but as I looked into his baffled, muddy eyes, I realized he didn't need to know. I kissed him, and we did what we had to do.

The next day, I quit my job. I didn't think Steve would come back, but it was better not to take chances. I told Mae I was pregnant, and I told Max I wanted the time to write a book. Both of those things may be true.

chapter fifteen

They never mentioned her name to him and he never asked. He didn't have to ask. He knew she was dead.

When he first came out of the hospital he had hoped to find her again, and prowled the streets in search of her, day and night. Gradually he accepted the truth, certain that if she had survived she would have come to him, or he would have found her by now.

They were fated to be together. It was his fault that she was dead. He had meant to die with her. Now, alone, he didn't dare kill himself.

Anyway, life wasn't quite as bad as he had thought it would be. Sallie and Angus got married, but they didn't send him away to school. They moved into a bigger house, and except for having to see a psychologist twice a week, Ben could pretty much do as he wished. He learned how to avoid Angus, and what he could get away with and what he couldn't.

By the end of the summer he had a baby sister. They called her Lily, and he loved her very much.

He would stand over her crib and watch for hours while she slept. He liked to make faces, to see her smile. When he was alone with her he would catch her vague, blue gaze and call her by her real name, and talk about the secret that they shared.

'Hello, Dinah,' he said softly. 'I'm Gabriel. You remember me. We belong together. Don't tell anybody else, but we're Gabriel and Dinah, and we belong together. We love each other, you and me. We'll love each other until we die.'

A selection of bestsellers from SPHERE

FICTION

A TASTE FOR DEATH	P. D. James	£3.50 ☐
THE PRINCESS OF POOR STREET	Emma Blair	£2.99 ☐
WANDERLUST	Danielle Steel	£3.50 ☐
LADY OF HAY	Barbara Erskine	£3.95 ☐
BIRTHRIGHT	Joseph Amiel	£3.50 ☐

FILM AND TV TIE-IN

BLACK FOREST CLINIC	Peter Heim	£2.99 ☐
INTIMATE CONTACT	Jacqueline Osborne	£2.50 ☐
BEST OF BRITISH	Maurice Sellar	£8.95 ☐
SEX WITH PAULA YATES	Paula Yates	£2.95 ☐
RAW DEAL	Walter Wager	£2.50 ☐

NON-FICTION

ALEX THROUGH THE LOOKING GLASS	Alex Higgins with Tony Francis	£2.99 ☐
NEXT TO A LETTER FROM HOME: THE GLENN MILLER STORY	Geoffrey Butcher	£4.99 ☐
AS TIME GOES BY: THE LIFE OF INGRID BERGMAN	Laurence Leamer	£3.95 ☐
BOTHAM	Don Mosey	£3.50 ☐
SOLDIERS	John Keegan & Richard Holmes	£5.95 ☐

All Sphere books are available at your local bookshop or newsagent, or can be ordered direct from the publisher. Just tick the titles you want and fill in the form below.

Name_____

Address_____

Write to Sphere Books, Cash Sales Department, P.O. Box 11, Falmouth, Cornwall TR10 9EN

Please enclose a cheque or postal order to the value of the cover price plus:

UK: 60p for the first book, 25p for the second book and 15p for each additional book ordered to a maximum charge of £1.90.

OVERSEAS & EIRE: £1.25 for the first book, 75p for the second book and 28p for each subsequent title ordered.

BFPO: 60p for the first book, 25p for the second book plus 15p per copy for the next 7 books, thereafter 9p per book.

Sphere Books reserve the right to show new retail prices on covers which may differ from those previously advertised in the text elsewhere, and to increase postal rates in accordance with the P.O.

THE HYPNOTIC POWER OF SOUL-CHILLING
TERROR . . .

Death Trance

Graham Masterton

Respectable businessman Randolph Clare, president of one
of Tennessee's largest companies, is challenging the
bureaucratic Cottonseed Association with lower prices and
greater efficiency. But then tragedy strikes – his wife and
children are savagely and brutally murdered . . .

In desperation Randolph makes contact with an Indonesian
priest who claims he can help him enter the world of the
dead. But there demons await, hungry for those who dare
make the journey. Not only do they want Randolph's life,
but are eager to condemn his family's souls to a hell of agony
far beyond all human imagination . . .

Don't miss Graham Masterton's other horror classics:
REVENGE OF THE MANITOU   THE WELLS OF HELL
THE DEVILS OF D-DAY   THE HEIRLOOM
CHARNEL HOUSE   TENGU
NIGHT WARRIORS

0 7221 6124 7   HORROR   £2.99